Leo's Chance

A Sign of Love Novel

Mia Sheridan

Copyright © 2013 Mia Sheridan

All rights reserved, including the right to reproduce, distribute, or transmit in any form or by any means.

ISBN-10: 1490381716
ISBN-13: 978-1490381718

COVER ARTIST: MIA SHERIDAN
FORMATTED BY MIDNIGHT ENGEL PRESS

This book is a work of fiction. Names, characters, places, and incidents are the product of the author's imagination or are used fictitiously. Any resemblance to actual events, locales, or persons, living or dead, is coincidental.

This book is dedicated to Darcy Rose for, among many things, teaching me that I'm braver than I ever knew.

The Leo

A passionate lover by nature and a brave fighter by instinct..

CHAPTER ONE

I lay in my hospital bed, staring up at the ceiling, swimming in my own grief. How had it come to this? How had life brought me to this place—not just this room in this building, but the unbearable state of my own heart and mind? I want to escape myself, I want to crawl out of my own head and become a shadow curled up in the corner, just a ball of emptiness. I had destroyed every person who had ever tried to love me, and the pain in that realization is so devastating that it feels crushing, constricting, too big to handle.

I hear a light knock on my hospital room door and before I can answer, it's pushed open slowly and Dr. Fox's head peaks around the door, white hair wild. "Morning, Jake," he says, smiling.

He walks in, letting the door swing closed behind him.

Dr. Fox is the hospital psychologist and he's been stopping by for two weeks now, but I don't have a word to say to him. I'm not interested in what he's selling. Period.

When I don't say anything, he looks at me for a minute and then says gently, "Still don't want to talk to me about the traumatic month you've had? You might be surprised that talking helps."

I exhale, still remaining silent. This is the last fucking thing I need, some shrink trying to tell me to cry it out and it'll all be okay. He looks like Einstein, which might be good considering I'd need a genius to even attempt to work through all my issues. I'm a fucking mess and I know it. Still, I'll pass. Thanks, but no thanks.

"So, what?" I finally say. "You're going to Goodwill Hunting me or something? It's not my fault, right?" I laugh humorlessly and look away. What a joke.

He's silent for a couple beats and then he says, "Well, I don't know, Jake. I read about your accident and it sounds like that was most definitely your fault. And I'd like to talk to you about that if you're willing. Your dad passing away . . . obviously, no. But either way, I'm not here to blow sunshine up your ass. If you want someone to pat you on the back and tell you you're not responsible for your own bad decisions, I'm not your guy. If you'd like to talk to someone who has helped people a lot worse off than some poor little rich boy who didn't get his way and threw a fit by smashing up his new Porsche, maybe I can be a listening ear."

He turns to leave and I'm seeing red at his words. I can barely move my broken body, both arms are in casts and my leg is suspended in the air, encased in a cast as well and my face is bandaged and swollen. But I manage to jerk my body enough to make him swing his head back around as he's turning and I clip out, "You presumptuous bastard. You think you know me based on a few things you have written down on a fucking piece of paper? You think people can be summed up in a line or two on a clipboard? I'm not some 'poor little rich boy!' I didn't grow up with more than a pot to piss in. I had just found out my little brother was dead—a kid I practically raised. You don't know shit about my situation."

He's silent again for a minute. "I do now," he says quietly. "Thank you for telling me. What was your brother's name?"

I hesitate for a minute, furrowing my brow and then turning my head to look out the window at the blue California sky. Holy shit, that sneaky bastard tricked me. Huh. I feel my lips twitch against my will. A seed of respect takes root.

I take my time answering, continuing to stare out the window silently for a minute or two after he's asked his question. He waits me out. "Seth."

"I'd love to hear about Seth if you'll tell me about him," he says.

I sigh. I haven't talked about Seth in so long. Ah, what the hell?

The only way that sweet kid is going to live on in this world is through me. I've fallen down on the job. I owe him so much. Still, I hesitate, but finally find the words. "I hadn't seen him in ten years. I'm adopted. He was my real brother. Or half brother. But my real brother in every way that counts. It's a long story."

"I have a Ph.D. in long stories." He smiles and I chuckle despite myself.

"I bet."

"How would you feel about me coming back tomorrow morning for an hour or so?"

I pause, considering. "I don't know, I'm kinda busy. I've got a pity party scheduled for eight o'clock followed by wallowing at nine."

He laughs quietly. "Ten it is then. I'll see you tomorrow, Jake."

He starts walking toward the door and as he's reaching for the handle, I call out, "Hey, Doc?"

"Yeah?" he says, turning to look at me.

"My name is Leo. My real name, I mean. It's not Jake. It's Leo."

He pauses for a minute but doesn't ask me to explain. "Okay. How about we talk about that tomorrow and you tell me what you'd like to go by. I'll see you at ten."

And with that he opens the door and walks out.

CHAPTER TWO

I watch Evie as she sits on the park bench, eating an apple, a novel open in her hands. She's so beautiful that it hurts a little bit to watch her and not approach. I think she's probably engrossed enough in her book that I can move a little closer and so I do, taking a seat on a bench close by, and pretending to talk into my cell phone. I'm desperate to see the details of her, to soak her in. But I have to keep my distance for now; at least until I figure out what I'm going to do, what I'm going to say. My heart starts beating faster. I can't mess this up. I've come so far and now the only girl I've ever loved is right in front of me. And she might hate my fucking guts.

I've been following her for a couple days now and I've ascertained that she's not married—thank God. I don't even want to think about how I would have handled that. But I don't know yet if she has a boyfriend or if she's dating anyone. I don't know if it'll stop me, but it'd be nice to know what I'm up against.

She works at the Hilton downtown and she doesn't own a car. I hate that she busses it everywhere she goes. It makes me feel better when I'm following in my car because I know she's safe as long as I'm watching. A small voice in the back of my head tells me that she's been doing okay without me watching out for her for eight years and I cringe inwardly, a spear of guilt stabbing through my chest.

She seems to be doing pretty well for herself despite the fact that she can't be making very much money. But she lives in a decent part of Clifton, a neighborhood near the University of Cincinnati, and she dresses nicely and is clearly doing a damn good job of taking care of herself. I'm not surprised. She's still the Evie I remember. I feel a fierce pride take hold. Hell, I had seen girls with far fewer problems than Evie turn into sniveling messes when their manicure appointments were cancelled. I had hung out with far too many of them myself. But who was I to judge? I had been weak, too.

The first time I saw Evie when I got back to Cincinnati, I had been waiting in my car, parked across the street from her apartment. She came walking out, dressed in jeans and a sweater, her long dark hair hanging loose down her back. My mouth got dry and my breath came out in a harsh exhale as I stared, frozen, watching her move down the street. I didn't know it was possible to hold your breath for eight years, but apparently, it is. She had been a beautiful girl, but she had grown into a stunning woman. She was still small and slender, but now with feminine curves that she hadn't had the last time I saw her. Emotions came slamming back, making it feel like it was only yesterday that I had kissed her on our roof, and told her to wait for me and that I would wait for her, come for her, love her forever. *But I had failed.*

As I followed her around, I was reminded of the strength of my girl, and I saw that she was still the caring, giving Evie I had known. She smiled at everyone and she stopped and helped when she could have easily kept walking. People who came into contact with her looked like they were holding themselves back from calling to her as they watched her walk away. I couldn't blame them. *My girl* . . . that's just not smart thinking, man. I had already been dangerously invested even before I got a glance of her and now . . . it was going to completely destroy me if she rejected me right off the bat.

After only a couple days of following Evie, I was pretty damn sure that I was already even more in love with her than I was when I was fifteen years old. Now I just had to figure out what the hell to do. I went over it and over it in my mind and I couldn't nail down an answer. My longing to talk to her, to touch her, was so all-consuming that I could hardly sit still. I went to my office every day and I had to force myself to concentrate on what I was supposed to be doing. The question, *what should I do* bouncing around in my head until I thought I'd go crazy. After years and years of pining for her so intensely, she was right in front of me, and yet she was still a thousand miles away.

****

When I was a kid, I used to hate picture day at school. Not because I gave a shit about that kind of thing, but I could tell Evie did and it fucking killed me. Any other day of the year and we could somewhat blend in with our worn clothes and messy hair. But on picture day, all the other kids would show up with new clothes, the girls with bows in their hair, envelopes of money ready to hand to the teacher. No one gave a rat's ass if they had a picture of their foster kid to hang on the wall. No one cared to document what I looked like in fifth grade or sixth grade or at *any* age—if they had, they would probably have cared that I was living in a stranger's house, too.

I would watch Evie watching the other girls and see how she would self-consciously bring her own hand up to her un-styled, half brushed hair in an effort to smooth it. She couldn't reach the back very well herself and no one else was gonna do it for her.

Then I would watch those endless dark eyes go dreamy and I would know that my Evie was weaving together a story for herself. Partly, that look broke me and partly, it made my heart swell with pride. I knew it was the reason that she didn't break or turn hard like I already had. I didn't think she dreamed because she was in denial about her own circumstances. She was the smartest, most observant person I had ever met. I thought she dreamed because it was how she took care of herself and how she rose above enough to retain that gentle spirit that made me love her so fiercely. Somehow she held onto the ability to brazenly believe that there was goodness in the world, despite her own devastating situation.

I guess the reason this memory comes back to me today as I follow Evie to work is because despite the fact that she's wearing a hotel housecleaning uniform, she walks proud and carefree as if she's perfectly content with her life and her situation. And she should be. She absolutely should be and I'm damn proud that she's gotten to this point. I just want to know more. I need to know more about who she's become. I need to know everything.

This is why I need to be ready and come to a decision about what I'm going to say, before I confront her. Fear of rejection churns heavily in my gut. I *refuse* to let her slip away from me before I've even had a chance to try to win her back.

Shit, I need a drink. *No, not gonna do that.* I'm gonna hit the gym and work off some tension and then I'm going to turn in early tonight. I saw in the paper last week that Willow's funeral is tomorrow and I'm planning to go. I'm sure Evie'll be there and so I'll have to maintain my distance, but I wouldn't miss it. I owe Willow my respect. She had a lot of demons but she was never unkind to anyone. Well, except herself. Right up to the very end. I think about how close I came to ending my own life, and I know that the only thing that separates me and Willow is that I get a second chance.

CHAPTER THREE

I park in the back of the cemetery and walk the long way toward the small group of people I know are gathered for Willow's service. I saw in the paper that a fund had been set up for the burial costs for the girl they described as having no family, and no friends who could afford the expenses. I called the funeral home and covered it all, including a granite headstone. Willow deserved more than an unmarked grave. I hadn't been there for her over the years, but I could do this small thing now.

I hang back a little, leaning against a tree several feet from the rest of the gathering as I wait for it to start.

My mind wanders to Willow as a little girl. Her eyes had held a wariness too deep for her young age. I had wanted to protect her, just like I had wanted to protect Evie, but Willow was always one step ahead of everyone when it came to her self-destruction. I didn't have the words back then, and I don't know that she'd have listened even if I did. But I wish I could tell her now that I understand. I know that you don't want to take your own life because death is appealing—but because *life* is excruciating. And you wonder what it's all for—all the struggling and suffering—what is the fucking point? Day in and day out, what is the *point* of hurting so damn much? She didn't want to die. She just didn't want to be in pain anymore. I know. *I know.* I've been there, too.

I think back to one of the times Willow showed up at my foster home, drunk and high on who knows what. I think she was twelve, maybe thirteen. It was right before I left for San Diego. I snuck out and walked her back to her foster home, only ten blocks away. I remember being so frustrated with her that night. It was like, no matter how many times I tried to make her safe, tried to protect her from the kids who didn't give a shit about her, she always ended back in the same spot anyway. It was exhausting.

As I was walking her home, she had looked up at me, eyes glazed and her voice slurred and said, "Leo, why are you nice to me?" And the expression on her face said that it was honestly a mystery she couldn't explain.

I had looked at her for a minute and finally answered, "Because I care about you, Willow."

"But, *why*?" she had asked.

"Because we're friends, okay?" I had said.

But really, I think the thing that made me feel protective of Willow was different than the thing that made me feel protective of Evie. I think I saw a part of *myself* in Willow. And that's how I knew that no matter how many nice things me or Evie or anyone did for her or said to her, she was going to keep believing the things that all those others who came before us had told her. My dad had beat my ass and told me I was a worthless waste of space and Evie loved me. Why was it so easy to believe that I deserved the former and that I didn't deserve the latter? I didn't know, but I knew Willow and I had more in common than I cared to think about at the time. I *got* her, even though I wished like hell I didn't. Still, I had thought I was stronger than her—until I wasn't.

I come back to myself as I see Evie walking toward the group from the opposite direction from where I came in. She's wearing a sleeveless, black dress and black heels and she has her hair pulled back. I can see the outline of her shape perfectly in the form-fitting outfit and I wonder what it would feel like to move my hands up her slightly rounded hips until they met at her small waist. I want that so badly it almost physically hurts.

The minister begins speaking and I'm listening to his words, but I can't move my eyes away from Evie. Every few minutes, she wipes tears out of her eyes with a tissue and it costs me not to run to her and comfort her in some way. I press my body into the tree to keep myself from going to her.

Fifteen minutes later, Evie moves to the front of the group to deliver the eulogy and as she takes her place, she looks straight at me, her brow furrowing slightly. Shit, what is she thinking? There's no way she could recognize me from this distance, could she? The more likely reason is that I look out of place in this motley looking crowd. Willow's taste in friends hadn't changed much over the years, I see. Evie stares at me for a beat or two and then her eyes shift back to the people in front of her. It's the first time our eyes have met in eight years and I feel it in the depth of my soul, the moment seeming to stand still and shimmer around me.

Still, my undoing happens several minutes later when Evie starts speaking and tells one of her stories for Willow. *Fuck me.*

"Once upon a time a very special, beautiful little girl was sent to a faraway land by the angels to live an enchanted life, full of love and happiness. They called her The Glass Princess because her laugh reminded them of the tinkling, glass bells that were hung on heaven's gate and would chime each time a new soul was welcomed. But her name was also appropriate for her because she was very sensitive and loved very deeply, and hers was a heart that could be easily broken.

"During the arrangement of her trip to this faraway land, one of the newer angels made a mistake, and a mix up occurred, sending The Glass Princess to a place she wasn't supposed to be - a dark, ugly area, ruled mostly by gargoyles and other evil creatures. But when a soul is placed in human skin, it is a permanent situation that cannot be changed. Although the angels cried in anguish for the fate The Glass Princess would have to bear, there was nothing they could do, other than to watch over her and try their best to lead her in the right direction, away from the land of gargoyles and evil creatures.

"Unfortunately, very soon after The Glass Princess arrived in this land, the cruelty of the beasts around her created the first large crack in her very breakable heart. And although many other less evil creatures tried to love and care for the princess—for she was very beautiful and very easy to love—the princess's heart continued to crack until it crumbled completely, leaving the princess heartbroken forever.

"The princess closed her eyes for the last time, thinking of all the evil monsters who had been cruel to her and caused her heart to shatter. But evil creatures, no matter how demented they are, never get the last word. The angels, always nearby, swooped down and carried The Glass Princess back up to heaven where they put her broken heart back together, never to be hurt again. The princess opened her eyes and smiled her beautiful smile and laughed her beautiful laugh. And it still sounded like the tinkling glass bells, just as it always had. The Glass Princess was home at last."

With her words, memories come slamming back so hard and fast that they almost feel like a physical blow. Suddenly I'm up on a roof, crying in the arms of the bravest girl I've ever known and feeling the only love I've ever felt, the only comfort I've ever had. I want to fall to my knees because her voice brings back not only the memory but also the *feeling* of those moments, and my longing for her jumps tenfold. I need to get the fuck out of here. How am I going to handle all this? I feel intoxicated with memories, drunk on emotion.

Evie makes her way back through the crowd and as she's talking to an older woman with bleached blond hair and ridiculous hot pink, stripper shoes, I walk around the tree and make my way to my car. As I'm walking, it becomes clearer than ever that I'm never going to get over Evie—a distressing thought when I consider that she may never be mine again.

I get in my car and sit there staring out the windshield for several minutes until I feel some emotional equilibrium return. Then I pick up my phone and call the funeral home and make an addition to Willow's headstone. "The Glass Princess" will be added below her name. I think Willow would have liked that. It says she was loved.

CHAPTER FOUR

Dr. *Fox walks into my hospital room and smiles in greeting. I raise my eyebrows at him. He's not supposed to be here until Thursday and it's only Tuesday.*

"Getting uglier by the day, I see," he says.

"Ugly is only a state of the soul, old man." *I grin my best sore-ass face, broken nose grin.* "If I'm getting uglier, you might want to look into another line of work."

He chuckles and pulls a chair up next to my bed.

I still have a splint on my nose and deep bruising under my eyes, and the inside of my mouth hurts like a bitch from where they went in to do more repair work on my cheekbone and my jaw. And I have another surgery scheduled for next month. But my arms are out of the casts, thank Christ. I can at least brush my own damn teeth.

My leg will be in a cast for another month and my ribs still need some healing time, but then I can start some physical therapy. I can't wait. I can feel my strength both growing and withering by the day.

I would have been sent to the rehab facility by now if the rod in my leg hadn't gotten infected. The whole ordeal is extending my stay but I don't really care. For the first time in eight years, I feel like I'm claiming back a part of who I am and if checking out of life for a while helps me do that, then maybe it's not a bad thing.

"Something came up on Thursday and so I thought I'd drop by today for twenty minutes or so if you're free," *Doc says.*

I raise an eyebrow. "I'm pretty much free, like . . . all the time,

Doc."

"Right." He chuckles again. "Then I guess a better question is, feel up to talking?"

"Yeah, sure. Actually, I've been thinking about what we talked about last time. About me putting Evie on a pedestal in my mind. I've been thinking about whether or not that's the case and I guess I came to the conclusion, that, yeah, in some ways I always did and I do now. But I think my reasoning behind it is valid and so I don't know if it's a 'pedestal' so much as she just deserves the respect. She always did."

"Okay, but you talk about who she is in present tense as much as past tense and you haven't seen the girl for eight years."

I sigh. "Yeah, I know. Maybe it's wishful thinking . . . maybe it's just a gut feeling. I don't know."

"Well, tell me what you've been going over."

I gather my thoughts for a minute before speaking. "Do you have any idea how brave it is to continue to wear your heart on your sleeve, to stay tender, when you've experienced the kind of lives me and Evie did? When you're surrounded by vultures, do you know how much courage it takes to walk around every day with a sensitive heart ripe for the picking? To continue to love? Shit, the easier thing to do is to turn hard. It's the route I went. It's the route most of the kids I grew up with went. I mean, how did she do that? I just . . . I always felt so proud of her for that. And so murderously protective." I laugh a humorless laugh.

Dr. Fox studies me for a minute. "It's always easier to build walls. You're right about that. And yes, it's remarkable that she was able to retain the sensitivity she did, and I hope that's still the case. But what I meant when I said you kept Evie up on a pedestal was that you seem to be under the impression that you weren't worthy of her."

"Because I WASN'T worthy of her."

"If you trusted her so much, wasn't she the one who was most qualified to decide that?"

I consider this for a minute, wondering for the millionth time, what DID she see in me? All those years ago, I showed her my true self more so than I had ever shown anyone. More so than I've shown anyone up to this very minute. I had never held back with Evie because she made me feel safe in a way no one in my life ever had. I CRAVED that. And she had never turned away. Not once.

"I don't know. I'll have to think about that." I sigh and run my hand through my short hair. They had to shave it to close the gash up on the back of my scalp and it's finally growing out.

"Jake," he says, and I raise my eyes to his face. The first day he came back to my room to talk, he had asked me what I preferred to be called. I had explained why I had started going by Jake and although I thought I might be ready to have someone call me Leo, I realized that I wasn't. Yet. That two syllable word of identity conjures up an emotion that is a relief as much as it is painful. Hearing my real name, even in my own head, feels like coming home. But I don't know what I have to come home to. It's so damn confusing. I have so much to sort through. Maybe I'll clear my schedule so I can get to that. I'm hilarious, even in my own mind.

Doc continues. "What I'm worried about is that you're putting all your self-worth in one person's hands. Evie loved you. It doesn't sound like even you doubt that. Neither one of us can know what her life looks like now and whether or not she'll be willing to let you back in, in any capacity. But that can't be what defines you, son. That can't be what makes you value yourself. That has to be there with or without Evie. Because even if she is in a place to accept you back into her life, and even if she's willing to do that, you owe it to her to be a complete man when you ask her to make that leap. You owe that not only to her, but to yourself."

"This is a lot of touchy-feely shit, Doc. I thought I told you I wasn't on board for that." I'm only partially joking.

He laughs softly. "All right, then let's get to the brutal honesty portion of our program. You need a shower, like, three weeks ago."

I laugh out loud. "Yeah, you try sitting on your ass in a hospital bed for three months. You might not smell as fresh as a daisy either."

He grins, the wrinkles by his eyes crinkling. "Don't they have pretty nurses to give sponge baths anymore?"

I laugh. But I don't tell him that in my mind, I'm on my way back to Evie. I can only pray that she'll let me back into her life. But regardless, letting other women touch me is something I did to numb my own pain. I don't want to be that man.

"So you got a hot date on Thursday or what?"

"No, actually I'm helping an old business associate with a project he's working on. You might be surprised to know that I used to work with computers when I was younger. Was good at it, too. I still do it on a consulting basis here and there."

"That is surprising. How'd you go from computers to psychology?"

"I decided that computers are too predictable. I like people better. They keep you guessing." *He winks.*

I laugh. "Man, that makes one of us. That's exactly why I DON'T like people."

"Ah, no, son. The complexity of the human heart is something to be awed by. If people always acted in a predictable way, determined solely by a set of data, you and Evie would have been much different people. Respect the mystery."

"Hey Doc, has anyone ever mentioned that you have a tendency to sound like a fortune cookie?"

He laughs out loud and stands up to leave. "I'll see you next week, son."

"See ya, Confucius."

CHAPTER FIVE

I have to give myself props. I could be a damn good P.I. I've been following Evie for a week and a half now and she has no idea. I've even gotten pretty close a couple of times. Not close enough, but still pretty close.

Today, I'm following her as she's walking home from the library where she's just spent an hour. So she's still a bookworm. I have to smile to myself. She always had her head buried in a novel when we were kids. She would practically skip to school on library day. She used to try to tell me about the stories she read and I could only laugh at her enthusiasm. She talked about the characters as if they were real people. Evie's own stories were always my favorites though because each one of them was colored with love. And since they were unwritten and unrehearsed, made up on the spot, you could count on the fact that they told the truth about how she felt about you. And there was always beauty in the way Evie viewed our fucked up little world. She made me believe, too. God, I miss that. It was . . . it was *hope*, that's what it was.

I pretend to talk on my cell phone as I walk on the other side of the street, several feet behind her. I watch her as she speeds up and walks right past her apartment building. What the hell? She rounds the corner at the end of her block and I can't see her any longer as her apartment building goes all the way to the corner and blocks the view of the street she's turned on to.

I wait as a couple cars drive down the street and then cross behind them, picking up my pace slightly. I stop at the corner and look around the building. When I don't see her, I turn the corner and walk halfway down the block. She's completely disappeared. Where the he—

"It's impolite to stalk strangers!"

I suck in a breath and whirl around at the female voice and there she is, Evie, standing right in front of me. "Jesus! You scared the shit out of me!" I breathe out. *Holy fucking shit.*

"I scared you?" she says, glaring at me. God, she's insanely beautiful. I almost fall to my knees right in front of her. *Get it together asshole. She already thinks you're some kind of demented stalker, which, come to think of it, you are. Shit.*

"You're the one following me like a creeper," she says, cocking her head to the side. "By the way, *pointer*, when you're stalking someone, you might want to consider being a little more discreet." She sweeps her hand in my direction indicating all of me. "Gawking at your victim in the middle of the street tends to be a giveaway." She narrows her eyes.

I hear what she's saying, half registering it, watching her lips move and knowing that I'll be expected to reply at some point, but the blood rushing through my brain is making everything except her seem very far away. My thoughts are all jumbled and my skin feels prickly. Fucking A, I'm not ready for this.

I stare at her for several seconds, trying desperately to collect myself. *She doesn't recognize me.* Thank God. *Fuck!* No, this is good. No, this is bad, very, very bad.

She puts her hands on her hips and my eyes follow her movements. "Don't despair though. I'm sure with some study, you could get better. There might be an instructional video or something you could pick up . . . maybe a book on the subject, *Creepy Stalker for Dummies*?" She raises one finely arched eyebrow.

Her words register and I realize that she's mocking me. I deserve it, obviously. I also realize that she's probably known I was following her for quite some time. I really and truly thought I was being discreet. This strikes me as funny and I burst out laughing. "Well, holy hell, you really are something aren't you?" I love it though. I love that she's feisty and funny. And being able to laugh at myself feels good.

I see her eyes widen slightly and her lips part as she stares at me, not saying a word. I'm desperate to know what she's thinking. She's sizing me up but there isn't a look of recognition in her eyes. She *definitely* doesn't know who I am. I knew there was a chance she wouldn't. I look different than I did when I was fifteen. *A lot different.* But still, something inside me quietly dies and I steel myself against the hurt.

After a minute, she says quietly, "Okay, well, the gig is up. Why are you following me?"

My blood runs cold. I need time. I need to think. I run my hand through my hair, buying a minute, and look up at her. "I've been that obvious, huh?"

I take a step toward her and she takes a step back. "I'm not going to hurt you," I say. She doesn't respond. But that small movement is all it takes. *That's it.* That movement hits me like ice water, fear sliding through my gut. *I'll do anything to keep her from backing away from me.*

"Yes, you've been THAT obvious. Enough games. I want to know why you're following me."

I pause for the briefest of seconds, panic coursing through my veins, but before I can really even think about it, the words, "I knew Leo. He asked me to check on you," pour from my lips. *I lie.* And now there's no turning back.

****

I watch as her eyes flare and she jerks back slightly and then freezes. "What?" she says, her voice cracking. But then I see her immediately gather herself. She's unhappy about her own reaction. I'm not sure what to make of this. "What do you mean you knew Leo?" she asks, her words strong and even now. She's gathered herself from her initial reaction. I don't know if this means that her first feeling was one of nothing more than surprise and she was able to quickly shake it off? Or if her reaction was something stronger than that, and she doesn't want me to know.

I'm all off balance, emotions slamming in to me too quickly to scrutinize, the feeling that I've just committed an *epic fail* forefront in my mind. *Fuck, fuck, fuck.* Can I freeze time and take a minute?

She turns around and walks to some porch steps directly behind her and sits down. She takes a deep breath and repeats her question, "What do you mean you knew Leo?"

I move closer, gesturing at the step next to her and she gives a slight nod of her head. I sit down and turn toward her, leaning my elbows on my knees. Her face is blank and she's staring just beyond me, into space. Jesus, this feels beyond shitty. Now I'm going to have to expand on my lie and I feel like a fucking douchebag. But my other choice is to expand on the truth, including Lauren, and *no*, I'm not ready for that. I know in my heart that if I wasn't ready to tell Evie the truth, the right thing would have been to walk away once I saw she was doing fine. But the thought of walking away from her again is unfathomable to me, even now that I've gotten myself into this fucked up mess. I speak slowly, picking my words carefully, trying to keep my lie as simple as possible. "Leo died in a car accident last year. We were friends, teammates in school. We all thought he might make it for a couple days, but he didn't. We visited him together and he pulled me aside and told me a little about you. He made me promise to check on you to make sure that you were okay, that you were in a good place, happy. He knew I was moving here to work for my dad's company, and that it would be easy for me to check up on you in person."

She's quiet for a minute before replying blankly, "I see. What exactly did Leo tell you about me?"

Not only am I hating myself for sitting here lying, but also the fact that she seems somewhat unmoved by the fact that I just told her I died is playing serious havoc with my heart. I'm having a hard time focusing solely on her though and not my feelings of regret over my dishonesty, so my read could be off.

"Just that he knew you in foster care and you were special to him. He said you lost touch but he'd always wondered about how your life turned out. That's really all."

I see her face flinch very slightly and I know that was a sucky thing to say. How would I feel if someone told me that Evie casually wondered how my life had turned out, but not enough to bother ever contacting me herself? I'm trudging through a river of shit of my own making. But it's either this or tell her the truth and watch her turn away in disgust. Either way, I'm fucked. At least this way, I'm sitting next to her on a step, memorizing her beautiful features up close and breathing in her fresh, very slightly flowery scent. God, I'm a selfish prick.

"I moved here in June, but it took me a couple months to settle in. Then I finally had the time to dedicate to being the creepster I had promised to be." I attempt a smile, hoping like hell to make her smile, too. She looks so lost.

She offers me a small smile in return and stands up. I jump up next to her. She wipes her hands on her jean clad thighs and says quietly, "I'm sorry to hear about Leo. It doesn't sound like you know a lot about our history, but Leo is someone who . . . broke a promise to me. It happened a long time ago, and I don't think about him anymore. There was no reason for him to send you to check on me. If he wanted to know how my life turned out, he should have contacted me himself before . . . well, before.

"All the same, it was nice of you to keep your word to your friend. And now you've done your job. Here I am, fine and dandy. Mission accomplished. Dying wish fulfilled." She smiles a small smile but it looks forced. Her words gut me and I almost physically reel back. Her indifference, feigned or not, kills.

"By the way, who do I have the pleasure of calling my own personal, creepy stalker?" she asks.

I find it in myself to smile, even though I'm still hurting from her previous words. "Jake Madsen." I watch her face closely for any sign of recognition. I don't think I ever mentioned my adoptive parent's last name but I can't remember for sure.

No sign of recognition appears on her face. "Well, Jake Madsen, a.k.a. creepy stalker, obviously you already know that I'm Evelyn Cruise. And you already know to call me Evie." She reaches her hand out to shake mine and when we touch, I feel the electricity jump to life against our touching skin. That same chemistry that we had when we were teenagers is still there. I want to grin with happiness at this undeniable proof of the connection between us, but I contain myself, simply staring at our clasped hands until she pulls away.

"Bye, Jake," she says, turning away.

"Evie!" I call, and she turns around. "You're gonna miss me, aren't you?" I'm smiling because there's no way she's going to miss me—I'm not going away. Annnnd . . . cue creepy stalker music. Fuck it. I don't care.

"You know, Jake, I think I will." She smiles a small smile and turns around and walks away.

CHAPTER SIX

I head back to my office and when I pull into my assigned parking spot in the underground garage, I realize that I don't even recall any portion of the drive. My brain is going over every second of my run-in with Evie. So much of me feels intense guilt for lying, but part of me is on a high for the time I spent close to her, brief though it was. I've waited what feels like a lifetime for the moment when I could feel her and know her presence in my life again. I'll have to tell her the truth, obviously, and, God I dread that. Just the thought of it chills my blood instantly. But if I'm going to explain why I never contacted her, I need to make sure that she cares enough to stay while I spew out my fucked up story. And then I'll just have to pray to God that she can find it in herself to forgive me. I bang my head against the seat back. After a few minutes, I sit up and get out of my car.

I pull my suit coat back on and head into the glass elevator that takes me to my office. I stop at the reception desk in the lobby on my floor, smiling at Christine, my receptionist.

Christine is in her forties, married with a son and a daughter in junior high school. She and I don't know each other outside the office, but I can tell by the way she talks about her husband and her kids that they're her world and that there's nothing she wouldn't do for them. She's everything to them that I had hoped Lauren would be to me when I moved to San Diego.

"Hey, there," she greets me, smiling back, tucking her chin length auburn hair behind her ear.

"Hey. How are you? What'd I miss?"

"I'm great! Nothing exciting going on around here. You gonna tell me where you've been disappearing to so much lately or what? You've had a gleam in your eye for a week now. There's a good story there. I can feel it." She rubs her manicured hands together and grins.

I lean forward on the counter above her and look around as if checking to make sure no one else is around. She leans in toward me, eyes wide. "Christine," I lower my voice and look around one more time for effect. "Can I have my messages?"

She stares at me for a beat and then her eyebrows snap down and she swipes the papers in her hand toward me. I laugh, leaning back to avoid being smacked in the face.

"Fine, have it your way. I don't have time to listen to your boring story anyway. I need to finish up here so I can get to Michael's game by five thirty."

I laugh at her boring story comment. "Why don't you leave now? You were here all Saturday morning for Preston's meeting. We owe you a couple hours. That way you can take your time."

She pauses. "You sure? That would actually be great because then I'd have time to stop by the house and change, too."

"Yup. Go." I smile and head into my office.

"Thanks! I'm just going to straighten up here and I'll see you tomorrow."

"Okay. Oh," I say, stopping in my office doorway and turning back toward her, "I'll be in a little late tomorrow. I have something to take care of in the morning. More secret espionage." I wink and walk into my office, closing the door behind me. I hear her harrumph.

I sit at my computer, going over the reports Preston sent me while I was gone. Surprisingly, I'm able to focus on them enough to make some necessary changes and send him a follow up email with my suggestions.

In a lot of ways, the day I was adopted by Lauren and Phil was the beginning of my downfall. But at the same time, I'm constantly aware of how lucky I am to be in charge of this company. I am honestly passionate about the business and in awe of Phil's brilliance and product design. I spend as much time as possible down in the lab, learning exactly how the technology works and what changes are being implemented to improve it. Phil handpicked all his lead engineers and so I know they're the best of the best. It's critical to me that I run this company well and through my success, pay homage to the man who wanted and tried his best to do right by me and whom I unfairly treated so poorly for years and years. It's the reason I put off finding Evie immediately when I got to Cincinnati. I needed to make sure that I was as mentally present as possible as I took on my new role. I knew that once I got a glance at Evie, my mind would be at least partially elsewhere. Just *thinking* about her and how close she was, played havoc with my emotions.

I was fucked up in a lot of ways over the years, but one thing I have confidence about is my work ethic. I've always been a hard worker. I always got good grades in school and I know I'm not a lazy person, like the good for nothing dirtbag who raised me most of my life. I take a deep breath as images of the man who called himself my father for the first eleven years of my life swirl around in my brain. It's still so fucking hard not to get stuck in the feeling his memory evokes. It's still so fucking hard not to let his disparaging words about me play on repeat in my brain. Dr. Fox brought me so far, but now I need to do the daily work of replacing the hateful ideas I was force fed from the time I could comprehend who I was, with something more positive. It takes daily diligence not to fall into the self-hatred trap. Disease can be deadly, and self-hatred is a disease, too. Secrets and shame can end a life just as easily as metastasizing cells and viral takeover. I *know* I'm not helping myself out by doing something that feels morally questionable, keeping something from Evie, but I need time. Not a lot, just a little.

My thoughts are interrupted when I hear a light knock at my office door. "Come in," I call.

A blond head peeks around the door, a smile on her full lips.

Gwen. *Shit.* If Christine had still been here, she'd have known to call my phone after a few minutes with a "pressing" call. *Damn it.* Why'd I let her go early? Now I'm trapped, like a rat in a cage. And Gwen is the hungry cat in this scenario.

She enters and then locks the door behind her before strutting in, her lean body encased in a skin-tight, navy blue dress. "Jake!" she croons. I stand up to greet her and she comes around my desk, holding her arms open. I lean in to kiss her on the cheek, her perfume assaulting me. It'd be a nice smell if she wasn't bathed in it. She turns her head at the last minute so that I can't help but to kiss her lips and she squeezes my shoulders. I lean back, smiling tightly and she takes her thumb and wipes her lipstick off my mouth, her own lips puckering up as she focuses on the task.

Every muscle in my body is tensed to move away from her. I need to be alone with my work and my thoughts. I'm not up for playing her games right now and past experience tells me that that is exactly what I'm in for. "Hey, Gwen. How are you?"

"Better now that I'm here with you, gorgeous." She smiles, showing me her perfect, overly white teeth as she takes a seat on the edge of my desk, her big, round breasts right at eye level. I take a deep breath and scoot my chair back slightly and look up at her. "Gwen, there are two chairs right there." I gesture my head in the direction of the chairs on the other side of my desk.

She ignores me, grabbing my tie and pulling me toward her. "God, look at you. All corporate. It's sexy." She slips her shoe off and puts her bare foot in my lap, wiggling her toes on my crotch.

That's it. I grab her foot and remove it, then scoot my chair back even further, my tie falling from her hand. Through a clenched jaw, I say, "Gwen. Enough." My blood is boiling. I can't stand forward women. It's mostly my own personal issue for obvious reasons, but that shit enrages me. "Unless you're here for something work related, you need to leave."

"Grumpy," she says, standing up, slipping her shoe on and

walking around my desk to one of the chairs. She sits down, crosses her legs and goes on, "We used to be friends, Jake. What happened?" She pouts, crossing her arms and sticking out her bottom lip. She literally sticks out her bottom lip like a petulant two-year-old. I almost laugh.

"I've already told you, Gwen, we can be friends. As long as you keep your foot, and other body parts away from my crotch, we'll get along fine."

"You used to like it when I paid attention to your crotch," she says, raising an eyebrow. "You know I'm good at it. Why deny yourself?"

I stare at her for several moments. I got myself into this mess by leading her on all those years. I used her to get back at Lauren and Phil. Any time there was a company sponsored trip and families went along, or her dad brought her with him for business in San Diego, I went out of my way to make sure we were "caught" together in the most compromising positions possible. She's one of the most shallow people I've had the displeasure of meeting, but the fact remains that she's a person, and deep down, maybe she has feelings. I've never seen them, but there's a chance that they exist. "Listen, Gwen, anything we had has been over for a long time. A really long time, actually. I'm trying to get my life back on a better track and I need to focus on doing that, okay?"

She narrows her eyes at me. "Fine. I'm glad to see you cleaned up, don't get me wrong about that. Just know that I'm not giving up on us."

I take a deep breath, conjuring patience. "This is why it's *really* challenging to be your friend. Do you get that? God damn." I run my hand through my hair. How many times do you have to tell someone something?

"Calm down, Jake. Fine. You need some space to go through your fourteen steps or whatever. I get it. I actually came here for a specific reason. I have the tickets for the autism fundraiser." She grabs an envelope out of her purse and places it on my desk. She stands up and fluffs her hair and makes a show of adjusting her dress down her hips. "Pick me up at seven thirty?"

Fuck. I almost forgot about taking Gwen to the fundraiser. I almost tell her that something came up and I can't go but I can't do that. It's a benefit for autism, for *Seth*, and there's no way I'm bailing on that, even if I have to put up with Gwen for a couple hours. It will be in public, and there will be lots of other people from the company there. It should be fine. "Yeah. Seven thirty. And Gwen? It's twelve steps."

She squints at me, pursing her lips. "What's twelve steps?"

"You said fourteen steps. I'm assuming you're talking about AA, which, incidentally, I'm not in. But it's twelve steps."

"Oh-kaaay. If you're not in it, then who cares how many steps there are?"

Uh, lots of alcoholics and their families probably do. People who grow up in homes like the one I did. "Never mind, Gwen. I'll see you Friday. And Gwen? Friends."

She sails out calling, "Whatever. See you then!" She turns at the door and pauses for a second. "Oh and I'm wearing red. You know, in case you want to match your tie or something."

"I'm not taking you to the prom, Gwen."

She smiles big and closes the door behind her. Clueless. I grit my teeth. Why do I have the feeling this is going to be painful?

CHAPTER SEVEN

The next morning, I get up early and shower and pull on jeans and a long sleeved T-shirt. I'll need to come home and change before I head to work, but after I check on Evie, I'm going to go visit Seth. I can't go to a cemetery dressed in a suit. I take a deep breath. This is not going to be easy.

When I was in the hospital, I had followed up with the lawyer who had located Seth for Lauren. I had held my breath when I called him, hoping against hope that she had been lying to me. I could see her doing something like that just to get back at me. But no, she had been telling the truth. When I heard the words, it felt like I lost him again. I had held it together long enough to ask him to find out where Seth is buried, and then I had hung up and let the tears for my baby brother fall once again.

I drive over to Evie's apartment, wondering if she's doing okay. I thought about her late into the night last night, tossing and turning, sleep elusive. I need to see her face and make sure that she's all right.

I park down the street, and as I get to her building, I see her locking up her apartment through the front glass doors. *Nice timing.* I lean against a car right in front and wait for her to come out. I can't help the grin that spreads across my face. I feel so fucking deliriously happy that she's back in my life. I realize it's on completely casual, practically non-existent terms right now, but it's a start. The happiness in that thought is so consuming that it's even easy to push away the fact that I'm here under false pretenses. The niggling reminder that that needs to be dealt with is there in the background, but forefront in my mind is that

Evie is right in front of me. After all these years, *she's right in front of me.*

She steps out and spots me and halts in her tracks, a surprised look briefly flashing across her face. She crosses her arms and tilts her head to the side as her eyes roam my body and finally land on my face. "Need help 'finding your puppy' I suppose?"

I laugh. "I was actually just going to offer you some candy. It's in my van over there." I grin bigger. I must look like a fucking loon.

Her face breaks out into a beautiful grin, too, and I swear I hear angels singing. *Get a grip on yourself, desperado.*

She shakes her head and starts walking and I fall in step beside her. From my peripheral vision, I see her inhale through her nose and then open her mouth and subtly take in a breath of my air. Holy shit! Did she just taste my scent in her mouth? I feel my dick twitch in my pants. I go over sales reports in my head trying to distract myself. *Do not tent your jeans walking down the street with her.*

For a minute I feel like I'm fourteen again, begging my body not to betray me in front of Evie who is unknowingly turning me on so much, I can hardly think straight. I want to start grinning again because for the first time in eight years, the thought of getting turned on feels clean and normal. The feeling of being turned on by her in the present conjures up the memory of being turned on by her in the past when sex wasn't all about guilt and shame. This stuns me. I didn't even know I could remember that feeling and Evie has brought it back for me in one day. I want to kiss her. *Stop!* Don't think about kissing her! *Sales reports, Excel spreadsheets, bar graphs.*

Evie breaks the momentary silence. "You know, I'm sure there are girls all over the city who would love the opportunity to be stalked by you. It really doesn't seem fair that you focus all your creepiness on me."

I smile. "I've decided I like focusing on you, though, Evie." Is she crazy? As far as I'm concerned, there are no other girls in this city.

She stops walking and crosses her arms. I stop, too, and take a quick glance at the perfect, small breasts that she's unknowingly plumping. *Equations, PowerPoint presentations, product testing.*

"Look, Jake," she says, looking serious, "you caught me by surprise yesterday, about a person I haven't thought about in a long time, but I'm okay. You don't need to check up on me anymore. My life is fine. It's not exciting, it's not glamorous. But I have everything I need. I'm, um, happy."

I run my hand through my hair wondering at why her statement ended up sounding like a question. I tuck away the comment about her not thinking about me in a long time. It stings.

"I just thought maybe you looked a little upset when you left yesterday. And I did that to you. I just wanted to make sure you were okay *today*, not in general, but today."

She glances over at me, pulling herself up straighter. "I was fine yesterday. I don't like to hear about anyone meeting a tragic end, even someone I don't know anymore." She frowns slightly and pauses but then goes on, "But it's nothing that a little ice cream won't take care of. That's where I'm headed. Want to follow me to the grocery store? One last stalking for old time's sake?" She winks.

Despite the fact that her words hurt and I'm becoming more and more sure that she let me go a long time ago, I rally and laugh at her joke. *I'm here now. I'm here now.*

"I don't think it's stalking if I get an invitation, but yes, I'd love to *accompany* you to the store."

She looks over at me and puts a hand to her chest, looking up at me through her lashes. "I don't know if I'm ready for this huge jump in status," she teases. "From stalker to chaperone in a day? You'll think I'm easy!"

God, she's cute. "Just lead the way, smart ass," I say. And then, before I even really think about it, I grab her hand. This whole situation is just so familiar and she's bringing feelings up in me that I thought I remembered perfectly but that I realize now were only memories in black and white. Reality is so overwhelming that I can barely keep up with everything I'm feeling. It's as if all my emotions for her are in living color now and coursing through my body at light speed. *I'm home.*

She jolts slightly though and pulls her hand away, reaching into her purse for her sunglasses and then popping them on and putting her hands on her purse strap so that I can't reach for her again. Damn. I spooked her. *Slow down.*

"So," she says, "What does your father's company do?"

I tell her a little bit about my company and how I started working with my father and then moved to the Ohio office when it started to suffer. *And because you're here, Evie.*

She nods as we turn the corner onto the block where the grocery store is. "Your father must trust you a lot to give you responsibility for such a big task so quickly," she says.

I feel myself stiffen at her words. This is still such a hard subject for me. "I never gave him much reason to trust me. But he actually passed away almost a year ago, six months before I moved here."

She's quiet for a beat and then I feel her small hand grab mine and my heartbeat picks up as she grins up at me. "I'm just glad you had something to fall back on after the crash and burn of your short-lived creepster career." She bats her eyelashes.

I can't help it. I burst out laughing. She was always so good at getting me to laugh at myself when I was in one of my moods and she still is. I've missed her so damn much. I want to tell her so badly, but I know I can't. Not yet.

We walk into the store and grab a cart and I watch her shamelessly as she selects items, trailing along behind her like a lovesick puppy dog. I'm fine with that. Several men do double takes as she walks by, completely oblivious. I have a quick vision of myself tackling them into a large display of cereal boxes; pink hearts, yellow moons, orange stars and green clovers turning into colored chalk beneath their faces as I slam them into the tiled floor. Magically delicious carnage. I snap out of it as we turn in to the ice cream aisle.

"What flavor do you like," I ask, opening the freezer door.

"Butter pecan," she says, opening a freezer door a couple down from where I'm standing.

I peruse the choices quickly and pull out a carton of butter pecan at the same time she pulls out the same flavor of another brand.

"Why that one?" I ask. "This one is twice the price. It's gotta be the best." I hold up my choice.

She shakes her head, "It's not about price, Jake. This one is the *World's Greatest Ice Cream*. Look, it says so right on the carton." She's completely serious.

I look between the two. "Evie, you do know that they can say whatever they want to on the package, right? It doesn't mean it's true."

She doesn't blink. "Well, see, you're right. But you're also wrong. I think that ninety-five percent of knowing you're the greatest is all about confidence. You might *suspect* you're the greatest, you might *hope* you're the greatest, but if you don't have the balls to *proclaim* yourself the greatest in bold packaging, and let your critics test you if they dare, then you probably aren't the greatest. Who can resist the guy who really, truly believes in himself?"

She throws the ice cream in the cart, turns, and starts walking down the aisle as I stare after her. And that's it. If I wasn't before, I'm ruined for life. Hopelessly. In. Love. The girl is *it* for me. Yeah, ruined. Happily ruined, standing smack dab in the middle of the ice cream aisle.

I try to pay for her groceries, but she glares at me and pushes my money away. I'm irritated. Something has shifted in my mind. She's mine and I want more than ever to take care of her. But she's independent and I know that she needs me to respect that. And I know that that would be true whether she knew who I really was or not.

We make our way back to her apartment. I'm hoping to God she'll invite me in when we get there. I want to spend more time with her.

"So, can I ask what you meant when you said you didn't give your father much reason to trust you?" she asks, a slight frown on her face. She's probably wondering if I'm a trustworthy person. I almost groan out loud, guilt washing over me.

I sigh. At least I can tell the truth here. I stare ahead as I say, "I was a screw up of a kid. I was selfish and messed up and I did everything my father hoped I wouldn't do. If it was self-destructive, I was first in line. Not exactly any parent's dream."

She looks at me sadly but doesn't say anything.

When we get to the front door of her building, she nudges the door open with her foot and passes through.

I feel my jaw tense. "There's no lock on the outside door?"

"Ah, no. I've called the landlord several times, but clearly, it's not his first priority. It's okay. This is a pretty safe neighborhood. No one's gonna step up and call it *World's Greatest*, but it's decent," she jokes.

I'm pissed. This is unacceptable. I make a mental note to call her landlord the second I get to my office.

We stop just outside her door and I set her grocery bags on the floor and wait for her to take her key out. She doesn't. "Um, so, thanks, Jake," she says instead, obviously not intending to invite me in. *Damn*. I can't really blame her though. I'm practically a stranger as far as she knows. "It was a way more enjoyable trip than I expected it to be." She smiles politely.

Both of our heads turn as a big, beefy black guy, probably in his mid forties, opens his apartment door and stands there with his arms crossed, looking at me suspiciously.

"Hi, Maurice." Evie grins. "This is Jake. I'm good. It's good, um, we're good."

Maurice continues to look at me as if he's considering whether to tear out my throat with his teeth or his bare hands. I try to diffuse the situation, putting on my most innocent smile and stepping forward. "Maurice," I say.

Maurice finally relents and shakes my outstretched hand. "Jake."

This is good. This guy looks like he could break a normal sized man in half and he's obviously protective of Evie. Until I can take over the job, Maurice will do.

"Ah, thanks, Maurice. So I'll see you later?" Evie smiles.

Maurice pauses another minute and then, "Right. I'm just inside the door here, Evie. You need me, you call, yeah?"

"Yeah, Maurice," she says softly.

Maurice closes the door to his apartment and I look back at Evie, glancing between her and the door. Still, no go. All right, plan B. I run my hand through my hair saying a silent prayer that she says yes to my next question. "Okay, I get it. I'm not invited in. Can I at least have your phone number?"

She pauses and I hold my breath. The last time I was nervous about asking a girl out, I was a teenager and it was the same girl.

"Give me your phone," she finally says and I exhale, handing it to her. She programs in her number and hands it back.

I grin at her and turn to walk away, saying, "I'm done stalking you, Evie. We've just elevated our status for real." She has no idea.

She laughs and calls after me. "You take all the fun out of everything. You know that, Jake Madsen?" I walk out the door grinning like a fool.

****

It takes me almost an hour to find Seth's small metal marker, half covered with grass and leaves. I squat down and push the debris aside, reading the words, "Seth Michael McKenna, April 7, 1986 to July 27, 2003." No "beloved" or "our little boy," nothing to give any indication that he was anything to anyone. But he was someone to me. My throat locks up as I pluck another leaf off that has just floated down from the large maple nearby. I rest my elbows on my thighs and say out loud, "Hey buddy." I let the silence stretch for long minutes, almost expecting to hear his giggle, his sweet voice saying, "Weeeo."

"I'm sorry it took me so long to get here. I talk to you a lot, I have a feeling you hear me. But I should have come here. Seeing where you are, it just feels so . . . real, I guess." I stare down at his marker for several minutes before I go on.

"I'm so sorry, buddy. I hope wherever you are that you can find it in your heart to forgive me." I pause, gathering myself. "You must have wondered where I was, all those years. You must have wondered what you did wrong. All your life, you must have wondered what you did wrong. And I wasn't there to tell you that you did everything right. Buddy, with what you were given, you did everything right. And I never came back for you. And I have to live with that. But you had to live with that, too, and it must have confused you and hurt you." Tears are sliding down my cheeks now, but I let them fall because Seth deserves each and every one of them. Fuck my pride. I sigh and collect myself a little, plucking at the grass. "Remember when dad came home that time rip roaring drunk and me and mom were so damn tense, walking on eggshells? And he turned away and you started mimicking him by teetering around and going squinty eyed?" I laugh out loud at the memory. "Mom thought you were just being you, she was too wrapped up in her own world to notice who *you* were. But I saw what you were doing and it cracked me up so much I started laughing out loud. Dad decked me because he thought I was making fun of him, which I was, actually. But, fuck, Seth, it was worth it because we were in on the joke together and that was fucking awesome. We *connected* and those were the moments I lived for with you. I wore that black eye around for two weeks, proudly. I hope you carried a few moments like that with you, too. I hope you know that I *saw* you. And I hope you know that I needed you, too, buddy."

I sit plucking at the grass, letting the memories wash over me, letting the past in, despite the fact that it hurts. It hurts so damn bad.

"What was that stupid little song that you used to ask me for every night? Baa Baa Black Sheep? Remember that? I swear I sang that damn song fifty thousand times." I chuckle but then I feel myself grimace with the hurt the memory brings. "I'd sing it fifty thousand more, buddy, if I could just have you back. I hope you know that."

I pause for several minutes, picturing my little brother's face, his smile, hearing his voice in my head. Then I recite very, very quietly,

"Baa, baa, black sheep, have you any wool? Yes sir, yes sir, three bags full. One for my master, one for my dame, and one for the little boy who lives down the lane. Baa, baa, black sheep, have you any wool? Yes sir, yes sir, three bags full. One for my master, one for my dame, and one for the little boy who lives down the lane."

I kneel down on the grass now and put my hands on the cold metal, tracing every letter of his name and the dates of his short life. "You mattered, Seth. In this world, you mattered. You mattered to me. You always will. I love you buddy. I want you to know that. You mattered." Then I stand up and I walk slowly back to my car.

CHAPTER EIGHT

I get to the office a little before noon and I sit in my car in the garage for ten minutes pulling myself together. It's been a long, emotional roller coaster of a morning. I put my head in my hands, massaging my temples even though I don't have a headache. Yet. I was so happy when I left Evie's, but now I'm just confused. Visiting Seth was hard and now I just want to call Evie and tell her about it. But of course, I can't do that. It's been eight years, but in some ways, I feel like it hasn't been any time at all. I wonder if she feels a comfort level with me, too, that she's having a hard time explaining to herself.

As I exit the elevator on my floor, Preston is walking down the hall toward me. Preston was my adoptive dad, Phil's, business partner, with him practically from the beginning, when the company was just a startup. He's extremely intelligent and an all-around good guy. I know my dad trusted him implicitly and I respect the hell out of him.

Even though Phil was an engineering guy just like Preston, Phil also had a really great knack for business, and so when he moved to San Diego to open an office there, the Ohio office suffered. It's what I've been working so hard to reverse as the new CEO and I think I've made some major improvements. We're now operating on solid ground.

"Jake!" he greets me. Preston looks like the ultimate engineer, skinny and geeky with thick glasses and a perpetual rumpled look, as if he sleeps at his desk. Hell, as far as I know, he does. Maybe that's how he seems to do an inhuman amount of work.

"I was just coming to see if you had a minute to go over some of these designs I just got from engineering." He holds out a folder.

"Hey, Preston. Yeah, of course. Come on into my office."

We walk toward my office and he waits as I stop and greet Christine and grab my messages from her.

"You're going to love these. The guys hit it out of the park with the new casing," Preston says.

We sit down at the four-person table in my office and go over all the designs, discussing our preferences and the details of the schematics. I focus easily on the work in front of us, lured in by the excitement and passion in Preston's voice. We don't agree on everything in front of us, but we discuss our differences easily and in the end, I convince him to take a chance on my design preference. He's right; the engineers hit this one out of the park.

As he stands, he grips my shoulder and smiles, saying, "You remind me a lot of your dad as a young man, Jake. He always had a knack for convincing me to take his side. And he was almost always right." He laughs.

He turns to leave, but when he gets to the door, he stops and turns back to me. "I hope you don't take offense when we call you 'The Kid.'" He smiles. "I know we joke about it, but in all honesty, you've held your own since the day you took over here and we're all very impressed. I knew your dad for over thirty years and I worked more closely with him than anyone else did. Jake, I know he'd be proud of you, too." He doesn't give me time to respond but turns and closes the door softly behind him. I sit unmoving for several minutes. Finally, I stand up and gather my paperwork. I catch sight of myself in the mirror on the wall over a credenza. It's only then that I realize I'm smiling.

****

Later that evening, I stand under the stream of hot water, letting the steam from the shower relax my tired muscles. I stopped at the gym after work and worked out until my body was spent and my restless mind was finally quieted, at least temporarily.

As the water rains down over my tired body, my mind goes to Evie and I wonder what she's doing tonight. I wish I had the right to know. I wish I had the right to call her up and tell her I want her with me tonight. I lean one hand on the tile in front of me as my other hand goes to my head, rinsing the shampoo out of my hair. Then I brace both hands on the wall and stand with my head directly under the spray, fantasizing about what it would be like for Evie to show up at my door . . . to kiss her hello and lead her to my bed. I feel my groin throb. My hand travels downward and I grip myself. I'm suddenly painfully hard and I hold back a groan as I stroke myself slowly. Pleasure, intense and hot, shoots through my body. I picture myself stripping Evie's clothes off, one piece at a time and drinking in every inch of her perfect little body. I wonder what she looks like naked, what color her nipples are, what they'd taste like. Sweet, I'm sure. As sweet as her mouth was when I kissed her on our roof all those years ago. I used to think about her naked constantly when I was a teenager, but I haven't allowed myself to since. It was too painful because I knew I'd never have her. But now . . . the mere possibility has the blood raging through my veins.

I pretend the water running down my back is Evie's hands soothing me, caressing me. I pretend that my own hand is hers, reaching around me from behind to stroke me, up and down, her little hand speeding up as the water splashes over both of us. I groan aloud. Her breasts are pressed up against my back, her body slick with the water raining down on both of us. She rubs them against me, moaning at the friction as they pebble against my skin. The sound of the running water mixes with our combined moans. "Fuck, baby that feels so good."

She slides around me and goes down on her knees, taking me in her hot little mouth. I watch her as she moves her head, sucking and licking, the water lubricating my cock so that she slides up and down effortlessly. "Oh baby, fuck, don't stop," I grit out. She moans her agreement, speeding up as I run my hands over her wet hair. Fuck, it feels so amazing. I feel my balls pull up tightly, my orgasm swirling through my belly. "I'm gonna come, baby," I choke out. She pulls back, fisting me now as I come harder than I've ever come in my life. Her hand continues to milk me slowly as I come down. *Holy fuck.*

I wipe the semen off the wall in front of me with my hand and I soap myself up one more time before standing under the spray for a few more minutes. I laugh quietly. Holy shit, if I come that hard just from the fantasy of her, what's going to happen to me if I ever really have her?

I towel off and collapse on my bed. I marvel at what just happened. Sex, even by myself, has never been more than a release for me. I can't honestly say I ever enjoyed it thoroughly because the emotions surrounding it have always been so negative for me. I've never *allowed* myself to fully enjoy it. It was always a means to an end for me—whether that end was for numbing purposes, to prove to Lauren that she didn't own me, or for a physical release, it was never, ever a fulfilling experience. I don't even know that I recognized that until this very moment. For the first time since I moved to San Diego, I had a good sexual experience and it was jacking off in my fucking shower to a fantasy of Evie. *Holy shit.*

CHAPTER NINE

I *flip blankly through the channels on the television mounted on the wall in front of me, finding nothing of interest. I turn it off and set the remote on the table next to me, as my room door swings open. I turn my head, my brows snapping down immediately. It's fucking Lauren. What the hell? The nurses know that she's on a "do not allow" visitors list. She must have sneaked past them somehow. I grab for the call button but Lauren swoops over and places it just out of my reach. She sits down, grabbing my hands and saying, "Jake, stop. I just want a minute. Please. Do you know what I've been going through, not being able to see you? Not being able to comfort you? I love you, honey."*

"You don't love me," I spit out. "What you feel for me is not love. It never was. It was sex. Sex that was wrong and dirty and manipulative and ruined my fucking life. And then ended Phil's life, too. Remember him, Lauren? Your HUSBAND? You need to get out of here."

She pauses, then leans over and tries to move a piece of hair off my forehead, I draw back from her hand. "No."

"Oh, Jake, of course I think of Phil. But that wasn't our fault. He never took very good care of himself . . . always working." She pauses, studying her fingernails. "It was going to be for the best that he found out about us. We should have told him years ago . . . What we HAVE, what we've always had, is not wrong or dirty. You just need to get over your guilt and you'll realize that. You don't have anything to feel guilty for. We fell in love. There's nothing to be ashamed of there."

I'm staring at her, my eyes narrowed. Jesus, she lives in her own world. "Lauren, you're delusional. I never fell in love with you. You were supposed to be a MOM to me. The sooner you get that through your head that I NEVER loved you, the easier it will be on both of us. This is not productive. You need to leave. If you won't give me the call button then I'm going to start yelling. You need to hear me for once in your self-absorbed life."

She's quiet a minute, then shakes her head. "No, you don't know what you're saying. They have you on so much medication. You're not thinking straight. One more time between us and you'd remember why we belong together. Remember it, Jake? Those nights in your room . . ."

I feel myself shutting down now. "I used to sneak down to your liquor cabinet afterwards and do four shots of bourbon just so I could fall back to sleep, Lauren. What does that tell you?" I had done it instead of the alternative, which was crying like a bitch, so confused and horrified over my body's betrayal.

She laughs. "I was thinking of you, too. It was hard for me to sleep, too, honey."

That's not what I meant but she's too self-involved to realize that. I pause for only a second. "MISSY! SUSAN!" I yell at the top of my lungs for the nurses who are on duty right now as Lauren startles at my sudden, booming voice. I hate feeling helpless in the presence of this woman, calling for my nurses like I'm a child. But I refuse to spend another second with her, especially like this, unable to move, like a fly in her spider web.

"Oh stop, Jake. Fine, I'm leaving." She stands up, but instead of stepping back, she leans forward and plants her mouth on mine, licking my closed lips, trying to gain entrance. Before I can make a move, the door flies open and Missy and Dr. Fox stand there staring at us. Lauren steps back, wiping her mouth and smiles brightly at me. "Don't forget to put me back on the visitors list, Jake. I'll be back soon." Then she breezes out, leaving all three of us staring after her.

Missy comes over to me and asks me if I'm okay, her eyes skittering away from mine when I look up at her. Obviously she saw my "mom" trying to make out with me in my hospital bed. Jesus. I grit my teeth in humiliation and shame. "I don't know how she got past us, Jake. We were all sitting right at the front desk. I'm so sorry," she says quietly.

"It's not your fault, Missy," I say. When that woman wants something, she uses any means necessary. Missy takes my vitals and then tells me she'll check on me in a couple hours, walking out and closing the door behind her.

Dr. Fox hasn't moved from the spot by the door. He's frowning at me as he walks over and sits down in the chair next to my bed.

"Hey Doc, do you mind if we re-schedule? I'm not feeling real up for talking right now."

"It seems to me that this might be a really good time to talk," he says gently.

I shake my head. "No, really. I'm not up for it. Plus, I'm not feeling very well. I need to sleep. I have another surgery scheduled for tomorrow morning . . ."

He's quiet for a moment, pursing his lips. "Okay, son." He puts his hand on my shoulder and I flinch slightly. He removes it and looks at me for another moment before moving away.

"I'll check on you tomorrow afternoon after your surgery. We can re-schedule a session for early next week, okay? But you call me if you want to talk sooner than that."

I nod blankly. I'm just so damn tired. I want to be alone. I want to sleep.

He walks to the door and looks back at me one last time. He looks as if he's struggling with himself over something.

As he closes the door behind him, I hear a familiar voice in the hall. Preston. He told me he'd visit me this week when he was in town for some meetings in the San Diego office. I've been slowly trying to get back to work, participating in some conference calls and going over reports on my laptop. I have so much to do to get myself up to speed enough to start running things in Cincinnati.

But I can't even think about that now. I feel overwhelmed, weak, *sickened.*

The voices trail away down the hall, growing quieter. Dr. Fox must have told him I wasn't up for company. Thank God. I'm not. I close my eyes, letting the depression that Lauren's presence always evokes wash over me. I fall into a restless sleep.

CHAPTER TEN

As soon as I get a break at work the next day, I call Evie. I need to see her. I feel an overwhelming need to hear her voice, just to remind myself that this is not a dream. She's back in my life. She doesn't answer and so I shoot her a text message.

Just as I'm heading into a board meeting, my phone rings and I see that it's her. I stop walking and move to the side of the hallway outside the conference room. "Evie."

"Hi, Jake," she says, sounding a little unsure. I exhale. God, just to hear her voice feels so damn good.

"Listen, I'm running into a meeting so I can only talk for a minute but I'd like to take you to dinner tonight."

"Oh," she says, sounding surprised. "Um, I—"

"Evie, it's a yes or yes question," I say jokingly.

I hear the smile in her voice as she says, "I—yes, that will work."

Thank God. I grin. "Great. I'll pick you up at seven."

"Um—"

"See you tonight, Evie," I say, hanging up quickly, not giving her a second to back out. Everyone looks up at me curiously as I walk into the conference room. I realize I have a stupid grin on my face and school my expression. *Focus!* But, is this real? Did I really just say, "See you tonight, Evie?" It takes effort not to grin through the whole damn meeting.

****

I leave work at five and head to the gym for a quick workout. I'm showered and dressed by six thirty. I know it's too early to leave, but despite the vigorous workout, I'm so restless I'm pacing the floor of my condo. Fuck it. I'm going to be early but I don't care. I'm over eager to see Evie and I realize that, but I don't plan to hide from her the fact that I want her. At this point, I think I'm probably incapable of playing it too cool. I don't want to scare her off but I also want her to know that I'm into her. I'm pretty sure she's at least attracted to me and for now, that's enough to give me the confidence to move forward. I'm a twenty-three-year-old man who feels like he's going on his first date. I have to chuckle at myself. But this is Evie. This thought both comforts and scares the shit out of me.

I tried to date a few women over the years. It never felt right to me to have purely physical relationships. That was nothing that ever brought me satisfaction on *any* level. But despite the fact that I gave it a shot once or twice, I always ended up feeling even worse about attempting to form an emotional relationship with someone. A physical relationship was one thing, but an emotional attachment always left me feeling the guiltiest of all, as if that was the ultimate betrayal to Evie. Not only was I left with an emptiness after each "date," but I was left disinterested as well, which made me feel shitty as hell on several different levels. No one ever came close to making me feel like Evie did. I was destined to compare every woman I met for the rest of my life to the girl who still owned my heart. It wasn't fair to anyone. After a couple dating attempts, I threw in the towel and vowed that I'd never be close to anyone again. I had betrayed Evie, and I deserved to live a life of loneliness. I *wanted* to live a life of loneliness.

I pull up in front of Evie's apartment building and sit in my car for several minutes. My body is humming with the thought of her being less than a hundred feet away from me, waiting behind her door. Heat builds in my chest and I know I have to kiss her, to taste her, before we get back in my car. I've never been much for kissing. Too intimate. But I want to kiss her as if feeling her lips on mine is necessary to life itself. I don't know how she'll react, but the deep need that fills me propels me out of my car and with single-minded determination, I pull open her broken front door and stride through. I called her landlord from work yesterday and that shit better be fixed in the next day or I will be on his cheap, lazy ass.

I knock on Evie's door, and I hear her moving around inside before she pulls it open. And suddenly she's standing in front of me, her long, dark hair hanging loose around her beautiful face and her eyes zeroed in on me. Then her eyes roam over me, and the appreciation that I see in them seals the deal. I am physically unable to resist touching her. I move forward and cup her jaw, pulling her into my body. I feel a growl moving up my chest like a fucking caveman. All I am is pure want, a possessiveness I haven't felt for almost a decade washing through me, sending waves of testosterone surging through my body.

I dip my head and settle my mouth on hers. I sweep my tongue inside and as her tongue meets mine, I almost groan at the taste of her. *Heaven*. My heaven.

She whimpers and lifts her arms around my neck, pressing her soft body into mine.

I'm like a starving man who is finally sitting before a banquet table of the most delicious food on earth. Ecstasy courses through my body as her tongue meets mine stroke for stroke.

I vaguely note that her hands are running through my hair and when I bring my hands down to cup her ass, she whimpers into my mouth and I can't help groaning back. This is the second most incredible kiss of my life. The first one was with the same girl.

My erection is straining against my pants and I know I need to cut this off before I come on myself like some over-eager teenager. Or before Maurice gets wind of this and crushes my ass like a bug right here in the hallway.

Reluctantly, I break away, breathing hard and forcing myself to step back. She makes a sweet little whimper in her throat and I can't help grinning as I say, "Damn, you can kiss." *But, I already knew that.*

She blinks up at me. She was as caught up in that kiss as I was.

She smiles sweetly. "Wow."

"Yeah," I agree, still grinning. I might never stop grinning again. "Hungry?"

She looks confused for a minute, but then says, "Yeah."

As we're walking to my car, she asks, "Doesn't the norm dictate that you were supposed to kiss me *after* our date?" She's smiling.

"Couldn't wait," I say, smiling back and winking. "It was either kiss you, or go insane." And damn if it isn't the truth.

Once we're settled in the car and I've pulled out of my parking space, I grab her hand and hold it between us. I'm having a hard time keeping my hands off of her, as if she might disappear into thin air, like a misty dream if I don't keep her attached to me in some physical way. Plus, the soothing effect of her warm, soft skin on mine is like a drug. I'm hooked. My confidence in who we are together is growing by the minute. Our chemistry is undeniable.

She shakes me out of my reverie with her words, "So, Jake, do you date a lot?" She's biting her lip as if she's worried about what my answer might be.

And here we are. I can't lie about this. I'm not even sure why I feel compelled to be completely honest about my past in this regard, but something in me feels that it's crucial and so I answer her honestly. "No. There have been a lot of women, Evie, but no, I didn't date many of them." I glance over at her to see her reaction but she's staring ahead, not giving me any clues. Not only do I want her to know that she's different, but I want her to know that I'm not that man anymore, and so I go on, "I'm not proud of that, but it's the truth. Does that bother you?"

She's silent for so long that my stomach starts knotting. Finally she says quietly, "Jake, I can't be your fuck buddy."

I have to keep staring straight ahead at the road not to burst out laughing. Is that what she thinks? Let me make this a hundred percent clear. "I don't want that with you, Evie."

"Oh. I just thought . . . I mean, I . . . Because . . ."

Shit, I didn't phrase that properly. Let me make this a hundred *and ten* percent clear. "What I mean is, when I fuck you, you're going to be mine. Is that clear enough for you?"

She keeps staring straight ahead, but I see her squeeze her thighs together in my peripheral vision. I almost groan out loud.

"Evie, look at me. You feel this, too, don't you?"

She hesitates for just a second before she looks over at me, nods, and whispers, "Yes."

I smile at her as I pull into a parking spot in front of the "Chart House."

I need to ask her about her past, too. I'm sure she's dated. How on earth could a girl who looks like her not have gotten lots of male attention over the years? The very thought of it turns my stomach, and I feel disgusted not only by the thought but also with myself for *having* the thought. I don't have the right. I should have been here making sure no other men so much as looked in her direction. I should have . . . I should have . . . stop. *This isn't productive right now.* Work with reality, not what ifs.

I shut off the car and turn to Evie. "Can I ask how many men you've dated, Evie?" I try not to hold my breath. Whatever she says, I'm responsible for. However many men she's been with, is my own fault. I need to accept that.

It looks like my question surprises her and I notice that she's blushing slightly as she says, "So many men, Jake, but I doubt you'd say I actually *dated* many of them."

I freeze. *What the fuck?* But then I realize she's mocking me. I exhale. "You're fucking with me," I say.

She tilts her head. "It's okay for you but not for me?" she asks.

No. It's not okay for either of us, but she wouldn't have made the mistakes I made. She would have found some way to be better than me. She always had. "Yes, because you're a better person than I am," I answer.

"Jake—" she starts.

"I just want an honest answer. I just want to know how many men have been in your life."

She sighs. She probably thinks I'm all over the map. Unsure one minute and caveman the next. But that's pretty much exactly what's going on inside of me. The two halves of me are dueling. I'm scared to death and possessive as hell. It's exhausting. But I have to know. Maybe I want to torture myself, I don't know. But I need her to answer me. After a minute, she says, "I've dated a couple guys. Mostly set-ups by my friend Nicole. No one seriously, and no one more than three times. The last guy I went out on a date with was a year ago. We went out for dinner once; he asked if he could take me out again, I declined. Is that specific enough for you?" She looks away.

I take her hand in mine. "And in high school?" I ask. Surely there had to be someone special after I moved to San Diego.

"High school?" she shakes her head slightly and laughs, but it sounds hollow to my ears. "No, I didn't date in high school."

It slowly settles into my soul that neither one of us has been in love since each other. Something inside of me takes flight, soaring. I lean over and turn her head toward me with one finger on her jaw and kiss her sweet lips. That possessiveness sweeps through me again.

We smile at each other for a few seconds before I take the keys out of the ignition and say, "Time for me to feed you. And talk about lighter stuff. I want to see you smile and hear you laugh. I want to know who Nicole is, I want to know what your favorite movie is, why you love to run so early in the morning, and what music is on your iPod. Wait there."

I let her out of my car and lead her into the restaurant.

We take our seats and I smile across at Evie, taking her hands in the middle of the table. She smiles at me and looks appreciatively around the restaurant. "This is beautiful. I've never been here," she says.

I can't help thinking about where we both came from and what we would have thought about eating in a place like this when we were kids. It's not the fanciest restaurant in town, but to us, it would have been like landing on another planet.

My mind goes to a time when my mom was zonked out on the couch in an alcohol coma. My dad had smacked her around for who knows what, *looking at him,* or some other grievous error, and after he left, she drank a bottle of Vodka and didn't wake up for two days. We had precious little food in the house as it was and we ran out completely the next day. I went around to some fast food restaurants and snagged as many ketchup packs as I could and made a horrific version of "tomato soup" to keep Seth and me fed until our mom came around enough to function. It sucked but I had someone depending on me and I did what I had to do. I was nine.

I long to share my feelings with Evie, to talk about how incredible it is for the two of us to be sitting here in this place, after where we came from. It's our connection and she would understand like no one else could. The fact that I can't leaves me feeling empty.

As we sip our wine, I say, "So tell me about your friend Nicole."

Her eyes warm and she says, "I met Nicole at work. She's my best friend and I guess you could say her and her husband Mike have kind of adopted me." She laughs.

I smile at her and she continues, "I spend holidays with them, things like that. It's nice. I never had that before I met Nicole." She takes a sip of her wine and looks slightly embarrassed.

"Where did you spend holidays before that?" I ask. *Why? Just to torture myself?*

Her eyes dart to mine and she says quietly, "After I got out of foster care, before I really got to know Nicole and her family, I spent them alone." She shrugs.

I'm quiet for a minute, hoping she doesn't see the sorrow in my eyes that I feel in my heart. "I'm sorry, Evie."

She smiles. "Why? It wasn't your fault. It was . . . lonely. But it wasn't the worst of what I've gone through, Jake." I frown and she pauses, tilting her head. "Wait, I thought we were supposed to be talking about lighter stuff." She smiles.

I find it in me to smile back, even though her comment about it not being my fault is echoing in my head. *It's entirely my fault.* "You're right. Nicole and Mike have a daughter?"

She grins and her eyes light up. Obviously the little girl is special to her. "Yes. Her name is Kaylee and she's the smartest, sweetest little thing in the world. She keeps us all in our places." She grins again.

Evie has surrounded herself with good people, people she loves and who love her back. I'm so happy to know that she has that in her life.

As we're eating, I ask about her job. She talks easily about it and laughs as she tells me a few funny stories about the worst things that people have accidentally left behind in a room she's cleaned.

"I've found more false teeth than I can count," she laughs and so do I. "I mean, how do you forget your teeth? Wouldn't you notice?" Her eyes warm as she's looking into mine. I love this. I love sitting here laughing with her, getting to know her again. I don't want it to end. A quiet voice in the back of my mind tells me that it probably will end when I tell her who I am. I feel my food trying to come back up my throat and swallow hard.

"You've done really well, Evie," I say, quietly. She has. Look at her, she has good friends, she takes care of herself, she's a hard worker, she's funny and warm and sweet.

She furrows her brows. "I'm a hotel maid, Jake," she says, as if I don't already know this.

I think of all the people who grew up the way we did and how most of their lives turned out. I think of Willow. *I think of myself.* "Don't ever be ashamed of the honest work you do to pay the rent. It's damn rare that someone who comes from the background you do, doesn't go on to repeat the cycle . . . drugs, early pregnancy, domestic abuse. Be proud of yourself. You deserve all the respect in the world. I think you're incredible," I say honestly.

She stares at me, her eyes getting moist before she looks away and says quietly, "Thank you." I stare at her, watching her blink away the tears in her eyes. Has no one ever told her that she's amazing? My heart squeezes painfully in my chest. If I'm given the chance, I vow to tell her at least once every day how incredible she is.

We're both quiet for a minute when she says, "Can I ask you about Leo?" She looks at me nervously.

I snap back to reality. Shit. I hate this. "Of course," I answer, hesitantly.

"Was *he* happy? Did he have a good life?"

Keep this simple. I already feel like an asshole lying at all, no need to expand on it. I think about who I was before my accident and mix just a little bit of the truth into my lie. "I don't know how to answer that. I didn't know him very well. I mean, outside of sports and partying, that sort of thing."

She nods and takes a deep breath. She's biting the inside of her mouth like she used to do when she was a kid. I know that's her "tell" that she's nervous or scared. "When he left, he promised he'd keep in touch and he never did. Do you have any idea why?" I think I see pain flash quickly in her eyes.

Yeah, I do. "His" life went to shit pretty immediately and he lived with a constant death wish for eight years. But he never stopped loving you. Not for a second.

"I'm sorry. I don't. I don't really know what his home life was like. And the first time he talked about you to me was in the hospital and I've told you the extent of what he said," is what I say instead. *Fuck.* I hate myself for not mustering up the courage to tell her the truth.

She nods and is silent for a minute but then she looks up at me and smiles shyly. "This might be a little bit of an odd thing to say, but, well, if he was going to send anyone, I'm glad it was you. I've had a nice time tonight."

Why does that hurt? Am I really jealous of myself? I push my fucked up emotions aside and smile back at her and say, "I'm glad he sent me, too. I thought I was doing him a favor, but it looks like he did me a favor."

After our plates are cleared, I reach across the table and take her hands in mine. "Can I take you out again?"

She nods yes and happiness spreads through me.

We drive back to Evie's apartment, chatting about the city.

"Where do you live?" she asks.

"Downtown, right near the new casino."

"Oh! Have you been there?"

"No. I haven't had time for too many leisure activities. Work has taken up all my time since I moved here." I smile. "Would you want to go sometime?"

"I'd like to see it. But I don't think I'd be any good at gambling," she says, smiling.

"No? Why not?"

"Not much of a poker face," she says, grinning at me.

I chuckle. "No, huh?"

She shakes her head, still smiling. "So, do you miss California?"

"I miss living near the ocean." Just to sit and look out at that vast body of water made me feel like maybe my problems weren't as huge as I felt like they were. It made me feel . . . humbled. That reminder got me through a couple really bad days. "But, no, I like the Midwest. I like the seasons." I smile.

She leans her head back on the headrest and says, "I'd love to see the ocean someday."

I think back to flying over the ocean for the first time and how badly I wanted Evie to be there with me. "I'd love to be the one to show you someday," I say quietly, glancing quickly at her.

She just smiles at me, remaining quiet. I guess it's a little too early to start making travel plans. I'm already getting better at reading Evie's face, her expressions coming back to me like a song that I haven't heard in years and yet still know all the words to. She's right; she doesn't have much of a poker face. I smile.

The first time I really noticed her, some nasty little bitch was giving her shit about her mom. I had glanced at Evie and the hurt and shame was right there on her face. I had sat there, frozen, unable to stop staring at this beautiful girl, her emotions clear and present in her eyes. It had been so long since I'd seen that type of vulnerability on someone's face. *I was mesmerized.* If pigs had flown over our dinner table, it wouldn't have surprised me as much as what I saw in Evie's expression. Hadn't she learned how to hide that shit? Didn't she know what *stoic* meant? You couldn't give your enemy that type of ammunition—it was emotional suicide. So why was I so damn *impressed?* Why did I feel my heart squeeze in my chest? I couldn't figure it out at the time. But I knew there was something about it that was pure beauty. Like seeing the sun suddenly break through the clouds. I wanted to raise my face to it and feel its warmth. She had looked over at me and caught me staring and by that point, I think I was already half in love, something new blossoming in my heart. "Why are you looking at me?" she had hissed, trying and failing to be tough. I liked that, too. I had studied her for a couple more seconds before replying, "Because I like your face." I couldn't contain the small smile that followed—the first one that'd been on my face for a really, really long time. *My gentle lion tamer.*

We drive the last couple of miles in companionable silence, both lost in our own thoughts, the radio playing softly in the background.

We pull up a half a block down from her apartment and I turn the car off but don't make a move to get out. Evie's looking at me expectantly, a small smile on her face. When I look at her, my heart lodges in my throat. "You are so beautiful when you smile," I say. *I missed you so much.*

I lean over, gently kissing her and leaning my forehead against hers. I realize vaguely that this is the exact same way we looked into each other's eyes the night we said goodbye.

We stare at each other for long minutes. Her eyes widen slightly and I can feel her pulse beating wildly at my fingertips. Suddenly, her eyes swim with questions, widening slightly. I freeze. And then I see them go dreamy. She's pushing the questions away. *I see her do it*. That look will forever be etched into my soul. That is the look of my Evie surviving. *She doesn't want to know.* Emotions are slamming through me; confusion, fear, *love*. She pulls away from me.

"What's wrong?" I ask, warily.

She exhales. "Nothing. This is just all kind of new for me." She smiles at me and somehow, I find it in me to smile back.

I walk her to her building. That look on her face keeps skating through my mind. I don't want to say goodnight. I need to do it quickly while I still have the strength to let her walk inside.

We get to her apartment door and I kiss her on her soft lips, smiling at her, whispering goodnight and heading back to my car. As wonderful as our evening was, I'm struggling. I wish to God I had someone to talk to about this. The person I really want to talk to is *Evie*, but obviously, that's not an option. The state of my utter aloneness hits me in the gut and I feel something inside twist tight and break as I pull away from the curb.

CHAPTER ELEVEN

I drive around for a little while, gripping the steering wheel with the effort to drive *away* from Evie, rather than *back* to Evie. I feel confused and needy as hell and this has never been a good combination for me. Feeling needy makes me feel weak and that makes me feel angry. It's been my lifetime struggle and I'm so fucking sick of always coming back to this place. My aloneness feels as if it always remains just beyond the surface.

Kissing Evie tonight was one of the best moments of my life, *literally*. But now it just makes me long for her even more and I don't know what to do with that. But I either continue on the path that I'm on and keep her in my life, or risk the very real possibility that she'll reject me if I tell her who I am.

I pull into a parking spot on the street in front of my building but instead of going up to my condo like I know I should, I walk a couple blocks down to a bar on the corner. I just don't feel like being alone. I just want to go somewhere where there are people, a crowd. I want to drown this feeling. A few shots of bourbon will do the trick. Temporarily.

I sit down at the bar and order two shots of Wild Turkey. It's what Lauren and Phil stocked. *Straight, No Chaser*. It's going to be my band's name once I actually form one, learn the guitar and go on the road. I almost snort to myself but suck it back before I become, crazy, party of one. I down one after the other, grimacing and signaling to the bartender to bring me two more. Four is the magic number. Not stumbling drunk, but don't fucking care buzzed. I've got *Numb Down to a Science*. That'll be my first single. The soundtrack for self-destructive tendencies everywhere. I grimace.

I order a beer so I can sit and nurse it for a little bit and as the bartender places it in front of me, a woman sits down next to me, smiling when I glance over. Chin length blond hair. Pretty. Definite cougar.

"Hey there," she smiles, turning toward me fully and taking a sip of her drink, something pink in a martini glass.

"Hey," I say back, not looking at her. I note that my voice is already thicker with the alcohol.

"I'm Alana." She reaches out her hand and I glance down at it before turning slightly to shake it. "Jake," I say.

"So what brings you here, alone, Jake?" She asks, tilting her head and sucking on her straw.

I pause for a minute, thinking. "Alana. I'm here because the love of my life is across town in her apartment and if I don't drink myself into a coma, I'm going to drive myself over there and knock down her door and make a complete jackass of myself."

She blinks, apparently stunned silent. Then a huge smile takes over her face. "Well, why the hell *wouldn't* you drive over there and make a jackass of yourself?"

I ponder that momentarily. "Because she'll tell me to go fuck myself and I don't want to fuck myself. I want to fuck her."

Alana blinks again. "Well, you sure say it like it is, don't you, Jake?" She's smiling though.

I shrug, taking another pull on my beer.

"Listen, Jake. I think the risk of looking like a fool is a hell of a lot better than living with regret."

I nod. If only it were that simple. We sit in silence for a minute before I say, "So what's your story, Alana?"

She sighs, taking another sip of her drink. "Well, *overall* story is pretty boring I guess. But we're in a bar, drowning our sorrows, so more appropriate is my *sob* story which is that I was married for ten years when I found out my husband was cheating on me with a married neighbor . . . his *soul mate*, he told me. We've been divorced for a year now."

I grimace. "Jesus. I'm sorry. Did you suspect anything?"

She's thoughtful for a minute. "Yeah, I guess I did. I mean, there wasn't anything specific, surprisingly. But I just felt like he was always off at home . . . Not abusive or anything . . . just, ran hot and cold all the time. I never really felt like he was very into me, I guess is a good way to put it." She shrugs.

"Well, then, Alana. Maybe you're better off now than you were with him. Maybe they did you a favor. Look at it as a second chance."

I take the last sip of my beer and signal to the bartender to bring me one more. "Want another one?" I nod my head toward her drink. She shakes her head no.

When the bartender places my fresh beer down, Alana says, "We all deserve a second chance, don't we? To second chances." She clinks her drink to my bottle.

"To second chances," I repeat, thinking of Evie. Do we all deserve a second chance? *Even me?*

After a minute she says, "We got married because I was pregnant and I always thought we probably wouldn't be together if it wasn't for our daughter. I wouldn't trade her for the world, but it's probably true."

I nod. "Life doesn't always go the way we plan it to go," I say quietly.

"No. That's for sure. My ex marries his *soul mate* this weekend. Tonight seemed like a good night to get a drink—or twenty." She laughs weakly. "It just feels so unfair." She frowns and looks down.

We're both quiet for a minute before I say, "Way I see it, maybe it's not so *unfair*, as *unfinished*. If you stopped in the middle of a lot of stories, they'd seem unfair. You're still in the middle of yours."

She studies me for a long moment and then nods and smiles. "I like that. The thing is, I was dating someone before I met Colin, my husband. We broke up over something dumb and then I immediately hooked up with Colin, got pregnant . . . and, the rest is history. But I never stopped thinking of that other man. I even looked him up on Facebook recently and saw that he's divorced, too, with two kids."

I look over at her. "Did you send him a message?"

She shakes her head. "No. I don't know . . . what if he still holds a grudge after all these years? What if he's just not interested?"

"Wait, didn't you tell me that it's better to look like a fool than to live with regret? Don't you take your own advice?" I smile over at her.

She laughs. "Isn't that always the problem? It's so easy to give advice to others. Taking your own advice isn't always so easy."

I chuckle. I guess that's the truth. Knowing in your mind what the right thing is and doing it can be two completely different things. Realizing what is right is the first step, but the follow through can get hung up on so many personal variables. I sigh and turn to Alana, taking the last swig of my beer. As I turn, I realize that I'm a lot drunker than I thought I was only two minutes ago. I need to get home.

"Alana, message that man."

I throw enough money to cover my drinks plus tip on the bar and stand up.

She looks up at me smiling. "Jake, I think I will. And you . . . you do whatever you need to do so that you're not drinking in a bar alone after your next date with that girl." She winks and I chuckle back.

"It was nice to meet you. You have a ride home, right?"

"Yeah, I'm taking a cab. I don't live far." She tilts her head. "It was really nice to meet you, too. I really mean that."

I smile and turn and walk out of the bar.

I make my way back to my condo and collapse on my couch, kicking my shoes off. I lie there for a few minutes, letting the feel of the alcohol lull me into a semi-sleep. Visions of Evie smiling at me across the table at the "Chart House" keep coming back to me, keeping my mind restless and eventually, I sit up and pull my phone out of my pocket. I've made a mistake with the alcohol. I'm not an alcoholic, I'm pretty certain of that. I've never had a problem having a glass of wine or two and stopping there. I don't think I really have an addictive personality, surprising, considering where I come from. But I'm smart enough to acknowledge that I've spent a lot of years using alcohol to self-medicate, and Dr. Fox was right when he said that numbing the pain had never worked. I'm always right back where I started in the morning, only with a fucked up hangover and even more regret.

I dial Dr. Fox's office number, even though it's after ten and I don't think he'll answer. The machine picks up and I hear his voice saying, 'You've reached the office of Dr. Edward Fox. I'm unable to take your call right now, but please leave your name and phone number, even if you think I have it, and I'll call you back as soon as possible. If you are in crisis, please hang up and dial 619-555-4573. Thank you."

I hang up without leaving a message. *Yeah, I'm in crisis.* My whole fucking life is one big crisis.

I sit on the couch, holding my phone in my hand, staring at the wall. Sometimes it feels like I'm a broken mess of pieces, always searching for a way to fit them all together.

Eventually, I make my way to my bedroom, find a bottle of aspirin in my medicine cabinet, and wash it down with water cupped in my hands from the tap. Then I strip and fall into bed in my boxers. In moments, I pass into blessed oblivion.

CHAPTER TWELVE

Surprisingly, I wake up feeling pretty good, physically and mentally. I shouldn't have drank last night to shut off my brain. I could have handled it better. But it's still an improvement over how I've done in the past. I'm moving in the right direction? I have a really big motivating factor, *Evie*. On my drive in to work, I pull out my phone and text her as I wait at a stoplight.

> **Me: I had a great time with you last night. What are you doing today?**

As I'm pulling into my spot in the garage, I hear my phone ding twice.

> **Evie: I had a really good time too. :) Working both jobs. Won't be home until late.**
>
> **btw, know anything about the lock repair on the front door of my building??**

I grab my suit jacket and briefcase, and type back as I'm heading to the elevator.

> **Me: I may have called and threatened your landlord with legal action if he didn't do door repair. Glad he**

stepped up. You should always feel safe.

My phone doesn't ding again until I'm stepping out onto my floor. Does she not like me interfering with her landlord? Too bad. There's no way I'm going to stand by now that I'm back and not make sure she's safe.

Evie: Well, thanks. I appreciate it.

"Billy!" Christine greets. It's her nickname for me. Once the rest of the board started calling me "The Kid," she told me she was going to put a badass spin on it and at least add "Billy" to it. "He was a cunning and deadly outlaw," she had whispered, making me laugh. "We'll hear the tremor in their voices when they call you 'The Kid' and we'll know why." Then she had whistled that Wild West Showdown tune and winked. Truthfully, I hadn't really minded the nickname, though. "The Kid" is a helluva lot better than "Incompetent Idiot," plus I think it has more to do with age than leadership ability and so I live with it. They all show me respect in the boardroom and I know I'm gaining more of it by the day, even with Gwen's father, Richard. I don't want anything I don't earn.

"Morning, Christine. How are you?" I ask, smiling.

"Great. The team is heading into the conference room right now. Coffee and bagels are already out. Your presentation is loaded on the laptop and the screen is down. Reports are at everyone's places."

"Thanks, Christine. We'd all be worthless without you."

"Tell me something I don't already know," she snorts and I grin at her.

I drop my stuff off in my office and shoot Evie a text in reply to her thanks.

Me: Anything for you. Headed in to a meeting. Have a good day/night at work. Can I call you tomorrow?

Evie: What if I say no?

I grin.

Me: I'll call you anyway. ;) Have a good day, Evie.

I'm glad to know that Evie is working tonight. Going to the benefit with Gwen is going to be bad enough as it is. If I knew I could potentially be with Evie instead, it'd be even worse.

****

It's a pretty uneventful day at the office and I'm able to start getting ready to leave by five o'clock. As I'm heading out, Christine says, "See you in your monkey suit later!" She's going to the benefit, too. It'll be nice to have someone there to chat with that I actually *like*. "Yeah, I'm taking Gwen," I say, grimacing.

"Why?!" She asks with a look of horror on her face. She's not exactly Gwen's number one fan. Gwen has been as much of a rude bitch to her as she is to everyone who she considers "beneath" her. For the tenth time today, I consider suddenly coming down with the stomach flu. I sigh. My loyalty to Seth wins out though and I resign myself, vowing to make it a quick evening, write a big check and be back at home before eleven o'clock. "Because I was trying to make nice and I ended up shooting myself in my own foot," I run my hand down my face, shaking my head.

"Jake, you don't need to try to be nice to that girl. I tried for years, every time she'd come by to visit her father, or during the time she had an internship here. She's just straight nasty, though. You can only be nice to someone for so long before your kindness starts making you feel like a doormat. I sure don't go out of my way to be her friend anymore. You shouldn't either. Plus, she doesn't want to be your *friend*. You trying just gives her more of an opportunity to get her claws in you."

I laugh a humorless laugh. "You're right. On all points." I smile at her. "Your kids are lucky to have a mom like you, you know that? I bet you give them great advice all the time."

"I give anyone great advice who will listen to it." She winks. "That includes you."

I grin at her. "Thanks, Christine. I'm glad you'll be there tonight."

"Me, too, and if you need a break from Phony Baloney, scratch the back of your neck and I'll pry her off you." She grins.

I laugh as I gather my stuff up and start walking toward the elevator. "Why am I afraid I'm going to have to take you up on that?"

****

I pull up in front of Gwen's father's home in Indian Hill and force myself out of the car. I'd rather be eating a Coney at Skyline *alone* than going to a catered, black tie dinner with Gwen. *No contest.* But here I am. Let's get this over with.

Even though I'm in a tux, I take the steps that lead up to their home two at a time and knock on the door with the gold, lion head knocker. It makes me think of Evie and I smile. I can't wait to call her tomorrow and—

The door swings open and Gwen catches me smiling to myself. *Damn it!* I do not want to give her the impression this is too pleasant for me. I go serious and say, "Hi, Gwen. You look nice." She looks like Christmas Barbie, swathed in tight, red velvet, adorned in gold jewelry and her hair in a big, blond, swirly up-do.

"Hey," she says, seductively, leaning against the doorframe. "Wanna come in for a few minutes? My father's already left for the benefit. We can practice being . . . *friendly*—" She raises her eyebrows.

I clench my jaw. "No, Gwen. I want to get there. As it is, we'll barely make the end of cocktail hour."

She doesn't make any attempt to hide her pout. "Fine," she says on a long sigh. "I'll just get my coat." She marches off to get it and I remain outside waiting for her.

She locks up and I open the car door for her and she slides in, making no attempt to pull her dress down when the high slit in it rides indecently high and lets me know she's not wearing underwear. I turn away quickly, slamming the door behind her. *What the fuck?* That stomach virus feels imminent.

"So, Jake," she coos, as I pull onto the street, "where's the after party? I haven't seen your new condo yet." I look over at her and she bats her eyelashes, smiling coyly. Did I really go through everything I did, all the hell, all the sessions with Doc, all the surgeries, all the struggles, to be sitting in my car, dying slowly of death by cloying perfume, with this clingy, uninteresting Fembot? Gwen is not the type of person I want as a friend, guilt or no. She's gotta be cut loose.

I completely ignore her comment and her blatant disregard for what I told her in my office this week, deciding the best tactic is to change the subject. "So how's your new job, Gwen?"

"Pfft," she half hisses, half sighs. "It's pointless." She studies her nails for a minute, a frown on her face. "Daddy wants me to 'gain an appreciation for hard work.' So annoying." She sighs again as if my heart should be breaking for her.

Jesus, she got a job at a prestigious law firm handed to her on a silver platter because her dad has connections. I'm practically sobbing my eyes out for her hard lot in life. It's not like I have much room to talk about getting handed a job, but I have the sense enough to know how fucking lucky I am in that regard.

I think of Evie, working her ass off as a maid, and doing it with dignity. She could teach Gwen a few lessons about an appreciation for hard work. I almost laugh out loud.

"What else would you do, Gwen? Shop all day?"

It's a rude thing to say, but, fuck, people like Gwen piss me off and my patience with her is wearing thin. She's so wrapped up in herself that she doesn't realize that the world extends beyond her own petty problems. She's too shallow to look around and marvel at all the gifts surrounding her, not one of which she actually had to work for. And I'm not even talking about the material wealth, I'm talking about a *family*, a safe place to land. I would have given my right arm for that, and Gwen complains about it. Fucking clueless.

She narrows her eyes at me.

"It's not a bad thing to support the economy, *Jake*. My shopping supports *jobs*. And by the way, do you think looking like this comes easily? I *work* at looking this amazing. It's a full time job in itself. There's highlighting, and waxing, and pumicing, and manicuring, and tanning and—"

I tune her out after that. Is she for real? Now I remember why I needed to be wasted to hang out with Gwen in the past.

I turn the music up and we ride in silence for the next five minutes, thank God. I'm fucking exhausted and I've only been with her for twenty minutes. We pull up in front of the Millennium Hotel and I leave my car with the valet.

As we're walking to the elevator, Gwen latches on to my arm. We get on the elevator and I shrug her off of me, giving her a pointed look. When I said friends, I did *not* mean friends with benefits. She's still not getting that.

We step off of the elevator and she latches back onto me. Jesus. Deep breath. *Two hours.*

I lead her over to the bar where I see a couple people from the company, including Christine, and we greet them. Christine introduces us to her husband Tom, whom I've never met and we all chat for a few minutes before a guy with a tray of champagne comes by. I take two and hand one to Gwen.

"Gwen," Christine says, when we've all taken a drink, "that's a lovely dress. It certainly doesn't give us any doubt as to what a lovely figure you have, does it?" She smiles brightly.

"Gwen runs her hands down her hips, smiling a big, fake smile. "Thank you, Christine. If you've got it, flaunt it, right? And if you don't . . . well . . ." She trails off, looking Christine up and down. Christine's husband almost chokes on his drink and I clench my jaw, thoroughly humiliated.

Christine looks like she's holding back a laugh though, and so I take a deep breath and say, "I'm going to find some appetizers. I'm starved." I turn around and I grit my teeth as Gwen turns with me, still latched to my arm.

I hear a small gasp and when I look up, *Evie* is standing directly in front of me in a serving uniform, a tray of appetizers in her hand. She looks frozen. My heart feels like it lurches toward her, and I can't help the smile that automatically spreads across my face. I want to run to her and scoop her up and kiss her all over her beautiful face. The unexpected sight of her is even more welcome after the last half an hour with Gwen. Oh shit, *Gwen*. Attached to my arm. *Fuck!*

"Evie," I say, pointedly taking Gwen's arm and removing it from mine. I feel her stiffen as I detach her but my eyes are glued to Evie who blinks and shoots me a fake smile. Shit.

"Jakey, do you *know* her?" I hear Gwen's bitchy voice coming up behind me, but I am physically unable to look away from Evie. *Jakey?* She's never once called me that before. I see Evie glance at Gwen, a look of hurt crossing her expression. This is one of the most fucked up situations I've ever been in. And that's saying something.

Her dark eyes are pools of hurt and confusion as she looks back at me and whispers, "Hi." I feel like a fucking jackass, even though I haven't done anything wrong. She doesn't know that. I need to grab her and pull her off somewhere so that I can explain this. Fuck, she's working. I don't want to jeopardize her job. I would never do that to her. Her job is very, very important to her. I know that.

I feel my jaw clenching as I answer Gwen, "Yes, I do know her. This is Evie Cruise." *The love of my life.* Evie glances over at Gwen questioningly and so I say, "This is Gwen Parker," gesturing my head toward Gwen's general area.

Evie nods toward her saying, "Hi," very quietly.

"I don't need an introduction, Jakey, I was just surprised that you know her," she says like the bitch she is, and then she hooks herself back onto my arm and grips more tightly when I attempt to move away.

The blood starts pounding through my brain and I feel my jaw ticking against my will.

Evie's eyes move to Gwen's arms gripping me and she says very quietly, her brow furrowing, "Right. Well, have a nice evening." And as she's turning away, I have to physically restrain myself from reaching out and grabbing her and hauling her off to my car. I can see that her hands are shaking and as she turns, her tray tips forward and I hear a loud, wet plop as a cracker full of caviar falls directly on the top of Gwen's foot. Bulls Eye! Score! I very, very barely contain the laugh that threatens, but that's quickly squelched as Gwen screeches, "Oh my God! Do you know how much these shoes cost? No, of course you don't! These are fourteen hundred dollar shoes!" And, Christ, that shit is funny, too, and I almost laugh again until I register the look on Evie's face. Her cheeks are flushed, eyes wide and she's humiliated. Fuck! My instincts roar through me and everything in me is screaming, *protect*! For so many, many years, that was my *job*, and I took it very seriously. Evie doesn't even have any idea how many times I got my ass kicked over her, or kicked someone's ass. I always preferred to do the ass kicking, but the outcome was somewhat irrelevant to me as long as the douchebag who insulted her, whether to her face or behind her back, learned why that was not acceptable. Mean kids always hone in on the weakest of their species, and who is weaker than a foster kid with low self-esteem and worn-ass clothes? Shit, we were like giant targets walking through school. That wasn't going to happen to Evie though, not if I had anything to say about it.

Before I can even react, the blond guy who brought the tray of drinks around earlier rushes up to Evie, whispers something close to her face and takes her tray, shooting me a death glare. Ouch. And who the fuck is he? I glare back at him, my jaw clenching even harder. *FUCK!*

Evie bends down to meet Gwen who is swiping at her foot and muttering to herself about minimum wage workers, and says, "I'm so sorry. Please, let me help you clean it off. If you'll come with me to the ladies room, I can use a cleaning cloth on it. I bet it will come right off."

"Fine!" Gwen hisses and I think it's probably good that Evie is leading her away from me because telling Gwen to go fuck herself would feel so damn good right now, and I honestly don't know if I could have helped myself.

The blond guy approaches me again, holding out a tray of champagne and I take two, downing them both, one after the other. I stare back at him expressionless as he shoots me one last, disgusted glare. Someone else who has Evie's back. Not surprising.

I stand staring in the direction of the bathroom, waiting for them to emerge, needing a glimpse of Evie to make sure she's okay.

Christine, who must have watched that whole exchange go down comes up and gently touches my arm. "You okay?" she asks gently.

"No, not so much."

She gives me a concerned look. "I'll make sure Gwen's occupied if you want to go talk to that girl."

I sigh, running my hand down my face. "I can't, Christine. She's working. I'd only make it worse."

She purses her lips and heaves a big sigh. "Okay." She pauses and then, "What's her name?"

I glance at her quickly. "Evie."

"Does Evie know you love her?"

I'm quiet for several moments. "She did once. But no, not now."

Christine is quiet, too, probably wondering what that means. "Well, then, you find a way to remind her."

I look at her fully now. "I'm trying."

I see Evie emerge from the bathroom first, a wounded look on her face as she scurries out the door of the banquet room. Fuck! Gwen is such a bitch! I hear Christine say warningly, "Jake—" but I don't listen. I storm off, and slam into the women's bathroom which I should have done ten minutes ago. What was I thinking leaving Evie alone with a calculating witch like Gwen?

She's standing at the bathroom mirror, primping, a look of satisfaction on her face. "Well, hello," she says, turning, and leaning up against the sink.

"What'd you say to her?" I demand, adrenaline racing through my body.

She scoffs and turns back to the mirror. "Who cares? She's some little serving girl, Jake. Seriously?"

I stare at her incredulously for several beats.

"That's it, Gwen. I'm done making nice with you out of sheer guilt. You're a spoiled, thoughtless bitch and so fucking boring, I can barely keep myself awake when you're talking. Christ, you should bottle your personality and sell it as a sleep aid."

She turns around slowly, her mouth dropping open and her eyes narrowing. She crosses her arms and hisses, "I thought you were classier than that, Jake, but I see that you can take the boy out of the ghetto, but you can't take the ghetto—"

I can't help it, I burst out laughing. All the anger, all the stress of the last thirty minutes just boils over into a fit of hilarity. She's so utterly and completely clueless, there's nothing else to do but laugh. "Did you just say 'ghetto,' Gwen? Holy shit, where'd you hear that? A 50 Cent song blasting out of the satellite radio in your Lexus?" It suddenly strikes me as so fucking funny, I almost double over. Instead, I lean against the wall, forcing my laughter back. I had actually forgotten she even knew I was adopted. She had never brought it up before. Probably helped her sleep better at night not to think about associating with someone who wasn't born with a silver spoon in their mouth.

Gwen is still staring at me, narrow eyed and seething as my laughter dies.

I take a step closer to her as I say, "You have no idea why this is funny Gwen, and you never will, but let me tell you a couple things. You have no idea about me. Not one. Fucking. Thing. And you don't know anything about her either and you never will. But here's what you do need to know. You will never come near me again, you got that? If I see you at an event, turn and walk the other way, and if I accidentally run into you on the fucking street, pretend like you never saw me. Now, unfortunately, we're sitting at the same table tonight, but there is no need for us to say another word to each other. If you need the fucking salt, ask someone else to pass it. When dinner is over, you will get a ride home with your daddy because, frankly, another twenty-minute car ride with you sounds intolerable. We clear?"

She stares at me for several seconds, her eyes still narrowed, before finally hissing, "You'll regret this, *Jake*. Consider our friendship over."

"Thank God." I walk out of the bathroom just as an older woman is going in.

"Oh!" she exclaims.

"Sorry, wrong door," I mumble.

I walk into the men's room and brace my hands on the counter of the sink for a minute collecting myself. Could this night have gone to any more shit? I splash some cold water on my face and as I'm grabbing a rolled up towel out of the tray on the counter, I notice the *World's Greatest Mints*. I stare down at them, a smile spreading across my face. I grab one and put it in my pocket.

CHAPTER THIRTEEN

I wake up the next morning and grimace at the memory of the night before. Sitting through dinner was torture. Every time the door to the kitchen swung open, my heart leaped into my throat. But I never saw Evie again. I gave the mint to her blond friend, who I was pretty sure was gay, after watching him swish his hips through the room. Straight men don't walk that way. He had looked at me dubiously when I handed him the mint for Evie, but he stuck it in his pocket anyway and walked back to the kitchen.

After dinner, I had written a check, bid on a few items up for auction, and then I had retrieved my car and headed home. I wrestled with myself over calling Evie, but I knew she probably didn't get off work until late and that the last thing she probably wanted to deal with was me. *Shit.* I could barely sleep, but I had to put her first and leave this until morning, even though every instinct in me was screaming to drive over to her apartment and explain myself. I started writing her a text message but after sitting there for a good five minutes not knowing what to say that would come across in the right way, I threw my phone on my bedside table and collapsed back on my bed.

I shower and get dressed, and then head over to Evie's apartment. I'm all worked up with the need to explain to her what the night before was about. I need to make this right if I'm going to be able to keep sane today. I ring her apartment from the front door buzzer and when there's no answer, I take out my phone, look up the Hilton's phone number and dial as I pace in front of her apartment. When I get through to the housekeeping manager, I tell him that I'm supposed to pick Evie Cruise up today but forgot the time she told me to be there. With no questioning whatsoever, he tells me what time she gets off work. That pisses me off slightly, even though I got the information I wanted.

Even though it's Saturday, I have a couple morning meetings scheduled with Preston and then the head engineers. We're up against a couple testing deadlines and so the team has agreed to sacrifice a couple weekends in order to meet them. As much as I'd like to obsess about Evie, I have to put my corporate hat on and be present for work. I owe it to all the people working extra hours for me. I finish up the first round of meetings just in time to catch Evie getting off work.

I drive quickly downtown and pull up near the bus stop that I know Evie takes, and park illegally as I wait for her to come around the corner. I don't feel nervous, just determined. I'm going to make her understand what last night was about. There's no other option. There is no way in hell that *Gwen*, of all people, is going to come in the way of what I had started to re-build with Evie. Un-fucking-thinkable.

After ten minutes or so, I see Evie appear around the corner of the hotel. Thankfully there's no one behind me as I pull up slowly next to her as she walks down the block. She looks over at me and I lean over the seat and smile. "Want a ride little girl?" I tease, trying to coax a smile from her, too. No go. She looks over at me as if I'm a fly that just landed on her dinner. Great. That's okay—I'm willing to work for this.

"Funny. No, Jake. I'm good with the bus." She keeps walking.

"Evie, we need to talk," I say seriously, but she doesn't even look back my way and instead keeps walking.

"No, Jake, we don't," she says.

Fuck me, there are cars parked along the street from this point forward so I pull to the side and get out of my car. I would leave my car in the middle of the street if I had to.

As I jog up to her, she sits down on one of the empty bus stop bench seats and cranes her neck to see if the bus is coming. Oh hell no, I *will* jump on that bus with her.

Because there are people milling around in front of her, I stand behind her and slightly to the left as I say, "Listen, Evie, last night was not what you think it was."

"Jake," she interrupts, "It's been a long day. I'm really asking you to just leave this, okay? You should have told me you have a girlfriend. You didn't. It's done. Walk away." Then she turns away from me. I can feel my blood start to boil, not because I blame Evie for her anger, but because it's fucking Gwen who is between us right now. It's too ludicrous for words. I clench my jaw.

"Gwen is not my girlfriend, Evie. I hope you'd think more of me than that after the time we've spent together."

"Jake, again, walk away."

"I'm not gonna do that, Evie," I say. No way in hell.

I see her heave a big impatient breath and purse those beautiful lips of hers. She's pissed. She stands up and gets right in my face, eyes narrowed. "Clue in, Jake. You don't know me. You think you do, but you *don't*. You think you know what type of person I am, but you have no idea. And so, you don't get to do this. You don't get to interrupt my life over and over again and then think that I will be grateful to you for gracing my life with your very presence. After last night, I think it's perfectly clear that there is no reason for you to be here. So I am asking you again if we can have this conversation another time like *never*?"

As she goes to turn away from me, I grab her hand and pull her back toward me, right up to my face. Oh hell no. This girl is going to listen to me if I have to pin her against the wall to make her do it. Would I really pin her against the wall to make her listen to me? Yeah, fuck yeah, I would. But I'm kinda hoping that scenario is not going to go down because then I'll really piss her off. I'd really rather have this conversation in my car, but I guess that's not going to happen.

"It wasn't my intention to do this on a street corner, but this stubborn girl is gonna make me," I say, mostly to myself. Okay, though. I'm flexible. I take a deep breath as Evie narrows her eyes at me again. But she's not trying to move away. This is a start.

I don't have to tell Evie who I am to let her know what was crystal clear to me simply from watching her live her life for a little over a week. I could very *well* have been a stranger and still figured out how amazing she is. "You think I don't know you, Evie? I'll tell you what I know about you. That week I was following you, I know that you took the goddamn BUS to an old man's house to drop off cookies."

Her brows snap down and she stares at me for a second. "Mr. Cooper?" she finally asks, shaking her head in confusion, her eyes losing some of the anger they just held. "He lived next to the house where I lived for four years. He was always nice to me. He's widowed. Lonely. He really likes my chocolate chip cookies."

"It's a two hour round trip bus ride, Evie."

She's still looking at me like I might be slightly crazy as she takes a deep breath. "Jake, I'm sure there's a point here but—"

"That guy across the hall was going to kill me before he let me even think about so much as making you uncomfortable."

"Maurice?" she says, scrunching her face up in confusion. God, she really has no fucking clue how she affects other people. "He's a really protective guy."

I keep going, trying to make my point, "Like the guy last night who practically melted me with the angry lasers coming out of his eyes after he thought I disrespected you in public?" I ask gently, my hold on her hand loosening because I don't think she's going to run now.

"Landon?" she asks. "He's one of my best friends, he—"

Jesus, am I not making this crystal clear to her? I've never met anyone who has a harder time understanding a compliment. I get it, believe me, I get it. But it's still fucking frustrating when you're the one trying to deliver the praise. It occurs to me that she probably hasn't had a lot of heartfelt compliments in her life since I left and it's no wonder she doesn't recognize one when she sees it. This thought makes an intense flood of possessiveness fill my chest and I make the vow to keep telling her how amazing she is every day until I leave this earth. If by some horror she rejects me once she knows my whole disgusting truth, I will have it written in the sky every morning over her apartment. It feels like the greatest travesty of justice on the planet for this girl not to understand the depth of her own beauty. For *my* girl not to understand the depth of her own beauty. "Evie, I think you're failing to grasp what I'm saying to you and so I'm going to spell it out for you here, baby."

I stare straight into her widened eyes as I say, "You say 'please' and 'thank you' to everyone, Evie. You almost bumped into a cocker spaniel being walked by his owner and when you ducked around him, you said, 'excuse me.' You said 'excuse me' to a dog. And I bet you didn't even think twice about that. And that's because your manners are so deeply ingrained in you, that that is second nature. And given what I know about your past, I'm gonna guess that no one fucking taught you that. That is just all Evie."

She's staring at me, unspeaking and so I consider that a good sign to continue.

"What I *know* about you, is that people who are lucky enough to have your trust and your friendship, it is clear that they would have your back to within an inch of their life and that is because you give them *you*, and they know that when they have you, they have a fuck of a lot.

"And, Evie, when you walk away from people, even strangers, you gotta know that their eyes follow you. And I'll tell you why, because I've felt it myself. It's because they don't want to see the light that is Evie, the light that is *you*, walking away from them. They want to see it coming *toward* them and staying *with* them."

"Uh—" she starts to say something, but I'm on a roll and frankly, this is my favorite subject and so I don't want to stop.

"So maybe I don't know what your favorite meal is, maybe I don't even know your birthday. But what I do know is *beautiful*, and Evie, what I do know lets me know that I want to know more."

The fact is, I *do* know her birthday. I know it as well as I know my own, but it wouldn't matter if I didn't. It wouldn't matter if I didn't know any more than what it took to figure out in a week and a half. And I know that for a fact, because it took me fifteen minutes to know she was someone I was going to fall in love with when I was fucking eleven years old. The day I first noticed her, sitting at that dinner table wearing her heart on her sleeve, she brought me back to *life* and made me hope. In those first few minutes, that's what she had done. And that's why my betrayal of her made me hate myself so goddamn much.

This all swirls through my mind at lightning speed as we stare into each other's eyes, standing at a bus stop on a city street. I'm lost in the depths of the dark brown windows to her soul.

"Um, Jake," she finally says quietly.

"What, Evie?"

"I missed my bus. I'm gonna need a ride."

Her words penetrate and I can't help the giant grin that I feel spreading across my face.

I lead her to my car and deposit her in the passenger side as I make my way around and get in the driver's side.

I pull onto the street. I need to make sure Evie is perfectly clear about Gwen, too. "I want you to listen to me about last night."

She glances over at me, biting the inside of her cheek. *Her tell*.

"Gwen's father is the CFO of my father's company. And when I say 'my father's company,' I really mean to say 'my company,' because that's what it is now, but that's a transition my brain is still working on." I didn't even realize that was true until I just said it, but it is.

"Anyway, I've known Gwen and her father for a long time and over the years Gwen and I have spent some time together here and there, although I always made it clear to her that I wasn't interested in anything more than what we had, and what we had was very little. Gwen made it clear that she was interested in more, and Gwen was raised to believe that she is entitled to what she wants and that eventually, if she whines enough, she'll get it."

She's quiet, just listening and I go on, "When I moved here, I tried to be a friend to her because, despite the fact that Gwen is a superficial bitch, I treated her disrespectfully over the years and in part that was because a side benefit of screwing Gwen was screwing my father, who was embarrassed at my treatment of a colleague's daughter."

I cringe internally, still ashamed of all the stupid shit I did over the years, but knowing why I did it. After a minute, I go on.

"I had arranged the event last night with Gwen months ago and I couldn't get out of it. It's a cause that is important to me and I didn't think it was any real skin off my teeth to bring Gwen as I'd planned. Three seconds in and I realized that I was mistaken on that front, and that was even before I saw you there."

She's silent for a second, frowning. "Gwen made it sound like things were *very* current with you," she says, staring straight ahead.

Oh, I'm sure she did. I never did find out *exactly* what Gwen said to Evie in the bathroom, but I'm pretty sure I can figure out that it was something to the effect of, *he's mine and you're less than dirt.*

"That's because Gwen saw the way I looked at you, she saw your beauty, and Gwen did what she thought would work to keep you away from me.

"I know that Gwen made you feel less-than because that is what Gwen does best, but, Evie, you could be wearing a gunny sack, rolling around in mud, and you would have more class in your little pinky than Gwen has in her whole designer-clad body. And Gwen knows that. And she hates that. And that is why she went out of her way to make you feel that way.

"It was killing me not to bust into that kitchen and pin you down and explain the situation to you, but you were working and I wasn't gonna make things worse for you."

She's quiet for a good minute and I see her looking around the inside of my car and then glance down at her uniform and I know exactly what she's thinking. She's letting Gwen's venom infect her and she's thinking that maybe she *is* less-than. After I just told her how amazing she is, she's letting the memory of Gwen's words take over. It pisses me off.

"Jake," she starts, quietly, "I might not be—"

I pull into a parking space, shut the car off and turn to her. "No,

Evie. Whatever you're about to say, consider whether it goes in direct contrast to everything I've just said to you in the past half an hour and if it does, just throw it out, okay?"

She stares at me again and then closes her mouth and quietly says, "Okay."

I grin at her. That's my girl. "Good answer."

As I'm walking around my car to let her out, I make a decision. She's mine. I need to start making that very, *very* clear. This type of stupid misunderstanding will not happen again. "I'm picking you up at six thirty tonight and I'm making you dinner. Do you eat steak?"

"Yes," she whispers.

Her eyes warm and she sways toward me, igniting a fierce possessiveness. "Do you work tomorrow?"

"No, day off."

I walk her to her door and she stands staring at me, and so I take her keys from her, open her outside door, and give her a little push inside. "See you tonight. And, Evie, pack an overnight bag." Very, very, *very* clear.

"What—" she sputters, but I let the door close behind me, not allowing her to argue.

CHAPTER FOURTEEN

Dr. Fox is sitting beside my bed in his usual spot, leaned back, one foot on his opposite knee, notepad in hand. He repeats the question he asked me minutes ago, that I still haven't answered. I'm staring out the window, anger simmering in my brain.

"Can we talk about Lauren?"

His voice snaps me back to myself and I realize I'm clenching my jaw against my will.

"There's nothing to talk about."

"I think we both know that's not true."

"All right, then, that subject is off limits."

"You need to talk about this, son."

"I don't talk about her. Ever. She doesn't exist to me."

"Saying it doesn't make it true. I think you already know that."

A cloud of rage has settled in my head now, and I'm fighting against the images that assault me, one by one by fucking one. I feel like I'm about to combust, my hands fisting in my lap, my entire body tense.

"Why is it that you won't talk about her?"

That's when I feel it happen. I snap. I think I even hear the sound effect of each thought in my head bending and finally breaking as the cloud overtakes every cognitive function. Suddenly I am nothing more than pure anger, my brain filled with, and controlled by, a roiling tumor of fury. And it's metastasizing by the minute, cells multiplying, spreading, and overtaking.

"Because I hate her!" I yell, picking my food tray up off the table next to my bed, and flinging it violently at the wall. Uneaten food splatters and the tray hits the floor with a clang.

"Who do you hate, son?"

"Lauren! I fucking hate her! I hate her!"

I sound like a toddler throwing a tantrum. I'm vaguely aware of this and yet my rage is so all-consuming, I don't care. Fury rules and I am just along for the ride.

I swing my legs off the side of my bed and start sweeping things off every surface in my room, grinding out, "I hate her. I hate her. I hate her," with every crash. My breath is coming fast now and I feel the words starting to hitch in my throat. I feel crazed with rage as I hobble from one side of the room to the next, yelling and destroying, a pain-cyclone of anger and bitterness. Hurricane Leo. Category five.

"Who do you hate, Jake?" Dr. Fox's voice comes to me through the red noise pulsing through my brain.

"I told you! I fucking told you! Lauren! I hate her! I hate her! I hate her!" I continue to half grind out, half yell, and half pant. My voice is coming to me from what seems to be very far away. I can't feel my body any longer. I feel like one big whirling ball of emotion, completely out of control.

In my peripheral vision, I briefly make note that a nurse with a stricken look opens the door halfway to see what is causing what must sound like a barroom brawl in my hospital room.

Dr. Fox holds his hand up to her in a stop gesture and nods to her, and she backs out of the room quickly, her eyes wide.

"I hate her! I hate her! I hate her!" I grind out, overturning the table next to my bed.

"Who do you hate, son?" Dr. Fox asks again, quietly.

I whirl around to him and my father's voice, that bastard who called himself my father, comes to me suddenly. I see his face in front of me, filled with disgust, swimming in my cloudy, fury-riddled vision. I feel the rage bloom larger in my chest and I pick up a chair and hurl it across the room. It bounces off the tall, plastic garbage can in the corner and clatters to the floor, one leg snapping off. "My father!" I bellow. "I hate him! I fucking hate that rat-fucking bastard! I hate every bone in his disgusting body! I want to fucking kill him! I want to bash his fucking head in!"

I continue chanting my mantra of hate, turning to my bed and punching the high, completely upraised end of my mattress again and again and again. I grunt with every blow, an inhuman growl coming from deep in my chest.

"Who do you hate?" Dr. Fox's voice comes from directly behind me, still gentle and controlled.

"Stop asking me that! I told you! Aren't you fucking listening to me? My father! My mother! Lauren! I hate them all! I fucking hate them! Fuck! Fuck them all! Fuck them! I hate them!" My voice cracks at the end and I'm breathing so hard that I feel like I might hyperventilate. A lifetime of built up rage over selfishness that steals dignity and cruelty that preys on the weak is coursing through my veins, a fire looking to consume me from the inside out.

"Who do you hate, son?"

My blows become softer, my defenseless mattress getting a momentary reprieve from my rage-filled beating. My breath hitches in my throat again, and now I can feel the tears burning behind my eyes, wanting to fall. This spurs my anger again and so my blows become harder and I am almost choking now. The rage begins to abate, and just beyond it is the grief and I feel it coming at me like a wave. I'm powerless to fight it. All I can do is wait as it washes over me, drenching the fiery ball of anger, putting out that flame, but dragging me under, tossing me, flailing and defenseless against its unrelenting power. It is bigger than the rage, bigger than the bitterness, bigger than the guilt, and I can do nothing but submit to it. I choke out, "Me! I hate me! I hate myself! I hate myself! I fucking hate myself!" And now the tears are coming, and I'm choking on my words and sputtering and punching and yelling. "I fucking hate myself! I hate myself! Fuck! Fuck! "I hear myself sobbing and muttering, and somewhere, from a distance, I think the words I hear are, "Why? Why? Why wasn't I enough? I'm worthless. Why did I do that? Why did I let her do that? Why did I do that? Why? Why? I hate myself. I hate myself. I hate myself. I'm worthless. I hate myself."

"Who do you hate, Jake?" Dr. Fox asks one final time.

"Me. I hate me," I say through panting, hitching breaths. "I hate me. Oh God. Oh God. I hate me."

Then I feel his hand grip my shoulder and he leaves it there as I bury my face in to the upraised pile of pillows that miraculously held their position through my pounding, and I finally wail for the first time since Evie held me in her arms on a rooftop under a summer, night sky and told me I had the heart of a lion. I wail for Seth, and I wail for all the hope I held onto day after day, year after year that my parents would find something in me worth loving, I give in completely and let the grief and longing for Evie consume me, wailing for my loss and my own feelings of self-hatred at my abandonment. I wail for what I did with Lauren, my disgust with myself, and all the hatred that has filled my heart for so many, many years. I wail until my voice is hoarse and I am drained of emotion. When my head clears and my own hiccupping and sputtering has trailed away, I come back into myself and note that Dr. Fox's hand is still gripping my shoulder tightly, anchoring me.

I remain still for several minutes until I feel calm enough to lift my head. I stand up straight and turn around slowly, looking at Dr. Fox. He has a somber look on his face, but there is absolutely no pity in his eyes, and I'm grateful for that. I let out a ragged breath and sit back down on my bed, quiet, letting my ragged breathing return to normal. After a few minutes I look around the room. It looks like a crazed animal tore it apart. I suppose that's exactly what did happen. I let out a humorless laugh and run my hand through my short hair.

"That must have looked really pathetic. I just made a total fool out of myself didn't I?" I grimace.

"Yes. Finally. Maybe we can get started now." His voice is gentle.

I look up at him and I can't help it. I laugh. And then I laugh harder at what we must look like right now. Me, a gimpy, swollen, *bandaged mess, sitting amongst the destruction of my hospital room, and Einstein there, white hair awry, sitting casually in his chair as if this happens every damn day. Both of us laughing now for some godforsaken reason I can't for the life of me even figure out.*

CHAPTER FIFTEEN

After another couple hours of meetings at work, I head to the grocery store to pick up dinner ingredients. I cooked for myself quite a bit when I moved out of Phil and Lauren's house and I enjoy it. I pause after gathering all the ingredients I need for dinner, and then walk over to the health and beauty section of the grocery store and throw a box of condoms in my cart. I don't want to be presumptuous with Evie and I'd sure as hell never pressure her, but it's good to be prepared. And I don't have one single condom anywhere. I haven't been with anyone in well over a year. I wish it had been in well over forever.

I'm almost afraid of how much I want her in my bed. I wonder if she's been with anyone sexually and the jealousy that flares inside of me makes me clench my jaw and move the thought aside immediately. Through the years, I pictured her with someone else sometimes just to torture myself. I felt like I deserved the agony it brought. It accomplished what I intended it to—it made me hate myself even more, but that's part of the person I'm trying to leave behind. Why shouldn't she have been with someone else? Still, it fucks me up to think about it.

Whether she's been with someone or not, she might not be ready to be with me, who as far as she knows, she practically just met. Still, the attraction between us is palpable and I know she feels it, too. And that brings a comfort level that even I wasn't prepared for. Either way, I just want her to stay with me tonight. I want her under my roof, where she belongs.

I drop the groceries off at my condo and quickly unpack them before having to rush out the door to pick up my girl. *My girl*. I smile to myself.

I drive over to Evie's wondering if she'll really even pack an overnight bag. It's not like I waited for an answer and I wouldn't be able to blame her if she wasn't ready. Thinking of having her all to myself in my condo, kissing her, touching her has the blood flowing south, and I adjust myself in my seat.

I knock on her door and when she opens it, I note two things immediately. One, she looks gorgeous, and two, there's a small overnight bag in her hand. My heart soars and I can't help the smile that takes over my face. She's going to stay the night with me. My heart starts hammering in my chest. Part of me feels like a nervous teenager, and part of me feels like throwing her down on the floor right here in the hallway and claiming her as mine. A small, overnight bag has me feeling simultaneously terrified and invincible.

She knocks on Maurice's door calling "'Night, Maurice!" as we're walking to the front and he calls back, "'Night, Evie," which reminds me that any Evie-claiming on hallway floors will most likely be frowned upon by Maurice.

We drive to my condo, and I tell her about my meetings that morning and a little bit about the deadlines the company is up against. She listens attentively, asking a few questions. It feels unbelievably good to talk to Evie about everyday stuff going on in our lives, and not everyday fucked up shit like what we were up against when we were kids. God, I've been craving this for what feels like my whole damn life. I used to dream about what it would feel like to come home to my girl at the end of a workday. Back then, I had no idea I'd be running a company, but I knew I would work hard every day of my life to give us more than what our parents had given us. I was going to make her safe, make her happy. I was going to make a *home* with her.

And now . . . I'm going to show her how deep my feelings are for her and make her trust down to her soul that I want to take care of her. Because I do. And then when I tell her who I am she'll know who we can be together.

We pull into my garage and I take her bag from her and walk her up the back stairway to the elevator, not letting go of her hand.

We walk into my condo and I glance back at Evie as I throw my keys on the table next to my door. She's taking it all in, a small frown on her face. I almost laugh. I don't like it either. It's sleek and modern and cold. "Corporate condo. You don't like it."

She looks horrified. "No, no!" she says, "It's really stylish. I was just thinking that it needs a little warmth. Maybe some colorful throw pillows or something." She looks down and starts biting the inside of her cheek. I smile.

"I agree. I just don't know how long I'll be in this place. I'd like to buy something eventually." I try not to let my mind go to a place where we are picking out a home together. *Slow down.*

I lead her inside and take her jacket and hang it up on the coat hooks in my foyer area. When I turn around, she's at the window, staring out at the city, the lights from the Horseshoe Casino shining in the distance.

A warmth spreads through my chest as I watch her standing in my condo. It's where she belongs. It's where she's always belonged. *With me.* The grief of all the years we missed out on hovers in the background but I push it away. That's not for tonight. Tonight is about us. Tonight is about *only* us.

I walk to her and wrap my arms around her, pulling her tight against me. I live in the moment, soaking it in, inhaling the smell of her hair, the feel of her delicate body wrapped in my arms, her warmth pressed against me. I remember this so well. It was always like this. She always had a way of soothing me, simply with her touch. How did I doubt it would always be this way? Then, now, a million lifetimes from this one. My Evie, my heart, my savior. *My lion tamer.*

I lower my head and brush her hair to the side and lower my lips to the back of her neck, nuzzling the satiny skin there. She shivers and I feel myself swell in my pants. "God, Evie, you feel so good. You smell so good. You undo me. And I haven't even had you yet. What will that do to me?"

I feel her stiffen. "Jake—" she starts, turning in my arms and bringing hers up around my neck until I'm staring into her eyes. "About that—"

"You're nervous." *Damn.* That's okay though. She can set the pace. This is her show.

"Yes. No. I mean—" She shakes her head, laughing a small laugh.

It *is* soon, I guess. I mean, it's not—it's four years overdue. I wish that life had worked out differently so that I had swooped her up on her eighteenth birthday and married her that very day. But as for the reality of now, we've really just begun. Still, I think she feels what I feel. Either way, I want it to be completely her choice.

"How about I make you dinner, we talk, hang out, and then if you want to sleep in the guest room, I'm okay with that tonight, all right? I'd like you in my bed. But I want it to be your call and if you're not ready, then you sleep in the guest room. I just want you here tonight, okay?"

Her eyes search mine for several seconds. "Okay," she whispers.

"Good," I say, my eyes moving to her pretty mouth, so incredibly kissable. I press my lips against hers, smiling as I take her bottom lip between my teeth, teasing her gently. She melts into me as I continue licking and sucking at her lips, but not going further. I want her to take the lead, to know that I'm giving that to her right now. She has no idea what this means to me to be able to do that, to willingly give a woman control sexually. Up until now, the whole point, most of the time, was to *be* in control, to take that part of myself back. But with Evie, I not only feel safe, but I'll do anything to make *her* feel safe, too.

Finally, after about a thousand years, she makes a frustrated little sound in her throat and slides her tongue into my mouth. *Oh, shit, that's so fucking sexy.* I moan deep and my cock jumps in my pants.

She slides one of her hands down my back and up under the hem of my un-tucked shirt and runs her fingernails lightly against my skin. I'm going up in flames. Nothing has ever felt as good as this.

Evie tilts her head and our kiss goes deeper, blood pounding harder and faster to my erection. The taste of her is like a drug and I'm completely lost in the feel of her against me, the taste of her, the very *idea* of her. I'm awestruck at these new feelings coursing through me. This is what physical closeness is supposed to be like. The very thought of everything I've experienced up to this moment is suddenly colored with even more sickness, and the beauty, the *rightness*, of this moment is highlighted against those cloudy flashes of ugly memory.

She runs her other hand up the back of my neck, into my hair, sifting and stroking, and I register that that feels great right before I register that her fingers are tracing my scar. *Fuck!* I tear my lips off hers, gathering myself.

"What happened to you, Jake?" she asks, frowning.

Tell the truth but keep it vague. Tonight is not for this. I pause before saying quietly, "Remember the stupid shit I told you I did to earn my father's contempt?"

She nods, still frowning.

"Some of that resulted in me tearing the back of my head open. Someday I'll tell you all about it, Evie, I promise. But how about right now I get dinner started?"

She frowns and reaches her hand up to my hair and traces my scar again. The tenderness of her touch is something only she has ever given me. I close my eyes and take her hand from my scar and bring it to my lips to kiss it. "So damn sweet," I say. Because that's exactly what she is.

I lead her to the kitchen and pull out a barstool for her.

"Can I pour you a glass of wine and take a few minutes to change out of this suit?" I ask her. I had only taken the time to remove my tie and un-tuck my shirt after dropping off the groceries since I was running a few minutes behind, and I didn't want her to wait for me. Also, after that kiss, I need to douse myself in a freezing shower if I'm going to be able to focus on cooking an edible dinner.

"How about you go change and I'll open the wine and do the pouring," she says, smiling.

"Perfect." I tell her where everything is and then walk back to my room.

I let the water run cold for a couple minutes before switching it to hot and soaping up. Ten minutes later I'm changed and walking back into the kitchen where Evie is now sitting at the counter with two glasses of red wine in front of her. She hands me one and says, "Red. Hope that's okay. Goes with red meat and all." She looks uncertain, sweet.

I smile and extend my glass to hers. "To beginnings," I say. *To new beginnings.*

As I start taking ingredients out of the fridge, I say, "Can I ask you a question? You told me the other night that you didn't date in high school. Why not?" I'm hoping she'll give me a better idea of what her life was like after I left. I know that I might be torturing myself with this information, but I need to know what she's been through.

She's quiet for a minute, seeming to consider whether she's going to answer me or not, when she puts her wine down and starts, "When I was fifteen, my foster mom, Jodi, was diagnosed with cancer and she and her husband decided they couldn't foster anymore. I wasn't close to either of them, they were mostly disinterested in us girls who lived with them. They weren't unkind, just sort of indifferent and checked out. They watched a lot of TV and didn't take a big interest in getting to know who any of us were. We co-existed and they mostly gave us what we needed physically, but emotionally, they were not parents to us, at least not in the way I define parenthood. But I was comfortable where I was, I liked the house, I liked the girls I lived with, and I thought life was as okay for me as it was gonna be in that situation.

"Anyway, when I was moved, I moved in with another couple and they made no bones about the fact that me and the other girls living there were drains on them, even though, as far as I could tell, the main reason we were there was for the checks we brought in. Me and Genevieve and Abby, the other girls who lived there, were mostly their slaves. We cooked, we cleaned, and we took care of their six-year-old twin boys who, it must be said, were good birth control for us girls if that was what they were trying to teach us. Our foster parents sat on their butts and if they wanted something, they hollered at us to run and fetch it for them. My foster mom, Carol, constantly made remarks about me, my body, my hair, my lack of personality, just being nasty. She was specifically mean to me, but she had an equal opportunity policy when it came to our care. She didn't spend one more cent than she had to on our needs, which meant that our clothes were constantly old and too small. At school, girls made fun of me because they thought I wore my clothes overly tight to get the boys to notice me. They called me a slut and worse and the boys treated me like one and so I steered clear of everyone as much as possible.

"I wasn't exactly brimming with self confidence as it was, but Carol made it her job to make me feel even worse about myself. This didn't exactly make me eager to put myself out there as far as making friends or dating. I ate my lunch in the library every day, and I went home after school and cleaned Carol and Billy's house. The day I turned eighteen, I got a job at the Hilton, and moved out with the intention of sleeping on Genevieve's couch for three months. She had moved out of our foster home and in with her boyfriend six months earlier and told me I could stay there until I had enough money saved up for a security deposit on an apartment. Two months into my stay, her boyfriend made a pass at me, Gen threw me out and I had nowhere to go, and so I worked during the day, went to the library after work and slept at a table in the corner for three hours until they closed and then wandered to several different coffee shops nursing coffees until it was time to go back to work, where thankfully, they have a shower in the employee restroom that they don't mind us using.

"I slept at a shelter downtown one night but an old man tried to crawl into my cot with me in the middle of the night, and someone stole the pair of shoes I had left at the end of my bed before I went to sleep. I couldn't risk someone stealing the money I had saved for an apartment, which I was carrying all in cash. I would have been right back where I started, and that was unthinkable."

I'm taking each and every one of her words into my soul, letting them dissolve into the very fiber of who I am, forcing myself to picture her alone and scared, sleeping at a table in the library, wandering around the city alone, nowhere to go. I want to start throwing things; I want to beat my fists into someone's face. I'm not sure who I want my victim to be. Probably myself. I need to be here for her though. I need to keep my own feelings of self-punishment for what I didn't do for her, at bay.

My mind flashes to a time when we were about twelve and thirteen and I saw a small form she had filled out from some "Giving Tree" crap that her foster parents had given her that some charity was collecting for foster kids. I had gotten one, too, but I had crumpled mine up and threw it away. I didn't want some well-off family picking out some shit for me and driving home in their minivan to eat roast beef around the family dining table, feeling like they were such super people, *giving back to the community*. Just the thought of it pissed me off.

But I got a glimpse of the one Evie had filled out when it fell from her backpack. She had flushed and quickly stuffed it back in, and I pretended I hadn't read it but I had. She had written in that she wanted her own pillow and pillowcase. I don't know why that was important to her and I never asked. Maybe because she moved around enough to feel like if she had one thing to take with her that was hers and permanent, something to provide comfort, it wouldn't be so hard. I don't know. But something about that broke me in a way that I couldn't explain at the time and I had gone home and picked a fight with this big thug of a kid that I lived with, mostly *letting* him kick my ass. I was usually able to get a few good licks in, even against kids a lot bigger than me. But that time I didn't even try.

When I told Dr. Fox about that, he told me that I was just picking up where my dad had left off because I thought I deserved it. Maybe. But he probably didn't know the excruciating pain of watching someone you love suffer and not be able to do a fucking thing to change it. The girl I loved wanted a fucking pillowcase for Christmas. It killed me and I hated my own powerlessness. I guess the only thing I *was* in control of was making the pain physical, rather than emotional, which is always the type of pain that feels unsurvivable.

The memory of that feeling comes back to me now because it's what I'm experiencing, sitting here in this kitchen, listening to Evie tell me what my abandonment did to her. Even though she doesn't know that that's what she's doing. I clench my jaw though and brace against the pain that comes in waves when I hear what she went through—she *lived* this, the least I can do is take it in and let it effect me fully, which is what I'm doing. But, fuck, it hurts.

She's silent for a minute, watching me, before she continues. "At the end of that month, I had enough money for a security deposit at any one of the apartments I had looked at. I called around and found the one that I could move into that day. I slept on the floor using my backpack as a pillow and a ratty, pink blanket I had had since I was a kid, until I could afford some used furniture. I got my GED that next year since I had moved out and started working before I graduated."

She watches me again carefully before picking up her glass and taking a sip of wine. I've been keeping my hands busy with the dinner prep so that I didn't pick up the nearest heavy object and hurl it through the window, and Evie nods toward the potatoes I'm rinsing. "Want me to do that?" she asks.

"No, I want you to sit there and relax and sip your wine and talk to me." And I have to smile now because despite the story she just told, she is sitting there relaxed and smiling. She amazes me and calms my own emotions.

"You've been through so much, Evie," I finally say.

"Yeah, but the thing is, in some ways I'm lucky for it."

"How so?" I'm confused.

"Well, how many people do you think walk into their apartment at the end of the day, small and simple as it may be, and look around and feel like one of the luckiest people in the world? How many people truly appreciate what they have because they know what it feels like to have absolutely nothing? I went through a lot to get where I am and I don't take anything I have for granted, ever. That's my reward."

And that right there, that is the best example of why this girl is the most exceptional person I've ever met. What she just did, turning ugliness into something beautiful—it's her gift. It's the thing I could never, ever do, no matter how hard I tried, instead letting the ugly take over and weave it's way through me until it changed who I was, making me bitter and rageful. And maybe that's exactly how Evie was able to love me—she looked deeply inside of me and was able to move past the ugliness to something that was good. I don't know. All I know is that she's the most beautiful thing I've ever seen, inside and out.

Finally, I say quietly, "I never would have thought to look at it that way." And I wouldn't have. It's why she makes me a better person. It's why she inspires me.

I finish some more dinner prep, and she sips her wine, both of us quiet for a couple minutes thinking our own thoughts. It feels so amazingly good just to sit here with her, making dinner and talking.

I'm thinking about the stories she used to tell when we were kids, and to keep her talking and to hear her thoughts on how she grew up, I ask, "Evie, the eulogy you gave for your friend, Willow. Tell me about that."

"I'm talking too much about myself, again. How does that happen every time I'm with you?" she asks, smiling.

"Indulge me, you're fascinating to me."

She rolls her eyes and smiles at me. "I used to tell Willow stories when we were kids and lived together in foster care. She loved them and even after we were adults and I would go over and clean her up from whatever mess she had gotten herself into; drug hangover, shit kicked out of her by a boyfriend, whatever." She waves her hand, pausing briefly before continuing. "Even as an adult she would ask me to tell her one of *her* stories. She would ask for them by name, even in a completely inebriated state sometimes."

"Sounds like she felt special in the ownership of them. She probably didn't have ownership of a lot. That's beautiful, Evie," I say.

And I know that it's true because that's exactly how I felt about the stories she told me. Just thinking about them made me feel good about myself and I needed that so desperately. Her stories were like medicine to my wounded heart. Then, and even thinking about them now, which I still do sometimes.

She stares at me silently for a minute, a soft look on her face. "In the beginning, it was just stupid kid stuff. I had a vivid imagination." She laughs a small laugh.

"It came in handy. Just a kid trying to comprehend the incomprehensible, you know?"

I nod. Of course I know.

And then I can't help myself. The question is out before I even give myself permission to ask it, "Will you tell me about Leo?"

She looks down and takes a sip of her wine. Shit, I shouldn't have gone there. "Jake, I've shared a lot tonight, and it felt good and that surprises me because I don't make it a habit of bringing up my past very often, but can we save Leo for another time? Is that okay?"

Something flares inside of me when I see the look in her eyes at the mention of my own name. I'm pretty sure I see sorrow there. She tries to hide it, but again, she was never any good at that. Something warm fills me, not only in the further realization that I'm reading my Evie again just like I used to be able to, but in the knowledge that maybe she didn't let me go all those years ago like she said she did. I stare at her, thinking more about how sweet and kind and loving she is. She looks up at me through her lashes and asks what I'm thinking.

I go around the bar and sit down on the stool next to her and she turns toward me as I take her hand, "I was just thinking about how much I appreciate you sharing with me tonight. And I was also thinking that from where I'm standing, you've done a pretty remarkable job of not letting your past make you hard. There's not a harsh or bitter thing about you, not a single thing, not your attitude, not the way you hold yourself, not your eyes, not your smile, not the way you treat people, always taking care of the people who are lucky enough to have your love, and that's just you. Life obviously took a lot from you and I know you've been cut deep, but the fact that you relied on yourself to make it through and that you didn't let it make you cynical or cold, that is all you. Own that. That's what I was thinking."

She stares at me for a couple beats before I see moisture glistening in her eyes and she smiles a shy smile. God, she's gorgeous.

I gesture for her to sit down at the table as I quickly set it and dish up the food and we dig in.

"Okay, truly impressed," she says. "This is amazing."

I'm glad she thinks so because if I have it my way, I'll cook for her every day for the rest of her life.

After we eat in silence for a couple minutes, she asks, "Will you tell me about your parents? How did your dad pass?" She looks at me nervously.

"Heart attack. It was sudden. He lingered for a week afterwards but got a blood clot. That's what actually killed him."

"I'm sorry, Jake." She pauses, still looking at me warily. "You must miss him."

"Yeah, I do. I wasted a lot of years with my dad that I can't ever get back," I say very truthfully.

"I'm sorry."

I think about my dad for a minute. There's still a sadness there for me but Dr. Fox helped me work through a lot of the guilt, not that it's completely gone, but I recognize that I've come a long way now that Evie's brought it up. "It's okay. Really. It wasn't okay for a long time but I've come to a place where I'm getting there. I realize now that there are a lot of paths in life. Some we choose and some are chosen for us. I was dealt some shit, just like a lot of us are, and I made a lot of poor choices, too. I have to take responsibility for those. But the only thing we'll get from trying to figure out where another path would have taken us are questions there are no answers to, and heartbreak that can't be healed. Regardless of how we got there, all any of us can do is move forward from where we are."

Just like when I talked to Dr. Fox, talking to Evie about this feels good. I'd like to go into it more with her someday because I know now that talking it through with someone who can understand is healing. Someday, though. Not tonight. I don't want to close myself off again after she's just given me so much of herself, but not only am I going to be unable to talk about a lot of this stuff, but it's still a hard subject for me. Getting it out is good but I want this night to be about me and her, not a bunch of shit. She's in a better place than I am regarding the pain of the past—tonight has made that very clear. Plus, mine is still on-going. Just thinking about Lauren's crusade makes me tense up. "I'll tell you all about it, Evie. You've already given me so much of you, and I want to give you me, but not tonight. Tonight, I want to enjoy dinner and enjoy you and not bring up a bunch of shit that's going to put me in a bad mood. Okay?"

"Okay," she whispers, looking at me with soft eyes as if she really does understand. I'm grateful.

I grab her hand and squeeze it across the table. We finish dinner and then she helps me clear the table and rinse the dishes.

She excuses herself to use the restroom as I finish tossing the pots and pans into the sink and dry my hands. Suddenly the reality of the fact that Evie is in my home and that we just shared dinner together like any other normal couple hits me hard and intense happiness fills me.

When she walks back into the kitchen, I grab her hand and lead her to the couch. My body is vibrating with the happiness her presence brings and I need to show her. I pull her down on top of me so that she's straddling me and *fuck, that's sexy*. Again, the awe that fills me in letting her be in a position of control and being okay with that is overwhelming. Her eyes fill with heat right before she puts her mouth on mine and licks the seam of my lips. I open for her immediately and she moans and *oh God*, I'm already painfully hard and that sweet little moan shoots straight to my cock. I take the back of her head in my hands and tilt it so that I can kiss her more deeply, the desire to possess her body so strong that I already feel out of control with need. We kiss, deep and wet, tongues tangling, tasting, moaning into each other's mouths and I don't ever want to come up for air. *She's* my air, my reason for existence, the only thing that matters to me in this life or any other.

I'm drunk from the taste of her, lust shooting through my veins, my entire body vibrating with the need to be inside her, to possess her, to make her mine. *Mine!* A growl comes from my throat and she moans back, grinding down on my lap so that my balls pull up tightly,

"*Fuck!*" I have to tear my mouth away from hers, breathing deeply. "God, Evie, you feel so fucking good."

"Jake," she says, breathing hard, too. "I'm not sleeping in the guest room tonight."

"Thank fucking Christ." *Thank fucking Christ. Thank fucking Christ.*

I stand up with her in my arms so that she wraps her legs around my waist. I carry her down the hall to my bed, my mouth locked on hers the entire way, the word *Mine!* reverberating through my head, the need to show her physically how much I love her, pulsing through my veins.

CHAPTER SIXTEEN

I carry her into my bedroom, deposit her in the middle of my bed, and then stand up and take off my shirt before rejoining her. My tattoo occurs to me for the first time. I know I can't show her yet, but I smile inside thinking that my lion tamer is both on my back and in my arms.

I've never in my life been this turned on. I'm vibrating with it. I think briefly that this is how it would have been if she had been my first—this is how it *should* have been. The grief in that thought hits me, but I push it aside. We're here together now. And I need to see all of her like right this fucking second.

I put my hands up her sweater, forcing her arms over her head, and pull it up and off of her before tossing it on the floor. I sit back and look down at her. She's wearing a red, lace bra and her skin is smooth and flawless, and I need to feel her against me—*now*.

"Help me out, Evie, I want to feel your skin on mine." *I've been waiting what feels like a lifetime to feel your skin on mine.*

She looks just a little unsure as she sits up slightly and unhooks her bra and pulls the straps slowly down her arms, and then drops it on the floor. I drink in the perfection of her breasts, small and firm, dark pink nipples already pebbled under my stare. "Christ, even more beautiful than I imagined," I whisper.

I lower my mouth to hers again, my tongue sliding into her sweetness, and revel in the feel of her softness against my chest, her hands wandering over my back. My hips start rolling instinctively, and she whimpers into my mouth, sending more sparks flying straight to my cock. I moan back, thinking that I need to slow this down if I'm going to last longer than three seconds. This is so fucking good, I don't ever want it to end, but I also want to make it good for her—and that means not coming on her stomach before we even get started.

I lean off of her and kiss down her neck as I bring one hand up to cup her breast and rub my thumb over her nipple. The slight weight of her is sheer perfection in my hand, the skin like satin. This woman was made for me in every way possible.

Her hips buck up against my raging hardness and I growl at the feel of her heat meeting mine. God, it's going to be like heaven to sink into her.

Desperate to taste her, I lower my mouth to her nipple and suck it into my mouth, licking and sucking as she trembles and gasps beneath me. I take turns at both, as her gasps become whimpers, her hips moving with each pull, her hands raking through my hair. My girl is so responsive, so perfect. *Mine.*

When one of her hands starts moving down my stomach, I suck in a breath and pull off of her breast to look down at her. She doesn't know the focus it's taking to take this slow, if she touches me there, it will be too easy to lose control.

I know the look on my face is probably intense as she gazes back at me, wide eyed, lips parted, too beautiful for words. "I'm a virgin," she says suddenly, her eyes studying mine.

Everything in me freezes as her words sink in. My heart squeezes in my chest and the blood starts roaring in my ears. Her eyes keep studying my face as she whispers, "Is that okay?"

Is that okay? Is that okay? "In the history of the world, nothing has ever been more okay," I say, the emotion I feel coming up my throat and making my voice husky, even to my own ears. Did she save herself for me? Surely not. I just got fucking lucky that life worked out this way, that no one has ever touched this beautiful girl except for me. And how is that even possible? I don't care. I just thank God and put my mouth back on hers, kissing her with wild abandon, licking and sucking at her lips. I feel greedy and possessive, more impatient than I was before to bury myself inside of her and claim her as mine. But I know I need to go slowly now for her. I need to make sure she's as wet as possible for me so that this isn't too painful for her. I need to make her come.

I unbutton and unzip her jeans and then kneel up and pull her boots off, one at a time. Then I quickly pull her jeans and her tiny red lace panties down her legs and toss it all on the floor. Then I quickly move back over her, claiming her mouth again and move my hand down between her silky thighs, urging them open. She shivers and I bring my head up, looking her in the eyes and whispering, "Open for me." She does as I say immediately, letting her legs fall to the sides.

"I'm gonna make it easier for you to take me," I say, and I see her eyes flare at my words. She nods slightly.

I press one finger gently inside of her and feel her body tremble. Jesus, she's so tight, so hot, so wet. My cock surges in my jeans, eager to take the place of my finger.

My thumb finds the sensitive little bundle of nerves high above her opening and I spread her wetness over it and then start moving my thumb on it in slow circles, while moving my finger in and out of her slick opening. She tilts her head back and moans, and seeing her pleasure is almost too much for me. I feel like I'm choking on lust, riding a thin line of desperation. It has never been like this before, ever. The beauty of this moment overwhelms me as I watch Evie on the brink of orgasm, lust and love surging through my body simultaneously.

"God, you're so beautiful. Is that good?" I manage to choke out.

"Yes," she pants out as I add another finger, stretching her, feeling her juices coat my fingers as I stroke them in and out of her.

When her hips start lifting up to meet my hand, I know she's almost there. *That's it, baby, come for me.*

"Oh my God," she pants out and I can't help the feral sound that escapes my lips. Seeing her on the threshold of orgasm is so beautiful and so intense. Her cheeks are flushed, her head thrown back into the pillow and her hips are undulating against my hand. Then her body stiffens for the briefest of seconds and she cries out my name as the orgasm washes over her. *That's it, beautiful girl*. Oh fuck. I need to be inside her now. Right now.

I sit back and strip off my jeans and boxers and toss them on the floor, and crawl back over her just as she's opening her eyes, a look of wonder on her face.

I'm practically shaking as I lean over her and pull a condom out of my bedside table drawer and kneel back and pull it on. I'm so hard, I'm aching, desperate with the need to pound myself into her. I remind myself to go slow though. I don't want to hurt her.

"Can I touch you, Jake? Will you show me how?" she whispers.

"Next time, baby. Hanging on by a thread here. If you touch me, we'll both be sorry," I say, my flimsy hold on control weakening by the minute.

I hold myself over her and guide the tip of my cock to her wet entrance. I lower my mouth to hers again, thrusting my tongue in her mouth, showing her with my mouth what I'm about to do with my cock. I groan in anticipation.

"Wrap your legs around me," I tell her. "Gonna do this fast to get the painful part over with, okay?"

"Okay," she whispers back, and I push myself into her in one thrust. Oh fuck, fuck. But then I grimace as she cries out in pain.

I remain still for a minute, letting her body get used to my invasion, and when I feel her relaxing around me, I start moving very slowly, relishing the feeling of her hot, wet embrace.

I want to be slow and careful but my cock is throbbing, screaming at me to *move* as the hot, slick friction of her body surrounds me.

"Baby, I gotta move faster. You okay?" I choke out.

"Yes," she whispers, and with her okay, I start thrusting into her, the feeling so overwhelmingly exquisite that I think I must be drowning in her. Drowning in a sea of bliss.

Her legs are wrapped around my hips, her hands moving on my back and over my ass, as she moans and whimpers beneath me, meeting me thrust for thrust. She's perfection and I'm lost. It feels so good, I don't want it to end, but I feel heat and pleasure circling in my belly, and I know that I'm not going to be able to hold out for much longer.

I bring my mouth back to hers and thrust my tongue into her mouth in time with the thrusting of my cock. That seems to ignite her as she arches her body up, and I feel the contractions of her orgasm along my length, milking my own orgasm to the very surface, my balls pulling up tight.

I thrust into her once, twice and then I explode with the force of an erupting volcano, shuddering and groaning and seeing stars from the intensity of my climax.

When I come back to myself, I'm circling my hips slowly, drawing out the last of the pleasure, and she's stroking her fingernails up and down my arms. I can't help the grin that spreads across my face as I nuzzle into her sweet smelling neck. Holy fuck. That was . . . that was . . . God, there are no words.

I bring my head up and gaze into her eyes.

"You okay?" I whisper.

"Yeah," she whispers back, a gentle, satiated smile on her lips.

I'd like to stay connected to her indefinitely, but I need to make sure she's okay and if there's any blood, clean her up. As I pull out, she makes a little mewling sound and I can't help grinning. "My Evie likes me inside of her." Good thing because I plan to spend a lot of time there.

"Let me get rid of this condom and get something to clean you up with. Stay there." Damn, there's a lot of blood. Something primal inside of me feels an intense satisfaction in the sight of Evie's virginal blood all over me. I'd never admit that out loud—seems cavemanish, I suppose, but it's the truth.

I make sure to face her as I pull on my T-shirt and boxers so she doesn't glimpse my back. Not yet.

I go to the bathroom and flush the bloody condom. Then I run a washcloth under warm water and bring it back into the bedroom. I smile because Evie hasn't moved a muscle, still lying naked and goddess-like in my sheets, a vision of beauty.

I sit down on the side of the bed and say, "Open your legs and bend your knees." She looks slightly embarrassed, but does as I ask, and I wipe the blood away and return to the bathroom to rinse out the washcloth and toss it in the laundry hamper.

When I walk back into the bedroom with a glass of water, Evie has put her tiny red panties back on. The sight of the small piece of red lace against her creamy skin sends an arrow of arousal shooting south, but I squash it. She's gotta be sore. I feel a momentary pang of guilt for not being gentler, but I had controlled myself to the best of my ability under the circumstances—I'd waited a long damn time for that. And I'd never experienced that level of pure lust. It was off the charts.

Evie takes a long drink of the water and smiles sweetly at me as she hands it back. I put it on the nightstand and climb back into bed with her, turning her and pulling her back against my chest. I nuzzle my face into her sweet smelling hair and cup her breast in my hand possessively.

Despite the fact that I've never cuddled in my life, this feels normal and natural and so very, very good.

After a couple minutes, Evie turns in my arms so that she's facing me and runs her hand down the side of my face, looking deeply into my eyes. I think I see—no, it can't be. It's too soon. But she cares about me, I think I can safely say that. My own possessiveness turns up a notch.

"You're mine now, Evie. Say it," I whisper.

Her hand stills and she continues searching my eyes, looking for what, I'm not sure. I hold my breath. "I'm yours, Jake," she whispers back.

I exhale, but in my fantasy, she had always called me Leo when she told me she belonged to me. I want her to know exactly who she belongs to and I long to hear her say it.

I smile at her and kiss her pretty lips gently. I want her to know how much that meant to me. "I've never experienced anything as beautiful as that," I say. And I mean that literally. She smiles back gently and then I pull her close and after a few minutes, I feel her breathing slow. She's asleep.

As I lay holding her, an emotion washes over me that I don't immediately recognize. The edges of my mind seem to grasp it as a memory, the fuzzy outline of something that I experienced long ago, but never since. I let it wrap around me like a cocoon, reveling in it, exalting in the euphoria it brings. I experience it wholly before I can name it, before the word comes to me: Joy. *Joy.* I pull her closer to me in the dark and listen to her even breathing; drawing in her scent and feeling the steady rise and fall of her chest against my own. Joy. I savor this moment, fully aware of my own happiness in the here and now. "You are my dream," I whisper to her in the dark. "You are my every dream come true." I relax and let the feeling of Evie in my arms seep into my soul. In moments, I fall into a deep, peaceful sleep.

CHAPTER SEVENTEEN

I come awake suddenly as I feel Evie's warm body separate from mine. I open my eyes sleepily and see her disappearing into the bathroom and close my eyes again contentedly, remembering the night before, and realizing that it wasn't just a dream. It was real. The best night of my life. She climbs back into bed and snuggles back into me, and when I feel the weight of her stare, I crack one eye open. She's watching me, a sweet little smile on her face.

I smile back. "Are you watching me sleep?" I ask, teasing her, my voice groggy. "Who's the creeper now?"

She giggles and snuggles her head under my chin. Mmm. This feels good. My sweet, warm, sexy girl's soft body is pressed against me, memories of what we shared last night swirling around my head, making my morning wood pulse in my boxers. I wrap my arms around her and pull her even closer.

I enjoy snuggling with her for a few minutes and then I feel her hand moving downwards. I suck in my breath. *Please let her be doing what I think she's doing.* And . . . oh God, yes, her hand moves gently over my erection, making me swell even further.

I flip her onto her back and move over her, eager to participate in her game. "You want to play, beautiful?"

"Yes," she whispers, her eyes heating. I feel her squeeze her thighs together. She's turned on, too.

"Do you feel a little sore or are you okay?"

She wiggles her bottom a little, grimacing slightly. "Just a little."

She looks disappointed and I almost laugh.

"Well, there are other things . . ."

"Yes," she whispers again, and that's all I need.

I bend down and trail my lips down her flat belly, stopping at her navel and licking around it, dipping my tongue inside. Every part of her tastes amazing. I still have my T-shirt on and so there's no risk of her seeing my tattoo. I can enjoy this as fully as I hope she's going to.

I pull her panties off and toss them aside as her heated gaze follows me, her lips slightly parted, her breath already ragged. God, she's the sexiest woman alive. I want to devour every part of her. I want to make her scream and come against my mouth.

I dip my head down and kiss the satiny skin on the inside of her thigh and she shivers, her legs falling apart, granting me access. *That's my girl.* I inhale the scent of her, a primal growl rising in my chest, as I smell our combined sex from last night, and a faint trace of my soap still on her. "I love you smelling like me," I say hoarsely, before I lower my face to her soft folds, circling my tongue over her little, pink clit. *Perfect.* She whimpers as I nip it with my lips, sucking on it gently before moving my tongue slowly over it again and again. I experiment with different movements and pressure, listening to her moans until I think I know exactly what she likes best.

That's when I start lapping rhythmically at her swollen tissue, first slowly and then faster and with more pressure as she writhes and moans. The sounds she's making, combined with the taste of her right against my face, the intoxicating smell of her, like an exotic flower, has me hard as a rock, and I can feel my cock surging forward in my boxers.

I hear her fisting the sheets next to her hips, and her breaths become pants, and she starts rolling her hips against my face, seeking more pressure. *Oh fuck, oh fuck.* This is so intense. She cries out as her orgasm starts, and as I feel it pulsing through her, I thrust my tongue inside of her, wanting to taste her, to feel her coming around me.

She cries out again, chanting my name over and over as her muscles clench and shudder, and that was by far the most erotic thing that I've experienced. By a mile. Probably a thousand.

I trail kisses down her thigh and bring my head up. She still has her eyes closed, her head turned to the side, hair spilling over most of her face. I grin as I crawl back up and kiss her neck before collapsing next to her. I pull her into me and she feels like a wet noodle in my arms. I grin again and close my eyes. But they snap open a few minutes later when I feel her hand go under the bottom of my T-shirt and rub over my stomach, tracing a finger along the muscles there. My cock jumps in my boxers.

She leans up over me and scoots my shirt up, and I watch her as she does this, the look on her face one of both concentration and nervousness. If she only knew the extent to which she affects me, she wouldn't have an ounce of anxiety in her mind. She really can't go wrong here. Her naked body in a bed is pretty much all I require. Whatever happens after that is only going to be good.

I reach my arms up and sit up slightly as she bites her full bottom lip and pulls my shirt up and over my head, looking sexy as hell. She tosses it on the floor, her rosy nipple coming close to my face as she bends over me. I lick my lips, wanting that small, perfect bud in my mouth. But this is her show now and I stay still. I love watching her take over, a peaceful contentedness washing over me, despite my raging hard on, at how far I've already come in just one night with Evie regarding my control issues in bed. My healer. My tamer.

She leans back and her eyes wander up and down my chest, right before she leans over and kisses and licks her way down, stopping at one nipple, licking and sucking it between her lips. I groan at the feel of her sweet little mouth on me and I feel her smile against my skin. All these sensations are so new for me, so many of them things I've never experienced before.

And then, *oh God, oh yes,* her hand wanders down my stomach and I beg her in my mind to keep going. I'm aching with the need to be touched, for her to take me in her hand, or her mouth. But I don't know if she's ready for the latter just yet.

"Teach me what you like," she whispers, heat in her eyes.

"Just put your hand on me. I just want you to touch me," I say, not caring that I sound desperate.

I lean up slightly and pull my boxers down so that she has access.

She scoots down and when she wraps her warm hand around my straining cock, it jerks in her hand. Oh, Jesus, just the feel of her hand gripping me feels so good, pre-cum beads on the tip. She takes her thumb and rubs it in slow circles expertly, making me wonder if she's touched another man before—or is that just instinct? Jealousy threatens, boiling up in my chest. I know I'm a hypocrite, but I can't help my reaction, even though I know it's unjustified. But then she looks at me questioningly, wondering what to do next, and I relax.

"Move your hand up and down, baby," I choke out. "Like this." I put my hand over hers and show her what I like. I see her clench her thighs together and her eyes widen at the sight of both of our hands on my length. I like it, too. There's something highly erotic about teaching her about my body, about her being so eager to know what I like. No one has ever cared about that before. Maybe we're both learning together.

She begins moving her hand, and it feels so fucking amazing, I clench my eyes shut and just enjoy the sensation of her hand stroking me, slowly at first, but then faster. I can tell she's moving her hand in response to my breathing and that turns me on even more.

I want to enjoy this, make it last, hold back on purpose, but it feels so good, I just relax and let my body have its way. I feel my cock swelling in her hand, my balls pulling tight as the sparks shoot from my belly, and I choke out Evie's name as I come almost as hard as I did last night.

"Oh God!" I moan out as her hand slows. Will it always be like this with her? Holy shit. I'll be dead by the time I'm thirty-two. But what a way to go. Death by orgasm. He came so hard he had an aneurism. Lucky bastard.

When I open my eyes, Evie is grinning proudly at me as if she's just found the cure for cancer. I can't help it—I burst out laughing. She's so fucking cute. And hot. And all mine.

We both keep grinning as I sit up slightly and reach under her arms and drag her over me so that she's lying on top of me, staring down into my eyes. "You're a natural," I joke, only not really.

She lays her head on my shoulder and nuzzles into my neck, and we lay like this for what feels like a long time, me just reveling in the feel of her, the perfection of the way her body fits against mine.

"I'm gonna run a bath for you while I make breakfast. Then you're gonna spend the day with me." There's no way she's going to be out of my sight today. Not after last night and this morning. No way. Plus, I want to spend more time just having fun with her. I haven't gotten enough of that yet.

"Hmm . . . Bossy," she mutters, smiling.

She gets up and starts walking to the bathroom and I put my hands behind my head, watching the amazing view of Evie's naked backside. I'm smiling as I sit up to pull on my T-shirt and boxers.

CHAPTER EIGHTEEN

I make breakfast while Evie soaks in the tub. I hear her humming to herself and I can't help the smile that stays permanently on my face as I get dishes out of the cabinet and food out of the refrigerator. Everything about this feels so right, like my life is finally back on the track it was always supposed to be on. Plus, I'm on a high after the most amazing night of sex I've ever had. Something that hasn't felt a day's peace since I left Cincinnati eight years ago is finally at rest, and the relief in that sensation is overwhelming. I'll never get enough of her. And the fact that this girl, the one I've loved with everything I am from the time I was a kid, is every dream come true for me in bed, too, is somehow miraculous, as if it's just one more piece of proof that we were created to be together.

Evie emerges from my room dressed and we eat breakfast together, laughing and teasing each other, and it feels normal and so amazingly good. I want to start every day for the rest of my life this way. Every once in a while, my deception comes racing to the forefront of my mind and guilt washes through me but I push it back. *Soon . . . we just need a little more time. Soon.*

Our teasing ends with her straddling me on the bar stool as I'm tickling her and nipping her neck and fake growling in her ear. Visions of her grinding down on me on the couch last night, and everything that came afterwards, come back and just like that, I'm ready to take her here, right now, on the bar stool in the kitchen.

I growl one more time for show but loosen my grip, laughing with her.

When she licks the dip at the base of my neck and kisses up to my jaw, I groan. The thought of sinking into her again is at the top of my priority list and I'd love nothing more than to cart her back to my bed and spend the rest of the day there. But she said she was sore . . . I groan again because I can tell she's turned on, too. "Evie, I thought you said you were sore . . ."

She sighs, sitting up. "I am. Maybe some Tylenol would take the edge off enough . . .?"

I stare at her for a beat and then burst out laughing, "Christ. I've brought a sex demon to life." And I say that with full approval.

She laughs as she's climbing off of me. I automatically frown at the loss of her body on mine. "Okay, so then what are you going to do with me today?" she asks.

"Ever been to the zoo?"

I think of the first time I went to the zoo in San Diego. I was seventeen and my life was shit at home. But I loved it. For a couple hours, I was a kid, doing something simple that I had never done when I was *actually* a kid. For a short time, I lost myself in doing something for no other reason than that it was *fun*. I want to give that to Evie, too.

She looks shocked for a second. "Actually, no. You're gonna take me to the zoo?" A beautiful grin spreads across her face.

I grin back and nod. "Cool. Do you have shoes that'll work for walking?"

"Yeah, I brought a pair of sneakers."

"Okay, good, I'll take a quick shower and we'll get going."

We finish up breakfast and I give her a kiss and head to the shower. I start the water and strip. As I'm turning to get in the shower, I catch a small glimpse of my tattoo in the mirror. If Evie were to come in and I didn't hear her... I feel a flash of guilt as I do what I have to do. I lock the bathroom door.

When I re-enter the kitchen, Evie comes to me, putting her arms around my waist and laying her head on my chest. As she lifts her head and smiles up at me, I kiss her on her forehead, whispering, "My Evie. So sweet." *My Evie. Mine.*

****

Watching Evie at the zoo is one of the most satisfying experiences of my life. I watch her more than I do any of the exhibits, a deep peace settling in my soul at being able to give this to her. I wish more than anything I could go back and erase the ugliness of her past and give her the fun, carefree childhood she deserved. I can't. But I can give this to her now.

I watch her though and it occurs to me that maybe it's for me, too. All those years of feeling so damn helpless, so incapable of making her life better, maybe this is healing for me as well. Perhaps, it's for me *most* of all. Because she always had a way of finding her own peace. That same pride that always fills me when I think of Evie's strength overwhelms me now.

As we're watching the elephants, Evie keeps her eyes on them as she says quietly, "Elephants grieve like we do. They shed tears and mourn their dead."

I look over at her. "Yeah? How do you know?"

"I read a book about them last year."

"You read a book about elephants?" I raise an eyebrow.

She looks over at me. "Don't make fun. I try to learn about different things. You never know when the topic of pachyderms is going to come up. I wanna be able to hold my own should a conversation like that occur in a social situation." She grins teasingly over at me and then turns back to the elephants.

"Pachyderms?" I smile.

"Various nonruminant animals… like an elephant, or a rhinoceros, or a hippopotamus…"

"Nonruminant?"

"Animals who have single compartment stomachs." She turns to me now, still smiling.

"Why didn't you tell me you were a walking animal encyclopedia? I would have had you leading this tour."

She laughs. "Not 'animal,' just 'elephant.' I haven't made it through any more books in the "Living Creatures" section of the library." She grins at me and the beauty of that full smile turned to me hits me square in the heart.

She shrugs, turning back to watch the big, majestic, apparently sensitive *pachyderms* as I gaze at her, finding yet another reason why I want to spend a lifetime with this woman. I don't know anyone else who would check a book out of the library on elephants just to learn something new.

I move around behind her, and pull her back against my front and wrap my arms around her as we watch the elephants for a few more minutes. "You hungry for lunch?" I finally say.

She nods, looking back around and up at me, smiling. "Will you buy me a hot dog?" she asks.

I laugh. "Yeah, Evie, I'll buy you a hot dog."

The Cincinnati zoo isn't as large as the San Diego zoo, but it's still beautiful with nice walking paths and roaming peacocks. We hold hands as we walk. I can barely contain the smile that wants to stay permanently on my face.

As we eat lunch, one of the colorful, roaming birds walks past our table and Evie gasps, jumping up and following it around with her phone, trying to snap a picture. She's dancing around with this wild look on her face and I can't help laughing as the stupid thing dodges her around tables and chairs and she follows it relentlessly. But suddenly, I swear that damn bird looks right at me, and then saunters over to her, stops right in front of Evie and spreads all his feathers, preening and strutting back and forth. I watch her as she sucks in a breath, a look of pure glee on her face and snaps picture after picture. I've completely ceased to exist. It's like I've disappeared. Fucking bird. I wonder if grilled peacock is any good.

She comes bouncing back, squealing, "Look!" and pushing her phone in front of my face so I can look at the dozens of pictures she snapped. I grunt, sick of that stupid bird already and when I look up, she's staring at me with an incredulous look on her face. "You're jealous of a bird?" she asks.

"What? No!" I snap. I just don't think I like peacocks very much.

"You're jealous of a bird," she says, a glint of amusement coming into her eyes. She glances back at her phone. "He IS gorgeous. Goddddd, soooo gorgeous," she moans out the words, throwing her head back.

"Hilarious," I say, trying not to smile now at my own ridiculousness. "That bird was trying to move in on my territory. I know a brazen male threat when I see one."

She laughs out loud, and I try my best not to laugh, but in the end, I grin up at her and we both laugh.

"You're ridiculous," she says, still smiling. *Yeah. Totally crazy. Totally crazy for you, Evie.*

She sits down on my lap and takes my face in her hands, and as we stare into each other's eyes, she glances down at my mouth and my body reacts, swelling in my pants.

"Jake—" she whispers.

"Evie—" I whisper back.

I lean my face in and plant my lips on hers, sliding my tongue into the sweetness of her ice cream flavored mouth.

When we come up for air, she puts her forehead against mine as we catch our breath and says, "I had a really, really nice day, Jake."

I study her face, so much racing through my mind, so much I want to say to her. I want to tell her that I'll do anything to make her happy, that anything I have is hers. But I can't. Not yet. And so instead, I smile and say, "It's not over yet, baby. Let's go see the tigers."

****

We leave the zoo close to dinnertime. I'm hoping that I can feed her and take her back to my condo. The thought of dropping her off at her apartment does not make me happy. I'll broach the subject at dinner though. I have to remind myself that she has a life and a job and that I can't try to completely take over like I'm tempted to. I don't see her taking kindly to that. Still, I'm going to have to make it clear that she's in my life now and her telling me she's mine means that she's in my bed more often than she's not. It's not going to be possible for me to take this overly slow. I hope she agrees.

I take her to Ferrari's, a small, Italian restaurant in Madeira that I've been to a couple times.

Once we're seated at our table, I order a bottle of red and tell her what I've had that's good. She closes her menu and raises her glass, stating, "To hot peacocks!" She's grinning. I snort. But I relent, and click her glass, grinning back.

Once we've ordered, I ask, "What shift do you work tomorrow?" I try to look nonchalant but I need to figure out her week so that I can book her up. I'd like to take her day planner out of her purse and just write JAKE across every single page.

"Ten to seven all week."

What I *want* to do is tell her to quit her job tomorrow and come live with me. She doesn't need to be working as a maid anymore. I wonder what she'd do if she had her choice.

"Ever think about doing anything else?" I ask.

Her eyes dart to mine. "You mean do I have ambitions to be more than a maid?"

"Yeah, I mean, you know I don't think there's anything wrong with what you do. You're just so smart, you could do anything. I was just wondering if you think about it."

These are things we never talked about growing up. The day-today struggles seemed so overwhelming at the time, just getting *out* of the system seemed like the main priority. What we'd do afterwards was something we'd think about later. Or at least, that's where my mind was. No one had ever asked me what I wanted to be when I grew up, but I'd thought about being a police officer when I was a kid. I thought maybe being part of bringing justice to victims would be satisfying to my personality. Or maybe all little boys want to be police officers and firemen. I don't know. And then I got adopted and after that, what *I* wanted out of life went by the wayside. I take a deep breath. It's just the way it happened. I can't change it now. I can only move forward. And that's what I'm doing.

She sighs. "Yeah, I do, actually. I'd love to go to college but that takes money. Money that right now, I don't have. But what I'd really love to do is write. I have this idea for a book . . ." She trails off, her cheeks flushing. She'd be an amazing writer . . . *God*, it's like she was born to tell stories. She has to know that, too.

"Do it. Why haven't you?"

"Well, I need a computer to be able to write. I brought a flash drive back and forth to the library for a while, but it's just too impractical. And when I was feeling inspired, the library was closed . . . you know. It just didn't work."

The waiter interrupts us, setting our food down. Evie digs in, closing her eyes and moaning, as she tastes the first bite.

"Good?" I ask, my mind going somewhere other than dinner.

"Mmm," she says, nodding.

"Will you stay with me again tonight?"

"I can't, Jake. I need to get ready for the week. I need to go home and get myself organized."

"Tomorrow night?" *Every night for the rest of your life?*

"Can't tomorrow night either. I have a catering job that'll go late. I don't usually do them on Monday nights but it's some sort of art showing at a gallery downtown." She glances up at me, narrowing her eyes. "You won't be there, will you?"

I laugh. "Wasn't planning on it but maybe now I'll have to see what I can arrange."

"Don't you dare."

I'm quiet for a minute, completely disappointed. "I have to travel to my office in San Diego on Tuesday but I'll be back Wednesday evening. Will you stay then?" I'm slightly pissed off that I won't see her for three more nights.

But she smiles. "Okay." I smile back.

We focus on dinner for a few minutes before she asks, "I'm assuming you went to college?"

"Yeah, I went to UCSD. I was in school and also working with my dad, learning all about the company since the plan was for me to start working there when I graduated. We just had no idea at the time that I'd be running the damn thing. That's when my dad and I finally formed more of a relationship than we'd ever had. I had moved out of our house and that was really the thing that allowed us to start over. It was the first time I was really something close to happy in a long time, being away from my parents, just 'finding myself' to use a clichéd expression."

I briefly think back to that time and stop myself from grimacing. Once I got out of that house, I had started doing a little better, seeing more clearly that my dad, Phil, was not to blame for what had been happening with Lauren all those years. The problem with letting go of that anger toward him was that I then had to accept the full responsibility of what had happened. The intense guilt I felt sent me into another spiral of depression that I was still in when I landed myself in the hospital.

She nods, watching me closely. "You're not close to your mother?"

Her choice of wording makes me almost gag. "Close?" If she only knew how close we really were. I cringe but answer her question in the way she means. "No."

I force my mind to go back to the conversation we were having before the topic of Phil and Lauren came up. "I want to pay for you to take classes, Evie."

She blinks, tensing. "What? Why would you do that?" *Uh oh, hostile territory here.*

I force myself to tread carefully. Obviously she doesn't like the idea. I don't blame her—it would have pissed me off to take charity from someone, too, if I had been offered it at any point in my life. But what I need to make her understand is that things coming from me aren't charity. I want her to know that I care about her and will do whatever I can do to make her dreams come true, not because I feel sorry for her, but because she's incredible. "Because I believe in you. Because I think you're smart, and I think you just need a small break to be able to reach for your dreams."

A memory comes to me suddenly of the Christmas I was eleven, right before I went to foster care. Christmas was like any other fucked up day in our house—no tree or presents or anything, but I knew what day it was and it pissed me off, and so I had left the house and walked around for a while, just to get out of there. I did that as much as possible, as long as I knew Seth was safe for a little bit. When I came back, there was this black garbage bag sitting on my house stairs with a red bow on it. I opened it up, kinda confused, and inside was this stuffed dog wearing a red sweater, and a football. I had no idea who had left it there, but to my eleven-year-old mind, it was some kind of magic. I knew the football was probably for me and the dog was for Seth, but something in me wanted that dog instead of the football, and so I gave the ball to Seth, even though I knew it made me a fucking pussy to want that stupid stuffed animal. But I knew Seth wouldn't care either way, and so I took what I wanted. I would have never admitted it to anyone and I kept it hidden from my dad, but I loved that damn dog.

I had taken that dog with me to foster care and kept it hidden under my bed, only taking it out at night to sleep with. A couple months later, I was in the grocery store with my foster mom and I looked at the bulletin board at the front of the store and there was a big call out for volunteers to deliver Christmas gifts to needy kids. When I looked closely, there were pictures of the volunteers from the year before, dropping off black garbage bags tied with red bows on porch steps.

Something in me crashed and burned and then shriveled. The shame and deep disappointment that washed over me in that moment was so intense, I almost started crying like a baby. It wasn't magic. It was *charity*. The thing was, I had known in the back of my mind that it wasn't magic, but before that moment, I could pretend I didn't. Now I had the *proof* staring at me from that bulletin board. I hated myself for hurting so damn much.

When I got home, I grabbed that dog and brought it over to Evie's and started throwing rocks at it in the empty gravel lot next to the house she lived in. When she came out of her house and saw me, she had grabbed my arm and asked me what I was doing, a look of confusion and concern on her face at what she must have seen in mine. I choked out the story, rambling about charity and magic and bullshit, still hucking rocks and then she had stood staring at me quietly for several minutes before bending down and picking up a rock of her own and throwing it at that dog, hitting it square in the head. We had looked at each other and cheered, and then continued throwing rocks until that stupid dog was nothing but a pile of demolished stuffing. Then she had wrapped her arms around my neck and squeezed me tightly. She made it better for me that day. She always made it better.

I snap back to reality as she shakes her head slightly at my offer of paying for her to go to school. "Jake, listen, that's a nice offer, but I've worked really hard to get where I am. I know to you my life probably doesn't look like a raving success story but I do okay, and I'll find a way to go to school at some point . . . I mean we just started sleeping together and I don't really know how all this works, but maybe we should wait to see where this goes before you start offering me large sums of money."

I get that it's hard to take things from other people when you've grown up like we did, but her comment about just starting to sleep together pisses me the hell off. "First of all, I thought I already made it clear that, actually, I do consider your life a raving success story, all things considered. And secondly, do I need to remind you what you told me in my bed not twenty-four hours ago, Evie?"

She blinks. "Um—"

"You told me you were mine, Evie. This is not some fun fuck. This is not casual to me. I thought I had conveyed that to you."

"So, what? You're like my boyfriend or something now?"

Yeah, exactly. "Boyfriend, man, lover, whatever label you like, you can use it, but what it means is that we take care of each other in and out of the bedroom. And part of me taking care of you means me offering to give you the money it takes to make your dreams come true." Hopefully that cleared things up for her. I realize that I tend to have a take-charge attitude with Evie. I'm not really sure what that dynamic is between us, but it was always there growing up, and something about it always seemed to work for us, it would calm her and calm me. I had a need to be in control, and maybe she had a need to give someone else control. Whatever it was—it worked for us then, and I find myself reverting back to it now, especially when I need her to really hear me.

"Just think about it okay?"

She stares at me for several seconds. "Okay."

"Okay."

We eat in silence for a few minutes as another thought occurs to me—and while I'm taking charge . . . "Also, you need to get on birth control. I don't want to use condoms with you."

She blinks and says quietly, "I'm already on the pill. I have bad periods. It regulates it. I've been on it for years."

I actually remember that. I remember her going to the school nurse every month, looking as pale as a ghost. "Okay, good. Now finish your dinner."

She's quiet for a minute and then, "Um, Jake, if we're not going to use condoms, I should probably ask . . ."

"I'm clean. I've always used condoms and I get regular check ups. I can show you paperwork if you want." Thank God I was always good about that. As a kid who grew up in a household where I wasn't wanted by anyone, I would have never risked an unwanted pregnancy. Ever. Still, shame engulfs me when I think of being with anyone other than Evie.

She's silent, studying me and I wonder what she's thinking. Finally, she reaches across the table and takes my hand in hers. "No, I trust you."

I let out a breath, relief coursing through me. I smile into her trusting brown eyes.

I drive her home after dinner and we kiss in my car for a few minutes, before I pull away, muttering, "*Killing me*." I want to groan in frustration. She gives me one last kiss at her building door, and then she turns and walks inside, shooting me a smile over her shoulder. I can't help smiling back, even though I'm not happy to be going home alone.

CHAPTER NINETEEN

I walk back into my room from physical therapy, feeling like I'm going to collapse. It feels good, though. Every muscle in my body got a workout and I could really tell a difference today. I felt stronger and surer, not back to normal by a long shot. But for the first time, I felt like I caught a glimmer of my old physical self.

I was moved to the rehab section of the hospital a couple days ago and I know that this means I won't be here much longer. That thought both makes me antsy to get out of here, and terrified to leave. This place has become like a safety zone to me in so many ways.

I glance at myself in the mirror as I head into my bathroom. I'm used to the minor changes that the surgeries made to my face now. They're pretty subtle, truth be told, but I wonder if these changes, coupled with all the other things that are different about me will make it hard for Evie to recognize me right away. I wonder how she's changed after all these years.

I take a long, hot shower, and just as I walk out of my bathroom, Dr. Fox walks in my room. "Hey, Doc." I smile.

He smiles, sitting down in his usual chair. "How's it going, kid? How was P.T.?"

"It was good, actually. Too much better and they're gonna kick me out of this joint." I smile.

He smiles back, but looks thoughtful.

"How are the moving plans coming along?"

"Good. I've got a condo lined up downtown, Cincinnati, and

Preston is preparing an office for me."

"Good, kid. And Evie?"

"I'm going to look her up once I get there. I just... I'm not ready yet. I don't know what I'm going to say, how I'm going to tell her what happened..." *I run my hand through my damp hair, frowning.*

"Speaking of all of that, son, I want to talk to you about something today that's perhaps a little out of my normal therapy realm." *He frowns, and is quiet for a minute. I wait him out. I'm pretty sure I know what he's going to say. I told him all about Lauren in the session after my freak out. It was hard, but I knew he had pretty much already guessed based on what he walked in on, and then what I had said while destroying my room.*

"I think you need to press charges against Lauren."

"No."

"Why not?"

"Well, for one thing, the statute of limitations is up for a statutory rape charge. Won't fly. I looked it up once as a way to try to . . . encourage her to stay away from me. Secondly, I wouldn't do that to Phil's . . . my father's company. Do you know what kind of bad press that would bring? Especially now that I'm running it? Anything attached to my name is attached to the company's name. The media would make a fucking soap opera out of that shit. Phil worked practically his entire adult life making that company what it is. It was his dream. After everything I did to him, I couldn't live with myself if I did that, too. Smearing his good name? Because that's exactly what the media would do, even though he had nothing to do with it. It wasn't just Lauren who adopted me. If her moral character is questioned as far as that goes, his will be, too, whether it holds water or not. No."

He's quiet for a minute, considering me. Then he says quietly, "I don't know if you see that what happened to you wasn't simply a case of statutory rape, son. That . . . woman adopted you, a damaged kid from the social services system, with the sole intent of molesting you. Do you see that? Do you see the perverted sickness in that? That she promised you hope and then, through her sick actions, instead, reinforced the message that you didn't deserve to be loved and cared about? Do you see that her crime goes beyond statutory rape?"

I look out the window. He's right, I have no doubt at this point that she brought me home intending on starting a sexual relationship with me when I was fifteen. I know because she told me. But what's done is done. Seeking a criminal investigation against her won't undo what happened.

"Still, no. I won't do that to my father. That's final. I can't do that to my father."

"Jake, what exactly do you carry so much guilt about when it comes to your father?"

I laugh a humorless laugh. "Well, fucking his wife wasn't very nice."

"That's you being crass as a way to deflect. And that's not what happened. An older woman who had taken you into her home manipulated you. You were . . ."

"Okay, Doc, I get it. I'm working that out, okay? We talked about that last session. I'm trying to let go of some of my own culpability. Not all of it, I won't do that, despite what you say. But some of it, enough to be able to forgive myself, all right? But as far as my father, he was never anything but good to me and I not only screwed his wife behind his back for three years, but I treated him like shit. I was so fucking angry with both of them, and I thought maybe he knew and let her play her little game with me. Or maybe I just convinced myself of that so I could hate someone else, blame someone else. But in the end, our secret killed him. He died because of me, because of us."

"Kid, he changed his will to leave his company to you, the same company you just told me was his dream, his life's work. He left that solely to you. Don't you think that speaks volumes?"

I run my hand through my hair again. "Yeah, I guess. But it just reinforces my decision to focus my energy on making him proud with the way I handle that gift."

"So you just let Lauren get away with what she did? With

harassing you, even now?"

"I'm moving to another city, Doc."

"People obsessed with someone don't typically let that stop them."

I'm quiet for a minute, staring out the window, considering what he's telling me.

"Can I tell you a little bit about the psychology of a woman who does what she did?"

I sigh. "If you have to. It won't change anything, but I'll listen."

He's silent for a minute. "Most older women who engage in sex with young teen boys have an arrested development. Psychologically, they see themselves as a teenager, therefore they don't feel guilt about the relationship, and generally justify it by saying they fell in love. They're unwell, Jake. Extremely unwell."

This sounds all too familiar. He goes on, "Male victims can show the same trauma that a female victim shows—depression, anxiety, acting out, relationship problems . . . The power imbalance and the fact that a boy's body usually cooperates are hugely confusing, hugely traumatic."

Okay, so I'm a fucking case study. Still doesn't change anything. I take a deep breath. "This is all interesting, but I can handle her now, Doc. I'm not fifteen anymore."

He sighs, looking pained. He's silent for several minutes, and I can practically see his wheels turning, but with what, I don't know. Doesn't matter. I'm not going to change my mind.

He stands up and puts his hand on my shoulder and squeezes gently before turning and walking toward the door.

"No parting words of wisdom, Confucius?" *I joke.*

He turns around, smiling, but still looking distracted. "Yeah, you're doing good, kid."

He walks through the door and I yell after him, "That's it? That's like a fortune cookie outtake."

But I don't hear him laugh as he moves away from my door, down the hall.

CHAPTER TWENTY

The next couple of days drag by for me, despite the fact that I'm slammed at work. I call Evie every chance I get between meetings and her two jobs. I hate that she's still bussing it around town but when I offer her my company driver, she declines. I'd like to insist, and I think if I pushed it enough, she'd relent, but I know that independence is important to her and I don't want to take away from who she is just so I get my way. Not on this point. This is not the hill I'm willing to die on. So my girl is riding public transportation around town. Not happy. But resigned. For now.

Monday is a crazy day, as I get ready for my trip to the San Diego office to meet with investors and to attend a dinner benefit that the company is sponsoring.

Evie's name comes up on my phone in the middle of a meeting and I excuse myself to take her call in the hallway.

"Hey, baby."

"Hi." I can hear the smile in her voice. "What are you up to?"

"In a meeting . . ." Preston sticks his head out and gestures to a schematic in his hand. He gives a thumbs up sign and mouths "Okay?" I nod back, knowing he's asking if it's okay to share it with the group. "Sorry, Evie, I can only talk for a minute. I miss you. You good?"

"Yeah, I'm good. I miss you, too."

"My bed has been cold . . . and there's nothing good to sniff on."

She laughs. "Maybe you should bring a warm batch of cookies to bed with you."

"Mmm . . . kinky. We'll have to try that."

She laughs again. "Okay, Jake, I know you have to get back to work. I'll call you on Tuesday when I get home, okay?"

"I'll be waiting. Bye, baby."

"Bye."

I walk back into my meeting smiling and wondering how I lived without her all those years. How did I do it? Then I realize, I *wasn't* living. I was existing. I was putting one foot in front of the other and simply getting by. On my best days, numb and on my worst days, miserable.

****

I fly to the San Diego office on Tuesday. Flying in over the water always reminds me of Evie and that very first plane ride to California. I'd been holding back a lump in my throat that kept threatening during the entire five hour journey. I missed her so desperately already. But I was also filled with a hope I'd never had before—a hope that I finally had a *family*, people who would help me and Evie start our life together when the time came. It would be so much easier now. I squash those memories. The darkness that hovers on the edge of those recollections is not somewhere I want to go right now.

I spend the day meeting with investors at an off-site conference room in a hotel on the bay. The view is breathtaking, not a cloud in the sky, the water sparkling, and sailboats dotting the horizon. But this is not home. Home is where *she* is and I can't wait to get back to my cold, gray-skied—when I flew out—Midwestern city. I smile to myself. Home. All along I thought home was a location, and it turns out home is a person. Home is Evie.

I'd like to fly back tonight but I have a benefit dinner that the company is sponsoring. It's for an organization that helps underprivileged kids in San Diego, a cause important to Phil that he did a lot of work for over the years, and perhaps the inspiration for wanting to adopt me in the first place. In any case, I feel like I need to represent him tonight. So I grudgingly don my tux and head there.

I mingle with some of the San Diego executives over cocktails, and as I'm turning to head to my table for dinner, I see Gwen walking my way. She's tried to talk to me several times tonight but I've been successful so far in evading her. Apparently, me telling her not to come near me again went in one ear and out the other. What is it with me and females who don't hear me? I clench my jaw and will her to turn the other way. She doesn't.

"Jake!" she calls.

I turn slowly. "Gwen. What are you doing here?"

"Oh, mom couldn't come. Daddy flew me in to be his date tonight." She smiles a big, dazzling smile.

Right at that moment, a photographer who has been taking shots of the guests mingling, comes up to us and asks for a picture. I briefly consider telling him to fuck off but don't want to cause a scene, and so I lean in to Gwen and say with a phony smile, "If we were anywhere but in front of a camera at a company event right now, you'd be watching me walk the other way." She laughs as if I'm joking. I'm not. As soon as the camera flashes, I turn and walk in the opposite direction. After a few steps, I hear Gwen call behind me, "It's because of *her*, isn't it?"

I stop, turning slowly. "Her?"

Gwen has her hip cocked, one hand resting on it. "The girl on your back. You can't let her go, can you?"

I look around but no one is close enough to hear what we're saying. I shake my head slowly. "No. Never could. Never will."

She smirks and crosses her arms under her breasts. "Well, good to know that it's not just me."

I stare at her for a minute before replying, "If that helps you sleep at night, so be it." I turn and walk away.

****

I leave as soon as I possibly can without it looking rude. It's early, but I'm looking forward to getting back to my hotel room and waiting for Evie's call. I walk into my room and throw my stuff on the dresser and start taking off my jacket when I hear a knock on my hotel room door. Who the hell could that be? Thinking it's most likely housekeeping with some question or another, I fling it open and Lauren is standing there. "Jake, before you close this door on me, please, can we just talk for a minute?"

I stare at her. "Lauren, there's nothing to talk about—"

"Please. I just wanted to see you for a minute. I've been waiting in the lobby for an hour. Please."

"Lauren, say what you want to say quickly, from right there. You have thirty seconds. And I'm being generous with that."

She purses her lips before saying, "Don't you see! This is OUR time, now, Jake. Phil is gone and we can be together now. We can have *everything* now, Jake. We—"

I grimace and take a step back. "Oh my God. There's something seriously wrong with you."

She steps forward. "No, the only thing wrong is that I don't have you. Jake, I need—"

"You need professional help. I want you to leave now, Lauren. Why do you ever think this will work?" I try to close the door on her but she holds it open, refusing to leave.

I grit out, "Fine. Have it your way. I'm not going to have a bodily struggle with you at the door. I'm going to go get in the shower, and LOCK the door. By the time I get out, if you're not long gone, I'll call security to cart you out of here. Do you understand me?"

"Jake please—"

But I walk back to the bathroom, slam the door loudly and click the lock into place. I stand leaning on the sink for a few minutes with my eyes closed. God, just the sight of that woman brings back the memory of being a weak fifteen-year-old kid whose control had been completely taken away. I run my hands down my face and then turn to the shower, turning the water up as hot as it'll go. I strip my tux off and leave it in a heap on the floor and step into the scalding water, standing under it as long as I can stand it before stepping out and blotting my red, stinging skin dry.

When I step back out of the bathroom, the room is vacated. I lay back on the bed, briefly considering calling Evie, but she said she was going to visit her friend tonight and I don't want to interrupt her. She said she'd call when she got home. I close my eyes, feeling like I just need to rest for a minute. The emotions Lauren brings up in me always make me feel so damn tired. I just want to shut out the world for a little bit.

****

I wake up, startled. What the fuck? I bolt upright, scrubbing a hand down my face. I don't think I even moved from the position I fell into on the bed. The clock says 2:58 a.m. It's almost six in Ohio. Evie never called me. *Shit!* What if something happened to her? That fucking bus. I knew I should have insisted on my driver. I'm pressing her number on speed dial before I even register picking up my phone from the bedside table.

My heart is hammering in my chest as her phone rings once, twice, three times. Then, finally, thank God, "Hello." Clearly I woke her up. My heart slows down but now I'm pissed. Why didn't she call me?

"Evie."

She hesitates. "Hey." Something's wrong.

"Hey, you never called me last night. I would have called you myself but I fell asleep waiting for you. I just woke up. I was worried."

There's silence for a second before she says, "Jake, I did call you.

A woman answered your phone. She said you were in the shower." I can clearly hear the hurt in her voice. I blink, confused for a second before it comes to me. *Fucking Lauren!*

She must have answered my phone before she left my hotel room. Fucked up timing. The lie that falls out of my mouth about having co-workers in my room for drinks and a female co-worker answering my phone makes me feel shitty because of the ease with which it forms. It's like a reflex to lie immediately when it comes to Lauren. I spent so many years keeping secrets when it comes to her. God, I hate this. I'm not ready for Evie to take on this burden, though. I can barely handle seeing Lauren for five minutes, and I've known what happened for years. *What is this going to do to Evie?*

I ask her if she's upset and she's silent for a second. "If that's the truth, Jake, then no, I'm not upset. I just don't see why she would pick up your cell phone and then not leave you the message." I close my eyes very briefly and grimace, hating myself.

"I don't know either, but they were drinking so that's my only guess. I'm sorry, baby. You must have been hurt," I say quietly.

I don't even want to think about what I would have done if a man had answered her phone while she was in the shower. Just the idea of it makes me feel murderous.

She sighs but finally says, "I was confused, Jake. It's okay. If that's what happened then it's not your fault."

I feel relieved but a hot arrow of shame is slithering down my spine. I want so badly to share this with her, but know that it is the very thing that ruined us then and may ruin us now.

I clear my throat. "I miss you. I can't wait to see you. Am I still picking you up after work tonight?"

"Yes. I'll see you then, okay?"

"Okay. Evie, I've . . . I've really missed you. I know it's just been a couple days, but I, I'm just really looking forward to seeing you." I just want her. Need courses through my veins.

"Me, too, Jake. See you tonight." Her voice is warmer now.

I disconnect and roll over, staring at the ceiling, wondering if Evie is going to be able to forgive me when she knows the truth.

****

My morning meeting is wrapped up quickly and I'm able to get a flight back to Cincinnati that leaves an hour earlier than my originally scheduled flight. After picking up my car in the long-term lot, I have plenty of time to head to the mall. I'm going to buy Evie a laptop. She's going to fight me on it but I'm doing it anyway. The need to make her life better in any way I possibly can is burning through me. Maybe it's the foresight that my time in her life is temporary. I hope to God not and just the thought of that sends panic racing to my gut. I'd fight it tooth and nail but if that unthinkable scenario does in fact come to pass, I'm going to know I did what I could to put her in a position to make her dreams come true.

I drop it off at my condo and then go to pick Evie up at work. I wait for her outside my car and when she comes out, she sees me and halts, a beautiful smile spreading over her face. My whole body relaxes. I didn't even realize how tense I was until I saw her. And now my pulse is strong and even in her presence.

"Hi," she says.

"Hi," I say back, still goofily grinning. We both burst out laughing and I can't not touch her for a minute longer. I swoop her up and breathe her in. "God, I missed you. I missed your smile and," I stick my nose in the sweet crook of her neck, "your smell, your body against mine at night."

"I missed you, too," she whispers back.

"You hungry?"

"Yeah, starving."

"Do you like sushi?" I ask.

"I do like sushi, but I can't go out dressed in my uniform."

"How about if we pick it up to go and bring it home?"

"Sounds great."

I drive to a little sushi place near my condo and run in and pick up dinner while she waits for me in the car.

When we walk into my condo, Evie halts, immediately spotting the MacBook I left open on my dining table with a red bow on top.

My heart picks up speed as I watch her take in the computer, finally looking up at me with a wary look on her face.

"Jake, you didn't—" she exclaims.

"Evie," I say, putting my hand up in a 'stop' gesture, "don't say anything until you hear me out. I know your first thought is going to be to say no to accepting this gift but please, just listen."

She raises an eyebrow but doesn't say anything.

"I want to do this but not because it's just for you, but because I think you're amazing, and I think that making *your* dreams come true will spread far and wide and not only affect you, but would affect me, too, and many, many people beyond that. Please let me do this for you, Evie, and all those people out there who will be changed when they read the beautiful words that are in your soul."

She takes a deep breath, her eyes tearing up and says on a small laugh, "No pressure, right?"

When she walks over to the computer and starts looking it over, I know she's going to accept it. I can't help the grin that spreads across my face.

"You make it really, really hard to say no to you, do you know that Jake Madsen?" She takes a deep breath and I know what she's feeling. I've been there, too. It can be a hit to your self-esteem to accept gifts from those who have more than you. I'm hoping like hell that her accepting this from me means she gets how much she gives me in return. Not monetarily, obviously, but in every way that really counts. She makes me happy. Unbelievably happy. And that's worth all the MacBooks at Apple headquarters.

"Thank you," she finally says, looking me in the eye. I smile back.

****

It's a chilly night and so I flick on the gas fireplace, pour a couple glasses of wine and set them on the coffee table, and then lay our food out on a blanket on the floor. "Sushi picnic?" she asks, smiling and sitting down.

"Yup. When eating sushi, do like the Japanese do." I smile, kneeling down on the blanket across from her. I put my palms together in front of my face and bow slightly to her. She giggles and bows back. Then I grab our glasses and hand one to her. "To what?" she asks.

I consider. "To dreams." I say, clinking my glass to hers.

She takes a drink and then says, "Thank you again for the laptop, Jake." I just smile at her. That's not the dream I was talking about but I let her think it is.

I open up all the containers—I got a little bit of everything since she told me to surprise her. She picks up her chopsticks and I unwrap a plastic fork. "Really, Jake?" she asks, inclining her head toward my fork. "When eating sushi, *eat* like the Japanese do."

"Babe, I don't eat with sticks. I want to get the food in my mouth."

She frowns. "Oh, come on, what's easier than picking up a big piece of sushi? It's not like you're trying to pick up individual pieces of rice. Look." And she reaches down with her chopsticks and expertly picks up a piece of Alaska roll, popping it in her mouth.

I look down at the food in front of us and then down at my fork and sigh. Then I pick up my chopsticks, break them in half and position them in my fingers. I reach down and position a piece of sushi between them and bring it toward my face. Inches away, it falls out and lands in my crotch.

My brows snap down as I hear Evie let out a very unladylike snort.

"Oh, that's funny, is it?"

She's looking down, clearly holding back laughter as she snags another piece of sushi with her chopsticks and pops it into her mouth, chewing and swallowing before saying, "Noooo, not funny at all. They take a little practice. Try again."

I fake glare at her, but pick my chopsticks back up and this time try a piece of tempura shrimp. I have it about halfway between the container and my open mouth when it, too, drops into my crotch.

Evie lets out a loud giggle.

"Okay, that's it. A fork it is." I pluck the food out of my crotch, noting my stained suit pants and toss it into a napkin sitting next to the containers.

"Oh, come on, it's like, bad luck or something to eat Japanese food with a fork. Okay, if you won't eat with chopsticks, I'll feed you. Open your mouth." She picks up another piece of the Alaska roll and lifts it toward me. I open and she feeds it to me, her eyes glued to my mouth as I take it from her. My heart picks up speed.

Her eyes lift to mine and I see the desire there. In just moments, the atmosphere has changed, humming with something thick and electric. She looks down quickly, picking up a piece of shrimp and bringing that to my mouth, too. This time, she lingers at my mouth with the chopsticks, sliding them out slowly after I've taken the food. I feel arousal swirling through my belly. Who knew sushi could be so sexy?

She feeds me several more bites and then takes a couple herself as I watch her chew. Focusing on her mouth is unbelievably erotic and I can't help leaning forward and tasting her lips. "You taste salty, like soy sauce," I say, smiling right up against her mouth. "Sweet and salty."

"Mmm . . ." she murmurs, smiling back and leaning closer for more.

We lick and taste each other's mouths for a couple minutes, and then I pull back, going up on my knees and moving around the food to where she's kneeling. I take her hand and move us both toward the fireplace, several feet away from the sushi picnic. We can finish that in a little bit. Right now, I'm craving something else.

I lean toward her, kissing her softly before leaning back and zipping her uniform dress down. Neither one of us had bothered to change yet. I keep eye contact with her as I bring it down her shoulders. Her dark eyes are wide and searching mine. She smiles gently as if she's happy with what she sees reflecting back at her.

I slide her bra straps down her arms and reach behind her to unhook it, kissing her down her neck as I lean back. She sighs with pleasure.

"You're so beautiful."

She looks down shyly. "You think?"

"Yeah. I think."

I take her face in my hands and return to her mouth, sliding my tongue in, kissing her deeply until we both pull away, panting.

When she spreads her hand over my erection, I suck in a ragged breath. I look into her eyes and the desire there almost undoes me.

She stands up and lets her dress fall to the floor. She's wearing nothing now but a small pair of white cotton underwear with lace on the edges. Something about them is so pure, yet so sexy that I feel myself unbelievably, grow even harder. She turns and starts walking away.

"Where are you going?"

She looks over her shoulder, smiling slightly. "I just remembered that I have somewhere else to be. I'll see you around?"

I chuckle as she switches off the light and walks back toward me.

She kneels back down in front of me and puts her palm on my cheek. I lean into her. "I wanted it to be you and me and the firelight," she whispers.

I nod, leaning toward her to kiss her again. I can't get enough of her mouth. I can't get enough of *her*.

I unbutton my shirt and pull it off, tossing it to the side. The flickering firelight is making shadows dance all around us, adding to the feeling of being alone with her in another world.

I lay down on the rug on my side and she lays down, too, facing me. Our fronts are pressed together as we continue kissing, the fire behind her.

I bring one hand to her breast and tweak and tease the hardened nipple as she moans and rubs her lower body against mine.

I pull back as I feel her unbuttoning my pants, and roll slightly onto my back so that I can pull them down and kick them off as she removes hers as well. We both lay back down and face each other again, now completely naked.

We stare at each other silently for several moments, something tender and beautiful in her expression. She brings her hand up to my face again and traces my lips with her thumb, whispering, "Can I ask you something?"

I nod.

"You said you never dated, never had a relationship with anyone." She's silent for a moment. "Why me?"

I stare into her eyes, searching them, wanting so much to tell her about all the reasons I'll never love anyone except for her, but knowing I can't, *yet*.

"Because you're everything I ever wanted," I whisper back. "Because to me, you're perfect."

She stares at me silently again before smiling and whispering, "Even this mole on my shoulder?"

I look down, barely able to see the tiny beauty mark she's pointing at in the dim light. "Especially that mole. I was on the fence about you before I saw it. That mole sealed the deal for me."

She laughs softly. "Okay, good. Thank you, little mole."

I smile and bring my lips back to hers. I reach down between us and slip my finger between her legs. *Oh, Jesus, she's so wet.* I moan into her mouth and she presses against me, wanting more of my hand. I slip my finger deeper into her warm wetness and use my thumb to dance lightly over her swollen bundle of nerves. She jerks slightly and whimpers into my mouth.

She brings her hand down to my rock hard erection and slides her hand gently up and down. I pull away from her mouth, groaning out, "Evie," as she continues to stroke me. We stare into each other's eyes, hers wide with desire, her lips parted, as our hands pleasure each other for several minutes. We watch each other's expressions change as the arousal rises. It's intimate and intense and I can already feel an orgasm circling through my abdomen. I close my eyes and clench my muscles until I feel it fade away. For the moment.

"Jake," she exhales, "I'm close. I want to come with you inside me." As she says this, she squeezes me lightly and rubs the pre-cum on my tip with her thumb.

"Ahhhhhh."

"Does that translate to, 'Okay, Evie?'" she laughs softly.

"Yes," I say, removing my hand from between her legs and hitching her top leg over my hip and scooting even closer to her.

I lean up over her to position myself at her entrance and push inside. Her tight heat surrounds me and the feel of her without a condom is beyond description. I'm afraid to move. But my body apparently isn't as my hips start thrusting practically of their own accord. I groan, "Oh God, baby, you feel so good."

She moans back, clutching me tighter to her. We move together, moaning and gasping and watching each other's faces in the dim glow of the fire. There's something primal and beautiful about making love in the glow of the flames, as if we could be in another era entirely and it would still be me and her, clasped together in this timeless dance of passion.

As her breathing becomes faster, I reach my hand down between her legs again and move my finger over her clit. I'm on a hair trigger here and I need her to come.

After only a couple seconds, she arches her back and presses into me and she's gasping through her orgasm. Watching her and feeling her spasming around me, tips me over the edge and I jerk inside of her as wave after wave of pleasure spike through me. We're coming together.

****

After we've cleaned up and changed, we finish our dinner. It tastes even better now after our mini workout. Evie even allows me to use a fork.

We pick up our picnic and then I move to the couch and switch on the TV I feel satiated and happy and some mindless television sounds good.

Evie goes over to the Mac and turns it on, sitting down at the dining room table. "Checking it out? Ever used a Mac?" I ask, looking over my shoulder.

"No, but I've always been pretty good with computers. I'll probably get the hang of it pretty quickly."

I get involved in the show, some real crime news show about a woman who disappeared and—

The sound of Evie's computer snapping down jolts me out of the story and I look over at Evie, whose face has gone pale. I stand up immediately.

"What's wrong, baby?" I ask. *Shit, what happened?*

She ignores me, walking to the door and starting to put her shoes on.

What the hell? "Evie! What happened? Why are you leaving?" My heart starts pounding.

"That woman in your hotel room was Gwen, wasn't it, Jake?"

"What?" I'm thrown. Where did this come from? My mind reaches back for the lie I told Evie after Lauren answered my phone. "No. Of course it wasn't. Do you think I would invite Gwen to my hotel room for drinks after the way she treated you?"

"Well, I wasn't exactly thinking you brought her to your hotel room for *drinks*, Jake. All I know is that you sure did look cozy whispering in her ear in the pictures from the benefit you were at Tuesday night."

It takes only seconds for me to connect the dots. Ah, God, she

Googled me and saw that damn picture of Gwen and me at the dinner in San Diego. Fucking Google. I hadn't thought of that picture once since it was snapped. I run my hand through my hair. How is it that Gwen of all people keeps coming between Evie and me? It's so ludicrous, I would laugh if Evie wasn't wearing that wounded expression.

"Evie, that was a company benefit. Gwen was there with her father. She tried to talk to me several times and I wouldn't have much to do with her. When she cornered me in front of a photographer, I leaned in and told her she was lucky that I wasn't the type to want to air my dislike for someone on film. She laughed as if I was joking, which I wasn't. That was that. I didn't talk to her again all evening."

She just keeps looking at me, searching my face. Finally, she takes a deep breath. "I want to believe you, Jake, I just . . . I don't want to . . ."

"Evie, listen, God, if you only knew . . ." I laugh a humorless laugh.

"If I only knew what?"

"If you only knew how ridiculous it is for you to think that I would ever betray you, much less with Gwen. Really, if you could get inside my brain, you'd be laughing, too."

"Jake—"

"Please, just trust me. Please don't go."

She continues to search my face, finally giving a very small nod of her head. I release my breath and lead her away from the door, throwing her coat back on the bench in my foyer.

CHAPTER TWENTY-ONE

Evie works a catering job the next night and tells me she's going to get a ride home afterwards. I want her to come home to me, but I'm trying to balance making her feel comfortable in our "new" relationship. This is the hard part for me because I'm so far beyond her emotionally, I think, but sometimes I see a look on her face that tells me her feelings for me are more intense than would make sense for a new relationship. I wonder if she finds it strange. I wonder if she's been questioning it at all. Then again, she doesn't have a lot of experience with relationships, so maybe she's not.

After a meeting at work that day, Preston takes me aside, a look of concern on his face.

"What's up? Everything okay?" I ask.

"Well, yeah, but I think you should know that Lauren has been making calls to the board. She's been asking to set up a meeting but she won't say why."

Ah, shit.

I pause for a minute, considering what she could want with the board and wondering if this is simply because I kicked her out of my hotel room a few nights ago. *Is this her new tactic to get at me?* I hold the majority of shares, so realistically, there's not much she'd be able to do. But because I'm the director of the board, I won't be part of the meeting and I won't know what she wants until after she's met with them.

"Okay, well thanks for letting me know, Preston. I'm sorry that family drama is affecting the company."

"It's doing no such thing. The company is doing great. It's you I'm worried about."

He pauses for a minute, looking at me, seeming to consider whether to go on.

"You know, I worked very closely with your father. When I visited him in the hospital after his heart attack, he obviously didn't know that you would be taking over the company as soon as you did, but he made it very, very clear to me that when that time came, he didn't want Lauren to have anything to do with this company. He asked that if there came a time when I was still here but he wasn't, that I look out for you. I hope that doesn't sound condescending. He didn't mean it that way. I just think that he felt like he had failed you in some way and he wanted to make sure that you knew you had someone on your side under any future circumstances."

Damn. I feel the emotion welling up in me and I push it back down for later. "Thanks, Preston. I appreciate—"

"No need to thank me. Just wanted you to know that I'm dealing with the board situation, okay?" And with that, he gives me a pat on the back and walks off.

****

I ask Evie to stay with me on Friday night. I have an idea that I hope will make her happy. Not only did we never get a chance to do the normal stuff *kids* do, but we never got a chance to do the things *young couples* do—all the things we might have done just for fun if we had actually gotten a chance to date when we were young and carefree. *If* we had ever been young and carefree. I'm also going to satisfy something in me from a long, long time ago. I'm going to buy her a dress and take her dancing. It still won't top dancing with her under the stars in an empty park, which, despite shaking with nerves and stepping on her feet, was the best dance of my life so far. Two foster kids dancing together in the park because they didn't have the right clothes to wear to a dance. Completely pitiful. But completely magical.

My mind goes back to that dance so many years ago and I can't help smiling. It had been so awkward, yet so intense, one of those memories that seems to be scalded into the very fiber of my being. Funny, I don't remember the songs that were playing, my head was so filled with static at her closeness, how good she smelled, how she moved against me. If I asked her, I wonder if she'd remember the songs. Those are the types of things I long to ask her, to reminisce about. *Our memories*. Some of the only good ones I have.

When I open my door for her on Friday, she looks beautiful but tired. That won't do. I scoop her up and tell her I'm going to run a bath for her so she gets a second wind because I'm taking her dancing.

She fights me a little bit on the dancing plan and gives me an exasperated look when I tell her I bought her an outfit. But she marches toward the bedroom to see what I picked out for her so I think that's a good sign.

I follow her back to the bedroom and watch her as she fingers the silky material of the dress and checks out the Jimmy Choo shoes. The saleswoman at the department store had put several in front of me that she suggested for the dress I chose, and I had noticed that one of the pairs was more than the fourteen hundred dollar price tag that Gwen had shrieked about after Evie spilled caviar on them. I had automatically chosen those. It was petty and superficial, I knew, but it made me smile to know that Evie would be wearing better shoes than that snotty bitch.

Finally, she turns to me with a smile. "I love it. Thank you. Did you really pick this out?"

"Well, I had some help from a saleswoman. But I did give her the color scheme I wanted, and I looked at the clothes you left here for your size."

"Peacock blue, huh?" she raises an eyebrow.

I shrug, grinning. "I like the color. Just don't ask me to take you anywhere near the zoo."

She laughs and I head into the bathroom to start her bath.

I make her some pasta as she's getting ready and when she emerges from the bedroom, I almost start drooling on myself. Holy shit, she's gorgeous. I've seen her body in nothing at all and I know it's perfect, but that dress highlights her best assets, her perky tits, flat stomach and firm little ass, without showing too much skin. "You're stunning." *I'm not sure if I want to take you out in public in that.* I momentarily regret not picking up that black, oversized sweater that I passed on the way to the eveningwear department.

"Thank you. I have a personal shopper who's well acquainted with my figure." She raises her eyebrows, but smiles.

Once she's sitting down eating, I decide to unveil the T-shirt I had made at a mall kiosk I passed when I was buying her laptop, just purely to make her laugh. I take off my long sleeved pullover and nonchalantly turn toward her so she can see written across the front in bold, black print, *World's Greatest.*

She almost chokes on the bite she's chewing, and brings her napkin up to her mouth, fighting back laughter.

"What?" I ask, innocently.

She points at my shirt. "World's Greatest *what?*"

"Oh, this?" I point at my shirt. "It's all inclusive. *World's Greatest Guy, World's Greatest Lover, World's Greatest Cook.* You name it, I'm the greatest."

"Ah. Well, I do appreciate your confidence. But you know, you've left yourself wide open now for your critics to test you." She raises an eyebrow.

"I only care about one critic. And I'm looking forward to being tested. The more testing, the better. Lots of testing would be good." I wink.

"You're completely ridiculous, you do realize that, right?" she says, shaking her head, but grinning.

I laugh. "Finish up. I'm going to go change while you're eating and then we'll get going."

"You're not going to wear your *World's Greatest* shirt to the club?" she yells after me.

"You don't really want me to advertise all over town, do you?" I call back. I can hear her laughing as I open my closet door.

I change in to some dressier clothes, and ten minutes later, we're headed downtown.

****

I take Evie to a club called Igby's that's relatively new and I've heard has an amazing interior that was completely gutted and re-done to resemble a New York City loft.

After we've gotten a drink, she mentions her friend Landon, the guy who was shooting death glares at me over the Gwen incident at the autism benefit. I know he's someone important to Evie, and I'd like the opportunity to make a better impression, so I suggest that she ask him to meet us here. She looks hesitant for a minute, but then agrees and about an hour later, he and his friend, Jeff, join us.

I buy a round of drinks and we all squeeze into the small table. I don't mind that Evie practically has to sit on my lap. I welcome the excuse to be as close to her as possible, especially in public. I've already caught several men staring at her for a beat longer than I'm comfortable with, and I want to make it crystal clear that she's here with me.

Landon leans toward me and asks, "So, Jake, you're from Cincinnati?"

I pause for a second, discombobulated, but then I realize that Evie probably hasn't had a chance to tell him too much about me, and he's just asking a simple question. So instead of saying, *yeah, I grew up in Northside just like Evie*. I say, "No, actually, San Diego."

"California? Really? I love San Diego. I've been there twice. I stayed in Pacific Beach with a friend of mine. Where did you live?"

"La Jolla." I take a drink of my water, chewing a piece of ice.

From a run-down foster home in Northside, Cincinnati to a mansion on the cliffs of the Pacific Ocean. And each was a different sort of hell.

He stares for a minute. Obviously he knows the area. He whistles. "Nice part of town. What brings you here?"

"My father's company has an office here. I started running things about six months ago."

Landon nods, raising his eyebrows and glancing at Evie.

Jeff says, "You must miss the sunshine."

I look at Evie. "Plenty of sunshine here, too." I smile at her.

"Cheesy," she laughs, but pulls my face toward her and gives me a quick kiss on the lips.

We look at each other grinning for a minute, and when I look over at Landon and Jeff, they're both looking back and forth between the two of us, huge smiles on their faces.

I pull Evie against my side and look toward the guys. "So, Landon, Evie tells me you're in school at U.C. What are you studying?"

"I'm getting my business degree," Landon says.

I nod. "Cool. When do you graduate?"

"Still a couple years away. I'm on the slow track," he says, smiling and taking a drink.

I nod again, smiling, too. "What about you, Jeff? What do you do?"

"I'm an engineer," Jeff says.

"Oh really? What type of engineering?"

He tells me he's a mechanical engineer and we talk for a few minutes about his job and what my company does.

After a few minutes, I hear a good song come on and I stand up, pulling Evie with me, and whisper, "I want you on the dance floor." I need to feel her against me. She looks hesitant but gives a little wave to the guys and starts following me.

When we make it to the middle of the dance floor, she puts her arms up around my neck and we start moving to the beat. The combination of our bodies moving against each other and the intense beat of the music is sexy as hell. I look down at her and her eyes are filled with the same thing I'm feeling.

"I should have known you'd be a good dancer," she whispers to me, and the feel of her breath at my ear sends a lightning bolt of arousal through my body. I press more closely into her.

Landon comes up behind Evie as the song changes and I take the opportunity to go to the restroom.

"Take care of her," I say to Landon as I hand Evie over.

When I return a few minutes later, I see a big, overly muscled meathead pulling Evie toward him as Landon tries to pull her in the other direction. A red haze comes over my vision and suddenly, I'm fourteen again and someone is pushing Evie around at school. Only now there's a sexual element to the bully's motives. It's all I can do not to tackle the asshole and pummel his face into the bar floor. Instead, I grab the back collar of his shirt and haul him back toward me.

I get right up close to him, and say, "Hey asshole, you need to learn what no means." He sizes me up for a split second. He's bigger, but I'm taller and my expression must tell him that I'm willing to push this because he says, "Whatever, man," and holds his hands up in mock surrender and pushes me back off him as he walks by me. *Stupid meathead.* I look over at Evie, and for a second our eyes lock and the rest of the club fades away as she tilts her head, looking dreamily at me. *She knows.* But just as quickly, she shakes her head very slightly and smiles brightly at me, crooking her finger to come to her. I do. When I reach her, she looks up at me and whispers, "My hero."

I look down into her slightly buzzed expression, shaking my head and smiling at her ability to disarm me. Sweet, beautiful lion tamer.

We dance next to the guys for another forty five minutes or so. Landon is funny as all hell and I can see why Evie likes him. Troublemaker by Olly Murs comes on and Landon starts doing these dance moves I swear I've never even seen before. We're all laughing at his show as people start to stand back to watch and cheer him on. I look over at Evie and I can't stop smiling, watching her as she laughs and has fun, living in the moment. Time seems to slow and the music fades out. There's only her, and I think, this, *this* makes my soul feel full.

The music comes slamming back into my head, and time resumes as Landon pulls Jeff forward, and now everyone is clapping for the both of them. Jeff isn't nearly the dancer Landon is, but he manages to hold his own. It's entertaining, but I'm ready to get Evie home to bed. The adrenaline rush from tearing the big guy off of her, and all the sweaty dancing has me worked up. All I can think of is getting her beneath me in bed and sinking into her tight, wet warmth.

As the crowd fills back in and Landon dances over to us, I lean toward him and tell him I'm going to get Evie home. He nods, saying, "It was great to really meet you." I smile and nod to Jeff a few feet away, and Evie blows him a kiss and waves to Jeff as I lead her off the dance floor.

Evie heads off to use the restroom and as I wait for her, I do a double take as a woman walks straight toward me. *Are you fucking kidding me?* A huge surge of adrenaline releases in my body. *Lauren.* She followed me here? I glance quickly toward the restrooms and walk straight to Lauren, grabbing her arm and turning her around so that she's forced to walk with me toward the front of the bar. She leans into me, hugging me as I practically drag her forward. I shake her off. "I'm done. I swear to fucking God, Lauren."

"Jake—stop! Wait, I'm in town to meet with the board tomorrow. You wouldn't let me talk to you in San Diego! I went to your building to see you and your doorman told me you were headed here. I didn't think you'd mind—"

"Yeah, I fucking *mind*. What about any of my words or actions in the past five fucking *years* gave you the idea that I wouldn't mind? And what the fuck are you meeting with the board about?" I'm gritting my teeth so hard that I'm barely moving my jaw as I'm spitting out each word to this crazed lunatic. She's gotta be living in a fantasy world in her own head. It's the only explanation.

I glance back toward the restroom, my heart hammering in my chest. Evie's going to be coming out any second. There is no way in hell that I can let Lauren know I'm here with a woman. She will attempt to cause a major scene—I'm all too familiar with the way she treated girls I brought around her when I was still living at her house. *Ugly*. If I saw her try some of that shit with Evie, I might have to kill her. And just having gotten Evie back in my life, prison doesn't sound all too appealing.

"I'll tell you, Jake. Please, I—"

"Fine, call me this weekend and we'll talk. If you leave now, I'll answer your call and we'll talk, all right? I'm with some friends here tonight and this is not the time or the place."

She furrows her brow and looks at me suspiciously for a minute, but then looks around and when she looks back at me, she says, "Fine. I want to meet in person though—I'll call you after my meeting. Make sure you answer, Jake."

And with that she turns and walks out the door of the club. I let out a breath and turn to look toward the restroom again, but still no sign of Evie.

I walk over to the bouncer and ask him if there's a line outside. He says yes which makes me feel better. If Lauren tries to come back in before we leave, she'll have to wait.

When I look up, Evie has almost made it all the way to where I'm standing. Shit, I didn't see her come out. I smile, hoping it doesn't look forced and take her hand.

"Ready?" I ask.

"Who were you talking to?" she asks, frowning.

Damn, she saw me with Lauren. More lies. I fucking hate this. I feel a depression sweep over me.

"Just some woman who was drunk, making a scene. The bouncers called her a cab and I just lead her to the door. Hold on, let me get a glass of water for you at the bar before we leave," I say, trying to distract her.

"I'm okay," she says. "You looked mad."

"Not really. She was just being kind of belligerent. She tried to make a pass. I said no. That was that." I don't know what she saw so I'm covering all the bases.

I tell her to trust me on the water and lead her over to the bar. I watch her drink it, trying to calm my frayed nerves. This night just went to shit.

She puts the glass down on the bar, smiling at me flirtily and saying, "Take me home. Before I have to beat more women off of you."

I laugh, hoping it doesn't look forced. Inwardly, I cringe.

We pull into my garage fifteen minutes later. In those few short minutes, Evie has managed to relax me a little as she chats and reminisces about our night and just seems so enthusiastic and *happy*.

I don't know what I'm feeling right now. I feel all keyed up, an intensity running through my body that I don't know is good or bad, or maybe both. I'm on a high from making Evie happy tonight, from the intense feelings of holding her body against mine for hours, from the music, but I'm also ready to burst out of my own skin at the rage I feel that Lauren won't leave me the fuck alone, at the guilt for lying to Evie. The lies are building up and it's getting worse and worse. It's all swirling inside of me and I don't know what to do with it. In the past, it was all negative and I would seek to numb it with a substance, but now there's that river of joy running through it all, muddling up my mind. I feel gentle and aggressive and so fucking confused.

I turn off the car and pull Evie to me, and take her face in my hands, pouring all my emotions into kissing her. We kiss fervently in the car for a few minutes before she climbs on top of me and *fuck*! This show needs to head upstairs now so I can fuck her properly.

I'm about to suggest just this when the sound of fabric tearing fills the car. What the hell? She leans off of me and the seam at my crotch is torn straight down the middle. Well, that's interesting.

"Oh my God," she breathes, "your boy part is like the Incredible Hulk."

Boy part? "Boy part?"

She nods, her eyes wide. "Is he angry?"

I'm trying really hard not to laugh. "Not yet. But if you keep referring to him as a 'boy part,' he could get there. He's all man. You don't want to see him get angry."

"Oh, I definitely want to see him get angry."

I can't help it then. I laugh out loud. "Come on, let's get you upstairs."

Evie walks in front of me to hide my gaping pants as we walk past Joe, the front deskman. I'll deal with him later regarding Lauren. Thinking of the whole situation tonight sends a bolt of possessiveness through me—my first priority is protecting Evie. Lauren will not mess this up. *No. Fucking. Way.*

We walk into my condo, stumbling against the wall, still laughing about my pants. I press her up against the wall and the testosterone starts pumping through my veins. My desire for her notches up several levels and the blood rushes downward. She's so fucking beautiful. I stare down at her and her face becomes serious as she stares back. "Jake, I've never really been silly a lot in my life and so I want to thank you for that. I know that sounds kind of crazy and maybe even a little dumb, but, really, it's a big deal to me so, honestly, thank you for tonight."

That's the best thing she could have said to me because that was the whole point. "I look forward to lots more silly moments with you, beautiful," I say back, smiling.

I press her harder into the wall and lower my mouth to hers. We kiss for long minutes, our tongues wrestling, licking and sucking at each other's lips. She tastes like Evie and chardonnay. I groan at the mixture, loving it, feeling like the residual alcohol on her breath is making me drunk, but I know that in reality, it's just *her* who intoxicates me. With the arousal, the feelings I had running through me in the car surge forward, and my body reacts, my tongue plundering, my hips rolling against her as she moans and whimpers, completely undoing me. I feel out of control, dizzy with desire, more aggressive than I've felt so far, a need to lose myself in her and claim her completely at the same time.

I lift her off her feet so that she's forced to wrap her legs around me and I press her more firmly against the wall. She reaches her hand down into my pants and strokes me, sending me reeling off the edge of sanity. All I can think of is pounding into her. I've completely lost control and I don't care. I relish it.

I hear another tearing sound and realize vaguely that I just tore her thong off. Damn thing was in my way. She breathes in sharply, and then moans loudly as I move my fingers around her wet opening, not penetrating, just spreading the wetness around in slow circles. I feel a growl come up my chest at the feel of her slickness. "Always so wet for me," I choke out.

She brings her arms up around me to hold on tight, and leans her head back against the wall, giving me perfect access to taste the sweet skin at her neck. I continue to finger her, spreading her juices up and around her clit. She's squirming and whimpering which fuels the desire for me to consume her. I hope she's ready for a rough ride because that's about all I'm capable of right now.

I lean my hips back and feel a burst of pre-cum when Evie whimpers in protest.

"Take my cock out, Evie," I say, feeling like my voice is thick and far away.

She reaches through the tear in my pants, into my boxers and takes me in her hand. The feel of her hand on me is almost too much. But she lets go quickly, and I grip her ass with one hand and position myself at her entrance with the other, and slam into her, none too gentle. She cries out and it brings me back to myself momentarily, and I still for several seconds as I stare into her lust filled eyes, making sure that she's okay. When I see that she is, I pull back very slowly and then thrust back into her again. The friction of her tight muscles wrapped around me feels so good that I let out an involuntary hiss. Evie closes her eyes and moans deeply, parting her lips and I lose it again, my body taking over, and my mind taking a backseat on the pleasure ride I'm on.

I crash my mouth back over hers and start thrusting wildly into her, hard and deep, slamming her against the wall. I want to possess her, own her, and confirm that she's mine. Convince myself that something beautiful in this world is mine, and only mine.

I feel another burst of pre-cum and a spike of overwhelming pleasure pulses through my abdomen. I reach down between us and roll my finger against her sweet spot, and she starts panting and moaning into my mouth as her orgasm rolls through her.

I rip my mouth off of hers and watch as the pleasure washes over her features, and it's so incredibly beautiful that the words, "Mine. Only mine. Only. Ever. Mine," pour unbidden from my brain to my lips as I continue to pump into her relentlessly.

My own climax swirls downward and my head automatically drops back, the intense pleasure taking over, and stars bursting in front of my eyes as I swell and jerk inside of her.

As the stars diminish and fade away slowly, control flows back in, and I wonder at what just happened. As unbelievably incredible as it was for me, I hope I didn't hurt her. Walls aren't exactly soft. But as I bring my head back up and gaze into her eyes, still gliding in and out of her slowly, the look on her face calms me. She looks awe-struck and satisfied, and very thoroughly fucked. Pride wells up in me, a fierce feeling of ownership.

"You are so beautiful," she says lazily.

I smile, letting her down to the floor very slowly. "You're the beautiful one," I whisper.

She leans up and kisses me sweetly, and I lead her to the bedroom.

Later, after we've cleaned up a little and fallen into bed, Evie is snuggled tightly against me, breathing deeply. I know she's asleep. "I love you," I whisper, needing to say it, even knowing she doesn't hear.

"Mmm, Leo . . ." she murmurs back. My whole body freezes, the steady beat of my heart pausing and then resuming as her words slam into me. *Oh my God. Holy shit.* My heart races furiously now, my brain cloudy, eyes wide in the dark. I don't know what to feel, but it takes me several hours before I fall into a fitful sleep.

CHAPTER TWENTY-TWO

Evie leaves for work the next morning, and I laze around for a little while before getting up and heading to the gym. I keep hearing Evie's voice in my head, whispering *Leo* in her sleep. I still don't know what to think about it. Does she still dream about me? What does that mean? Is there something inside of her that still holds on to the boy that I once was? Is that going to make it easier or harder for her to hear the truth about me?

I work out for a couple hours and then head home. I'm also keyed up because I know that Lauren is meeting with the board today—and I don't know why. Whatever it is, I can pretty much guarantee that her only motivation is to have something to control me with, and that knowledge alone fills me with a sickening anger. How long am I going to have to deal with her crazy shit? How can I ask Evie to deal with any of this? It never fucking stops. And I know for a fact that if Lauren realizes that Evie is back in my life, it will only get worse. A lot worse.

Dealing with Lauren today or any day is about the last thing I want. But I have to know what she's up to. My personal feelings aside, I owe it to my company to know what she's planning. Best to meet her in public before I leave to pick up Evie. If I didn't want to know what board business she thinks she has, I suppose I could avoid her call like I usually do. But then she'll try to show up while Evie's here and, *oh Christ*, now I just have a headache. I sit at the bar in my kitchen with my head in my hands for a few minutes, just considering this mess. Then I get up and take a shower, shave and work at my desk in workout pants and a T-shirt for the remainder of the afternoon.

I have Lauren's number programmed to go straight to voicemail, so I check my phone every so often until I see that I have a message. When I listen to it, it's Lauren and I call her back.

"Jake, I'm on my way up." She doesn't even wait for me to say hi.

"What the fuck, Lauren? I didn't tell you to come to my condo. Who let you up anyway?"

"The front deskman let me up—I told him who I am. Of course he did."

Ah hell—I forgot to talk to Joe. I'm going to ream his ass when I go down there.

I step out into the hallway just as the elevator dings. Lauren steps off, giving me a huge grin. I don't smile back.

"Still a moody teenager, I see," she says, breezing past me into my condo.

She looks around. "I love it, Jake." She goes over to the window and looks out at the view. "You know I'd move here if you want me to. I'd prefer you move back to San Diego with me but—"

"Lauren, why are you meeting with the board? Why'd they have to sacrifice a Saturday for you?"

She sighs, stepping closer. "Jake, I met with the board today to let them know that I'm contesting the will. Phil wasn't in his right mind when he left the majority of the shares to you. My lawyer has advised me that I have a very good case. I made an appeal to the board to halt all financial decisions until I reclaim ownership of the company, which I will."

I stare at her for a couple beats. I wondered if she'd try to make this play. "It's not going to happen. Phil's will was ironclad, and he was very much in his right mind. You have all the money you'll ever need. You know the only reason you're doing this is to try to control me. Life was pretty good for you when you had control over me, wasn't it?" I grit out.

"Oh, Jake," she sighs. "What this is about is me getting what is rightfully mine. I was married to that workaholic for twenty years. Do you know how much I sacrificed? Until you came along, I was lonely all the time. You need to let go of the unnecessary guilt. Phil being gone makes it easier for us to be together. It's the truth. It's just how it happened. You don't need to feel badly about it. It isn't possible for two people to be as attracted to each other as we are and it not be right."

"Lauren, this is a waste of my breath because you hear what you want to hear, but I was never attracted to you—at least not for more than twenty very confusing, ultimately horrifying minutes eight years ago, during an episode that was the beginning of the end for me. The most fucked up part of what happened between us is that a part of me complied with you because I didn't want to disappoint you. I had been a disappointment all my life and I thought... I thought I was finally going to have a family who cared about me. A very fucked up, very confused part of me just wanted you to like me, under any circumstances. And somehow, I think you knew that, preyed on it even. When you talk about what's "rightfully yours," I get the feeling you're referring to *me* more so than the company, Lauren." I'm practically spitting the words at her, my jaw tight. She won't hear me, but maybe I needed to say that anyway, not for her, but for myself.

She looks defeated for just a second, and I wonder if maybe my words penetrated, but then she comes closer to me, and tries to put her hand on my cheek. I block her, moving away. "You don't have to act like this. Let me make it better, honey." Then she leans up on her tiptoes and tries to press her lips to mine. I step back, and put my hand up in front of me. *Done*. It always comes to this.

"Don't start this shit. I explained to you in San Diego the nature of our relationship and that is that there isn't one, okay?"

"You lie to yourself, Jake. You can't just make this go away. You can't just make *me* go away."

"The fuck I can't. Get out."

She steps toward me again and tries to wrap her arms around me.

"Get the fuck OUT!" I yell, the anger spiking inside of me now.

Why did I even waste my breath with her? I swear to God, she's psychotic.

She looks down and whispers so softly I can barely hear it, "I'm never going to get you back, am I?"

I don't even answer. What's the point? Her saying that doesn't mean anything—she'll just come at me in some other way once she regroups.

I stride over to my door, flinging it open. Holy *fuck*, Evie is standing there blinking at me from the hallway. My adrenaline is pumping through my veins and this is the worst possible scenario I can think of. How much did she hear? I can't even remember what was said, I'm so filled with anger and now fear. "Shit. Evie. What the *fuck* are you doing here?"

Her face goes pale, her mouth opens to say something and then closes as her large, expressive eyes fill with hurt. Fuck, fuck, FUCK! I want to roar and smash something.

I clench my jaw, struggling to keep control as Lauren walks out my door and halts in her tracks when she sees Evie. She looks between the two of us and then clips out, "Really, Jake? Already?"

This is a nightmare. Evie *cannot* find out about Lauren in this way. I close my eyes momentarily, fighting for strength, and say as calmly as I possibly can, "Get out."

Lauren ignores me, as usual, and walks over to Evie saying, "I'm Lauren," in the bitchy, condescending voice that means something bad is coming.

Evie blinks and starts extending her hand, whispering, "Nice to meet you, I'm . . ."

"Mom!" I yell. Evie cannot say her name. Lauren never met her, but she sure as hell knows her name since I said it about a thousand times on our way to San Diego. She knows that Evie is the name of the girl on my back. I doubt if she'll recognize that *this* woman is *that* girl, especially since she's only seen my tattoo a couple times, but I can't have her hearing her name. I know that calling Lauren 'mom' will get her attention. She's always hated it.

"If you don't get out, swear to God, I will call security to haul you downstairs." My hands clench and unclench at my sides.

Lauren pouts momentarily but pulls herself together and says, "Fine, Jake, have it your way."

I've never had it my way, not with you, you crazy bitch.

Then she steps onto the open elevator, turns and looks directly at Evie and says, "You're just one of many. You should know that."

Evie lets out a small sound that, quiet though it is, slams into my chest like a ten-ton wrecking ball. Appalled shock runs down my spine.

I stand where I am for several long seconds, trying to get a handle on my control, trying to rein in the swirling rage, wanting to choke on the overwhelming disgust at having Lauren and Evie in the same hallway.

Evie is the first to move, walking over to the elevator and pushing the button. Her movement snaps me out of my angry trance and I feel a surge of panic. *She's going to leave me now.*

"Evie! Where are you going?"

"I'm leaving, Jake. Obviously you don't want me here. I'm sorry, I got off work early and I thought, I mean, I thought it would be okay. I called you . . ." She trails off, her eyes filling with tears, undoing me.

"Evie, baby, please. Let me explain. I'm so sorry. So fucking sorry. I keep messing up." I run my hand through my hair, trying to figure out how to make Evie understand. I pull on her hand very, very slightly, hoping she'll follow me into my condo. She remains still for a minute, studying my face before she lets me lead her inside. It isn't lost on me that she leaves her things right next to the door. She's going to let me explain, but she's ready to make a quick getaway, should it be necessary.

****

We sit down in my living room and I begin. "First of all, I'm so sorry I made you feel badly for coming here. You can show up here anytime you want to. I never expected my mom to . . ." I sigh, "We're . . . estranged. Things are not good between us, which I guess you could tell." I laugh humorlessly. There is nothing remotely funny about this situation.

I tell Evie about Lauren being in town to appeal to the board, and that despite having told her I want nothing to do with her, I need to deal with that issue.

I explain to her about my complicated relationship with my mom, only leaving out details of why. Even talking about Lauren at all is difficult for me. I've spent so many years trying to pretend the situation doesn't exist, trying to stuff the feelings away and numb the pain of what happened in that house. It obviously didn't work, but it was a way for me to try to move past it. I find that even telling Evie the nature of my relationship with Lauren, and that she was the reason for me acting out in high school and my stilted relationship with my dad, is very difficult.

Despite the fact that I don't give Evie a lot of details, this is a hundred times harder than telling Doc all my darkest secrets. For one thing, Doc was my psychologist, Evie is . . . Evie is everything to me. The fear of her turning away when she hears even a portion of my truth is terrifying on a very deep level.

I want her to understand where my lashing out at her came from. It wasn't right. I know that. But it came from a place that had nothing to do with Evie, not really.

"When I saw you standing there, I couldn't believe that you were even about to share her *air*. She's a ruthless bitch and she'll do or say anything that she thinks will further her own agenda. I wasn't mad that you were here, I was mad that you were even in the *vicinity* of that pit viper. And that was not your fault, but I lost it, and I'm so sorry." I plead for her understanding with my eyes.

"Jake," she says, "I feel like when you're talking about yourself, you're talking to me in code. I get the gist of what you're saying but you really haven't told me anything."

She's completely right of course, and I feel shitty about that, but this is all I can give right now. Telling her everything about my hatred for Lauren means telling her who I am, and I just can't muster up the courage to do it in this moment. I'm a coward. When it comes to her, I'm a coward. But, if anything, I want her to know how sorry I am.

We're both silent for another minute before I squeeze her hands and say, "Forgive me for talking to you like that, for making you feel that way? God, for that whole fucked up situation?"

She takes a deep breath and looks at me for several moments, frowning slightly before saying, "Yes, I forgive you. And you don't have to apologize for your mom, Jake. I know better than anyone you can't help who your parents are."

"Thank you," I say quietly, bringing her hands to my mouth and kissing her knuckles. "I never want to do anything to hurt you, Evie. Everything I do, it's because my feelings are so strong for you . . . I . . . Christ, I'm so out of my element here and there are all these fucked up things . . . Just, be patient with me?"

And then my sweet Evie does the one thing that no one has done for me in eight years, the one thing I couldn't have even asked for because I didn't know how much I needed it. She puts her arms around me and holds me close.

CHAPTER TWENTY-THREE

I order dinner while Evie takes a shower. I screwed up and I know it. Talking to Evie the way I did weighs heavily on my mind. My anger was at Lauren and I took it out on her. And I'm still asking her to be patient with me. How much longer will she be willing to do that? She knows I'm holding back from her, and yet she's trusting me anyway. I think she senses that my feelings for her are honest, but she must know that what I'm holding back from her has the potential to change her mind about me. I'll hurt her either way. And I'll lose her either way. I stare out at the city unseeing, misery roiling through my gut.

I feel Evie's arms wrap around my waist from behind and I sigh, leaning back into her warmth. She lays her head against my back, and I take her hands in mine from the front. I want her comfort. *Crave* her comfort. We stand like this quietly for several minutes, me finding peace in her warmth and her sweetness. Being held in her arms is like a balm to my heart.

I breath deeply, letting Evie's magic wash over me—nothing in this crazy, messed up world feels quite so bad when I'm standing in her embrace. Nothing feels like it can't be overcome when I feel her love surrounding me. I want to turn around and fall to my knees at her feet and declare my undying love, tell her that I would charge into battle for her, do anything and everything to keep her. *Will you tell her the truth? Will you risk losing her?* A small whisper resonates in the back of my mind. I hold onto her more tightly.

After a little bit, she gives me a squeeze and slides her warm hands up the bottom of my shirt. I feel her lean down and then I feel her lips kissing and licking up my spine. I can feel her smiling against my skin. As she moves higher, I tense. My back is off limits, for now. *Someday soon, baby, I'm going to tell you about how I missed you so fucking badly, I needed you etched into my skin permanently to even make it to the next breath.*

I turn around so that my stomach is at her face, and she looks up at me and presses her lips against it. "Evie," I breathe. I still feel guilty about my words earlier, and I feel like I should pull her up to me and stop her from proceeding with what I see in her eyes, but try as I might, I can't bring myself to do it. As we make eye contact, a live current rushes between us and blood rushes downward, hardening me immediately. I want to make sure that she's okay with this.

But when she smiles up at me and goes down on her knees, unbuttoning my jeans, my mind blanks and it's sweet relief. She takes my zipper down and pulls my jeans and boxers down my legs, springing me free. I feel the cool air against my erection and I want her mouth on me so badly, I ache. "Put your mouth on me, please, Evie," I beg, all rational thought gone.

She looks at me with big, dark eyes and then leans into me and licks the underside of my erection. *Oh God, oh God.*

She takes me in her mouth, fluttering her tongue across the underside of my cock, and then sucking gently, and I can't help the involuntary thrust of my hips. She owns me right now and I love giving myself to her completely. The relief in being able to lose control to her is overwhelming.

Her hair falls over her face and I brush it aside and hold it there, wanting to watch. The physical sensations are incredible, but the visual of Evie's lips stretched around my cock is so exciting, I already feel spikes of pleasure racing through my belly, tightening my balls and making me groan involuntarily.

As she takes me fully in her mouth, she looks up at me and I feel a burst of pre-cum. She takes the base of my erection in one hand and starts sucking me rhythmically, and I'm completely at her mercy.

"Oh, fuck! Evie . . . your mouth . . . Like that!" I grind out, my voice heavy with lust.

I push my hands all the way into her hair, pulling it at the roots and holding it back from her face so I can see more of her. She moans and keeps sucking and stroking with her mouth, her eyes closed now.

I feel myself jerk in her mouth, and I can't help thrusting my hips toward her face, out of control with the pleasure and the sight of her taking me in, her lips stretched around my length.

I don't want it to end but I'm so far gone, I can't hold back. "Oh God! I'm gonna come, baby," I warn her, but she doesn't take her mouth off of me, which makes the orgasm that was building hit me hard and fast, pleasure exploding as I jerk again and again in the grip of her warm mouth.

I groan through it, watching her as she swallows all of it, milking me in her mouth until my body stills.

"Holy fuck."

She tucks me back into my pants, smiling up at me. I'm bleary eyed and disoriented. What just happened? The buzzer from the front desk sounds. I shake my head, confused, as she looks up at me. Oh right, our food. We both simultaneously look at the door and then back at each other and both burst out laughing.

****

After we've eaten and I've showered, I take her back to the bedroom and return the favor from earlier. It's just her and me—and for just tonight, none of the other bullshit matters. We're just Evie and Jake, a couple falling in love, or in my case, already deeply in love, enjoying the comfort and pleasure our bodies can give. Afterwards, I lay satiated and happy on the bed after another mind-blowing orgasm.

I smile up at the ceiling, pondering on the layers of my love for this girl. "What's that for?" she asks, smiling over at me.

"I knew it'd be like this with us," I say, grinning now.

"You did, did you?"

"Yup. Knew it the first time I kissed you." *On our roof, eight years ago.*

That kiss had blown my mind at the time. I had anticipated kissing her for so long, but still, the way the air seemed to sparkle around us when our lips met had taken me by surprise. I realized then that my connection to Evie went beyond my love for her. I loved her deeply, yes, but there was also something purely physical and electric that sizzled to life when our bodies touched. I didn't know at the time how rare that is, but I know it now.

She smiles back at me and leans up and kisses me gently on the lips. "I'm gonna go clean up. I'll be right back."

She finishes in the bathroom, and I pull on my boxers and T-shirt and get in under the covers.

When she gets back, she pulls on her underwear and tank top and slides in next to me, taking her spot in my bed. I spoon her from behind and put my arm around her, cupping her breast possessively, in what has become our sleep position. She looks over her shoulder at me and smiles, and I lean forward and kiss her, and then lean back and put my leg over her hip.

She pushes back against me. "Your leg is too heavy. It's making me feel trapped."

"You *are* trapped. I'm going to keep you here in my bed indefinitely, trapped under my body, having my way with you."

She giggles. "Indefinitely? We'll need to eat at some point."

"I have a half a pack of gum in my bedside table. We'll cut each piece into tiny portions and ration."

"You'd live on rationed gum to have unlimited sex with me?"

"Not just sex. I like everything we do in my bed . . . the snuggling, the talking, the sniffing." I stick my nose in her neck and inhale and she giggles. "I just want you with me twenty-four hours a day. Right here."

"Aw, that's so sweet."

I pause. "But mostly sex. Mostly for the sex."

She laughs and pushes my leg off of her, and turns around still smiling. She snuggles into me and I wrap my arms around her, kissing her on the top of her sweet-smelling head. I don't know exactly how long it takes me to fall asleep, but I know I do it smiling.

CHAPTER TWENTY-FOUR

I'm just finishing up my P.T. when Doc walks in the gym. My physical therapist, Mark, is already working with someone else, and I'm on my own, doing a few extra exercises to help my range of motion.

"Looks like you're just about back to normal there."

I stand up, pulling a small towel around my neck and taking a drink from my water bottle. "Yeah, I am. I feel good. Patched up inside and out." I grin.

He smiles back. "All packed up?"

"Yeah." I run my hand through my hair, landing on the scar on the back of my head. "It's gonna feel weird to leave this place. I almost feel like I started a new life here. And now I need to go out there and start over again."

"Not start over. Just continue on. I'm not worried about you." He smiles and claps his hand on my shoulder, squeezing it before pulling away.

I blow out a little puff of air. "I'M worried about me. What if I screw this up, Doc?" And by "this," I mean all of it—the company, Evie, the rest of my life.

He shakes his head. "You won't. You know why?"

"Why?" We've started walking out of the gym and turn down the hall toward my room now.

"Because when a person is on the right path, they know it. And, Jake, you're a survivor, a fighter. You'll fight to stay on the path you're on now. The path that you know you're MEANT to be on. Did anything *about the last eight years feel right to you?"*

I take a deep breath. "No. Not a single thing."

"You get that feeling again, you turn the other way, okay?"

"Yeah. Okay, Doc."

As we walk, I think back over the last eight years . . . arriving in San Diego, so much hope . . . that first horrifying week, hating myself every fucking day after that.

A visual of myself veering off a path laid out in front of me flashes through my mind.

I think about high school. I think about how differently I was received in that school in California than I had ever been in any school before that—first as a kid who got free lunches and then later, as a foster kid. I think about liking how that felt and hating myself for liking it. I think about trying out for sports and being good at them, getting popular, girls liking me. I had dozens of so-called "friends" and yet not one of them really knew me. Always a thread of misery running through my heart. Always a loneliness I couldn't completely shut out, always a longing I could never fill. I think about drinking at parties, doing drugs if they were there. I think about how when it came to sex, anyone could have me, which in some fucked up way, meant that no one had me. All those rich kids seemed to live that way, too, passing each other around, living for the next party. But I was the worst of them all because I knew better, because I was a fucking sell out. I realize now that although I didn't have much in Ohio, the one thing I did have was hope, and once that was gone, despite the fact that I finally had every material possession imaginable, I had nothing. Nothing at all.

I think of moving out of Lauren and Phil's house, going to college, but still carrying around that self-hatred that would never let me get enough of a finger hold to climb out of the pit of despair that I was constantly in. And so I made all the same mistakes then that I had made in high school. I had meaningless relationships that only made me feel more miserable, always trying to claim something back, but never knowing exactly what. I drank when it got so bad I didn't know what else to do, and finally, the straw—Seth. Roaring out of that driveway on a mission of death. I could admit that now. And Evie, God, Evie. Missing her every second of every day and hurting so damn bad because I knew she'd never forgive me. But maybe, just maybe I had been wrong. I was going to find out. I was finally strong enough to find out. Please, please don't let it be too late.

We stop in front of my room door.

"You know I'm only a phone call away, right? If you need anything—anything at all, you pick up that phone and you call me."

I feel emotion well up in my chest. Goodbyes suck. And this man has changed my life in a profound way. "Yeah."

He smiles. "Okay."

I pause for a minute and then say, "Doc, I just . . . Shit, this is hard." I pause and run my hand through my hair as emotion overwhelms me. He waits me out. He's always been good at that. "I wanted to say, you know, I never had a father. At least not one that taught me how to be a man. And I know you're my doctor, but you've been more than that for me. The other doctors here patched me up but you . . . you saved my life."

He clears his throat and squeezes my shoulder again. "You did all the hard work, kid."

I nod, clearing my throat, too.

"Go finish packing. And Jake?"

"Yeah?"

"Go get that girl of yours." He grins at me and walks away.

CHAPTER TWENTY-FIVE

I plan a trip to San Diego to meet with company lawyers about what Lauren has set in motion. Anger encompasses me when I think of what she's trying to do. She has no interest in running the company. She never took an interest in it once in all the years I've known her—not until it was something that she could hold over me. Her motives are transparent. But unfortunately, her manipulative reasons won't matter in court. I need to talk to my lawyers and find out if she's come up with something that might hold any water. I doubt it, but I owe it to all my employees and board members to be fully briefed on this situation.

    I haven't seen Evie in two days and I'm craving her, so this trip pisses me off for more than one reason. She mentions to me that she's cleaning the penthouse this week if it's occupied, so first thing Tuesday morning, I get an idea and swing by the Hilton on my way to the airport to rent the penthouse until Wednesday afternoon. Wednesday night seems an unacceptable amount of time to wait to see her. I'll have to take the red-eye back but that's okay.

    I meet with my lawyers on Tuesday, and we go over Phil's will, including the timing of the change. The lawyers feel confident that Lauren doesn't have a leg to stand on, but the fact remains that it will still be expensive to defend, and could drag out for quite a while. I clench my jaw, thinking of all the unnecessary time I'm going to have to spend in San Diego, away from Evie, working through this bullshit. I think of all the time I'm going to have to spend with Lauren in a courtroom and across a table from her and her lawyers. It's exactly what she wants, and

I feel like punching my hand through a wall at the thought of her manipulation. Can I just get on with my fucking life already?

I didn't give the office the name of my hotel this time so at least I know Lauren has no way to pay me a surprise visit. I only check in to a room at all because I don't feel like hanging around the airport until midnight when my flight leaves. I need to have some dinner and sleep for a couple hours if I'm going to be awake enough to surprise Evie. I smile with the thought.

Evie's at work, but I text her and let her know that I'm done with my meetings and checked in to the hotel. I order room service and take a long, hot shower. There's a knock on my door just as I'm pulling on some clothes. I freeze, my T-shirt halfway over my head. There's no way . . . I walk over to the door and look through the peephole. It's room service again. When I open the door, the teenage waiter starts rolling a cart in with a single, covered plate in the middle. "Ah, I didn't order anything. You must have the wrong room."

"He looks at his ticket. "Jake Madsen, room eight forty-two?"

"Yeah. But I really didn't order anything."

"Someone else called this in, sir."

I furrow my brow. "Okay. Ah, well, thanks." I grab a twenty out of my wallet and hand it to him.

"Thanks!" he says, looking at the bill and ducking out the door.

I lift the cover off the plate and there's a pile of warm, chocolate chip cookies. *Evie.* A grin takes over my face. Just as I'm replacing the lid, my phone rings, and I see Evie's name on the screen.

"Hey, baby," I answer.

"Hi." I can hear the smile in her voice. "What are you doing?"

"Missing you."

"Did you get my delivery?"

I grin. "Yeah. The sheets are all smeared with chocolate and crumbs. And I'm still left dissatisfied."

She laughs. "I'm sorry. I thought they'd be a satisfactory stand in for me."

"Uh uh. Not even close. Any chance a cart is going to roll in with you on it next?"

She laughs again. "I wish. What time will you be back tomorrow?"

"Not until late."

"Oh. Okay." She sounds disappointed. I smile to myself.

"How did your meetings go?"

"Pretty well." I sigh. "I didn't mention this because it's just another example of my dysfunctional relationship with my mom, but . . . she has some issues with my father's will. It's what she was meeting with the board about in Cincy. I met with company lawyers today to find out if she has a case at all and what it's going to take to fight this in court."

"Oh. Jake. That's . . . I'm sorry. What does she want out of it?"

"Essentially, she wants control over the company, over me. But my lawyers are confident that she's not going to get it. Still, I'm going to have to be here more than I'd like." I don't succeed at keeping the bitterness out of my voice.

She pauses. "Maybe I could come with you once or twice, if I'm not working during one of your trips. You know, to support you. If you think it would help . . ." She trails off, sounding unsure.

Emotion wells up in my chest and I'm quiet for several beats. "Jake?" She asks quietly.

"You'd do that?

"Would I do that? Yes, of course I'd come with you—"

"Support me."

She's quiet for a minute. "Of course I'd support you.

I let out a harsh exhale, and something deep inside warms and softens, seeming to unclench, like a muscle that has been held in a perpetual cramp. "I don't deserve you, Evelyn Cruise."

"Probably not. Those cookies were also meant to serve as a warning of what you'll be stuck with if you don't treat me right. A lifetime of chocolate stained sheets and dissatisfaction."

I laugh, and we continue to talk about what she's been doing for the last couple of days, including making dinner plans for us with her friends Nicole and Mike. After a little while, I can hear in her voice that she's fading, and so we say our goodnights.

On Wednesday morning, when I arrive in Cincinnati, I barely have time to stop home and shower before changing and driving straight to the Hilton. I use the keycard I was given yesterday to enter the penthouse.

When I hear three loud knocks on the door, I don't answer. I stand in the doorway between the bedroom and the bathroom and wait. My heart picks up in excitement as I anticipate Evie appearing in the bedroom doorway. I make some quiet noises so she'll know someone is here.

"Hello?" she calls out and I just grin, not answering.

The minutes drag as I hear Evie doing something in the other room. I crane my ears, listening to her quiet footsteps on the plush carpeting, stuffing my hands in my pockets and waiting, suddenly feeling a little nervous. How will she react to this surprise?

I see her peak around the doorway, a walkie-talkie in one hand and a bottle of some type of cleaner in the other.

I keep grinning as she spies me, a look of shock first and then pure happiness fills her face.

She drops the items in her hands and launches herself at me, letting out a little shriek of happiness as I catch her. I laugh in surprise and spin her around as we both laugh and kiss. *Evie, Evie, my girl, my heart.* I imagine that this is what it would have been like if I had come for her when she turned eighteen. For just a minute, I pretend that we're just two kids who had a rough childhood but were lucky enough to find each other, and now it's just her and me against the world, starting over. Our whole life is in front of us—no secrets, no guilt, no shame.

She takes my face in her hands, laughing against my mouth as she kisses me again and again. I kiss her back with just as much passion, spinning her once more. Everything about her feels like home. The only home I've ever truly had.

After a few minutes, our laughter dies and we go still, simply holding each other close, soaking in the moment.

Finally, I let my grip on her loosen and she slides to the floor, gazing up at me. "What are you doing here, Jake?"

"I wanted to surprise you. When we talked on Sunday, you told me you were cleaning the penthouse all this week if it was occupied, and my evil wheels started turning. I rented it on Tuesday morning before I left town. How long does it usually take to clean it?"

"You rented this room so you could spend the time with me it takes to clean it?" she says, furrowing her brow.

"Yup."

She looks up at me quietly for a second.

"Um, how long to clean it? If the guests are really messy, an hour and a half?"

"They're dirty slobs."

"Oh, okay, then, maybe I could push it to two hours."

No time to waste. I start unzipping her dress.

"What are you doing, Jake?" she asks.

"Not wasting any time."

"Um, Jake—" she starts, but doesn't finish her thought, as I kiss down her neck. That's fine. There's plenty of time to talk later.

She looks at me with heated eyes and a small smile on her lips as she takes my hand and leads me to the upholstered chair on the opposite side of the room. She pushes me down and I watch her, wondering what she has in mind. I was *hoping* things would lead in a specific direction. Me, Evie, a bed . . . several days of missing the hell out of her. But I didn't know if she'd feel comfortable with that while she was supposed to be working. Apparently, she does. *Thank God.*

She climbs on top of me, straddling me and takes my face in her hands, looking into my eyes for several beats before lowering her lips to mine, nipping at me and sliding her tongue into my mouth. I smile against her lips. My Evie is finding her inner sex goddess. Something in me roars to life—a fierce possessive pride in the fact that she's only known *my lovemaking*, only learned what she knows from *me*. I take control of our kiss, tilting her head so that I can go deeper into her sweetness, the taste of her exploding on my tongue and making me harder. My body is gripped in an onslaught of desire, my erection swollen to its fullest beneath Evie's core. I ache to be inside her, to sink into her so deeply that we don't know where she begins and I end.

I yank the zipper on her dress down, lowering it until I've exposed the smooth skin of her shoulders. I bring my mouth back to hers as I lower it down her arms. When the swell of her hips stops the material from going any further in this position, she breaks our kiss and stands up, keeping eye contact as she lets it fall to the floor.

My eyes feel heavy, need coursing through me as I lean back in the chair, draping one arm over the back and watching the show which threatens the control I'm barely keeping in check.

Evie unhooks her bra slowly and lets it slide down her arms and drop to the floor. Her panties are next and she hooks her thumbs through the waistband and just as slowly, drags them down her legs to land on the floor with her bra. She kicks off her shoes and steps out of her panties. My eyes have been following each piece of material as it falls down her body, and now they roam back up over her, standing before me in all her naked perfection. My gaze meets hers and I see hesitation mixed with desire. Somehow the fact that she's a little nervous makes what she just did all the sexier.

I reach down and unbutton my pants and take my zipper down, never releasing eye contact with her. I want to reassure her by showing her what she does to me. As I spring my erection free, she finally breaks contact and follows my hand with her eyes. Her eyes turn glassy as I stroke myself. Oh God, that's not a good idea. I'm barely hanging on by a thread here. The small whimper that comes from Evie's throat inflames me. "Touch yourself, Evie," I choke out.

The hesitation I saw in her eyes seems to have vanished. She does what I say immediately, touching her nipples lightly, and then bringing one hand down between the v-shaped, short dark curls and fingering herself as she moans, her lips parting. That thread of control I've been holding onto snaps.

"*Fuck!* I need to be in you now, baby," I manage, grabbing her by the hips and bringing her back to straddle me again, her knees on the chair next to my hips. I bring her down on top of me, thrusting with my hips in a force that impales her completely. Her internal muscles clench me briefly right before she pulls up and then slams back down on me. Stars blink in my head. *Oh God, that's good.* I grunt at the surge of pleasure that streaks down my spine.

I watch her as she experiments with this new position, riding me, taking her pleasure from my body and it's so fucking hot that I don't know if I can hold out much longer.

As she moves up and down on me, stroking us both toward orgasm, I bring my mouth to her breast, sucking the nipple into my mouth. As I lathe the hardened peak, I roll its twin between my thumb and pointer, and then switch sides. When I lean back, a growl comes up my throat when I see that her nipples are dark and wet from my mouth and her lips are red and swollen from my kisses. For some reason the sight inflames me, a primal satisfaction rising up in me at the evidence of my lovemaking on her body.

As I feel my climax rising up in me, I grab her hips, guiding her harder and faster, taking what I need. "Christ! Fuck!" I grunt out as the pleasure explodes through me.

I take her mouth as she begins to peak, kissing her passionately as we both moan and grasp at each other.

We are still in each other's arms for several minutes until our breath is steady again.

"What are you doing to me?" she finally asks.

I grin at her, chuckling quietly. "What are you doing to *me*?"

We clean up, and then fall onto the bed, Evie snuggling into me and squeezing me tightly as I wrap my arm around her.

"Did you take the red-eye out last night?" she asks. "You must be exhausted."

"Yeah. I thought I'd get a little sleep on the plane, but I sat next to this guy who wouldn't stop chattering all night long. He was afraid to fly and I think talking kept him from panicking."

"Oh God, that's awful—for both of you!"

"Yeah. Every time there was even a small bump, he would grab my thigh. Only in his panicked state, his aim wasn't great every time, and he grazed my 'boy parts' more than once."

She laughs. "That's probably close enough that you can cross joining the mile high club off your bucket list."

I laugh, too. "Probably."

"Seriously—is it *on* your bucket list?" she asks, raising her head and lifting an eyebrow.

"Nah. But if it's on yours, I could sacrifice." I grin down at her.

"I don't know. I've never even flown before. I'll let you know."

"Okay."

I pull her close and kiss the top of her head. "What's on your bucket list, baby?"

She's quiet for a minute, before she says softly, "Having a family."

My hand, moving slowly up and down her arm stills as her words wrap around me. It's the only thing I've ever wanted, too. With her. Only ever with her.

She must take my silence as discomfort because she says, "I mean, someday. In the future. If it happens. Not, like—"

"Evie, stop. You don't have to qualify your answer. Wanting a family, especially when you've never had one is completely understandable."

She lifts her head and looks up into my eyes, and finally nods. "I just didn't want you to think I was proposing to you or anything," she says, smiling now and laying her head back on my chest.

I laugh. "I would have said yes. Just for the record."

"Good to know," she says with a smile in her voice.

"But not for less than three carats."

She laughs. "I knew you were just a gold digger."

"Hey, a guy's got to have standards."

She lifts her head and looks into my eyes, "Sometimes I wonder if I'd even be any good at being a mom. It's not like anyone ever showed me how."

I look back at her quietly for a minute. "I think some people just know things in their heart, Evie. You'll be a great mom," I say, knowing with certainty that it's true.

We're quiet for a few minutes as I resume running my hand up and down her arm, and feel the comfort of her heart beating against my side where she's curled up.

Visions of her carrying a baby in her arms, *my baby*, run through my mind. I pull her tighter to me.

"Oh, hey, I got you something."

"What?" she asks, sitting up a little.

I lean over and grab the jacket that I had placed at the end of the bed when I first came in. I reach into the pocket and take out the small item wrapped in tissue paper and hand it to Evie.

She takes it, glancing at me with a small smile on her lips. She unwraps it and holds up the small, delicate shell, a smile breaking out on her face. "A shell! I've never had a shell! Thank you. Did you find it or buy it?"

"I found it. At first glance it's not the fanciest shell around, but do you see the spiral on the side here? It's called a whorl. See. Ninety-nine percent of whorls go in a clockwise direction. This one is counterclockwise." I pause as she studies it.

"I took a walk on the beach between meetings yesterday and when I saw the shell, I picked it up for you. Then I noticed its whorl. Never found one like it before."

She looks down at the shell and traces the spiral with a delicate finger.

She looks up at me and smiles. "Did you check out a book on shells? How do you know so much about whorls?" She raises an eyebrow.

I laugh. "No. I don't know. I just picked up that information somewhere. I can't even remember where."

I watch her with a small smile on my face as she looks back at the shell, studying it. I go on. "The thing about sea snails with counterclockwise whorls is that they can only mate with other sea snails whose shells coil in the same direction."

Her eyes meet mine and she frowns. "How do they ever find a mate if their type only make up one percent of the snail population? Seems impossible."

I nod. "Well, lucky for the counterclockwise whorled snails, their predators use a hunting technique that only works on their opposites, the more common ninety-nine percent. If their predators try to eat them, they find they can't and end up dropping them instead. This little guy, his design, *the way he's made,* allows him to survive another day. And that's another day to find his mate. He's rare, but he's a survivor, and so is the other sea snail he's looking for."

She's looking at me dreamily as I talk, a small smile on her lips, and I feel hypnotized by her beautiful, dark eyes. She looks down at the shell in her hand and says quietly, "Hmm . . . I wonder if this one died before finding his mate. Poor little guy."

I smile. "I like to think that she was somewhere washed up on that beach, too, and that they had lived a long and happy sea snail life together."

She smiles back and then looks back down at the shell, tracing the whorls again. When she looks up at me, she says, "This was a nice surprise, Jake. Thank you."

I hold her on the bed for a while longer before it's time to get up and straighten the room and let her get back to work. Today's going to be a long day. I'm exhausted. But it was totally worth it. Completely.

CHAPTER TWENTY-SIX

After our conversation in the suite at the Hilton, I can't get the images out of my head of what it would be like to have a family with Evie. I didn't think a lot about what that would look like when I was fourteen and fifteen, even though I took it for granted that it *would* happen—and I never let myself go there after that. It would have been unnecessary and torturous. In my mind, I could never have her again. What would be the point of picturing my and Evie's little brown-eyed kids running around when they would never exist? But now . . . just talking about the dream of a family with Evie has brought it to life for me. Not just the misty, faraway dream, but also the specific vision. I can't get it out of my head. She didn't even say she wanted that with *me*, but I want to let her know that I want that with *her*. And I can't do that without telling her who I am.

I want to move forward so badly, I can hardly think straight. But, in order to move forward, I have to tell her the truth. She now knows what we can be together. *This can't go on.*

If she decides she doesn't want to be with me after she knows the truth, I've also set her off her path to making her own dream come true. I can't do that to her for one more day. I love her. I want her to have everything she wants, even if it's not with me. A flash of fear shoots down my spine at the thought but I steel myself. *Do what you know is right.*

I've made sure she's attached to me so that she's less likely to want to leave. Jesus, how much more selfish could I be? I'm the poster boy for deceitful assholes everywhere. If she hates me even more now, I won't blame her. Not only am I going to lose her, I'm going to go to hell. The fear and shame I feel churns heavily in my gut.

I want so badly to tell her I love her, but how can I do that when I'm being so selfish? Love isn't selfish. I've loved her all along, but I refuse to *say* it to her until she knows my name.

A week after surprising her at her job, I call Doc while she's at work.

"Jake!" he greets me. "How are you?"

"I'm okay, Doc. Work's good."

"And Evie? How are things going with Evie?"

I haven't spoken to Doc in person since Evie surprised me that day. I had emailed him a brief note and told him that I had re-connected with her, but nothing beyond that.

"Good. But Doc," I pause before continuing, "she didn't recognize me. I lied to her and told her Leo died and I'm someone who knew him."

There's a minute of utter silence. I swear I hear a pin drop on the other end of the line. "Jake." He sounds disappointed. *Fuck.*

"I know, Doc. I know. Believe me, I know."

"And you still haven't told her the truth? Why?"

"Because I'm a worthless coward who took what I wanted. And I wanted her, and I thought that was the only way I could keep her from leaving. I panicked and I lied, and now . . . I know I have to tell her but I'm so fucking scared. See, a worthless coward."

He sighs. "Son, you're not a worthless anything. But you know you have to tell her the truth so you give her a real choice. Give her the choice to choose you or not, the *real* you."

"And if she doesn't choose me?" My voice almost cracks but I pull it together.

"Then you know you did what's right and you show your love for her by letting her go. You respect her by letting her choose the life she wants and letting *her* decide what she can forgive."

We're both silent for a couple seconds when he asks, "You on the right path, kid? Do you feel at peace inside?"

I'm silent for a second. "No." I sigh, running my hand through my hair. *I'm so close though . . .*

"Step back on it then. Tell her the truth."

I let out a sigh. "Okay. I know this, I do. Just doing it is . . ."

"The right thing is not always the easiest thing. But I believe in you. I believe you're stronger than you give yourself credit for. But you already know that." I hear the smile in his voice.

"Okay, Doc. Hey, I gotta run—thanks, okay?" I need to hang up before the lump in my throat rises any further.

"Okay, Jake. You can do this."

"Okay. Bye Doc."

"Bye, son."

That Friday night I make love to her in the dark, pouring all my emotions into worshipping her body. I acknowledge that I'm attempting to memorize every part of her in case I have to use my memories to last a lifetime. I'm going to tell her tomorrow. She's made dinner plans for tomorrow night with her friends, and I can't let this go on any longer than I already have.

I hold her in my arms that night until she falls asleep, and then I lay there in the dark, letting her scent and the feel of her soak into my soul. Will this be the last time I get to do this? Will I be able to make her understand? Will she be able to forgive me?

Finally, I ease myself out from under her sleeping body, and go out to the kitchen and pour myself a drink and take it out on the balcony. The fresh air clears my head and the alcohol starts making me sleepy after a little bit. I'm about ready to return to bed when I feel Evie's arms wrap around me from behind. "Can't sleep?" she asks in a sleepy voice.

"Yeah. I thought a nightcap would help. Go back to bed, baby. I'll join you in a minute."

"Okay," she agrees, giving me a little squeeze and walking back to bed.

I had arranged a spa day for Evie the week before, thinking it would be nice for her to relax before we went out for dinner. I don't cancel it the next morning. I want her to enjoy this, and I realize I'm buying myself a few more hours. *A few more hours when I can still call her mine.*

We get up and eat a light breakfast and she leaves for the spa. I shower and pull on jeans and a T-shirt before returning to the living room to wait for her. I do some work on my laptop for a few hours, but it's hard to focus and so finally, I put it away and simply sit. I don't try to figure out what to say when she gets back—the exact order of the words won't matter. I don't even know if she'll let me explain beyond who I am and that I've been lying to her all this time. Will she cry? Will she be angry? Slap me? I hope she does. I deserve it. I feel nauseous and scared, but I know what I have to do and I'm going to do it. I'm scared, but resolved.

The buzzer from the front desk startles me and I snap out of the trance I've been in for the last hour. I pick up and the other front deskman, Carl, says into the phone, "Mr. Madsen, Ms. Cruise is downstairs. She looks . . . unwell. Shall I send her up?"

"Yes, of course," I say, putting my own emotions aside as worry for her grips me. She was supposed to text me so I could send a car for her. Did something go wrong at the spa?

When the elevator door opens, Evie steps off, looking pale and shell-shocked.

My heart stops. "Evie, baby, what's wrong?" I ask, putting my arms around her and leading her into my condo.

I close the door behind us and turn her toward me, taking her face in my hands. "Evie, talk to me, love, what's wrong?" My eyes roam up and down her body, looking for an injury of some sort, something to explain the look on her face.

"Take off your shirt, Jake," she says, expressionless. For a minute I just look at her, not comprehending. What does my shirt have to do with this?

"What? Baby, I don't understand."

"Let me see your back, Jake," she says, gazing into my eyes now, fear, stark and vivid washing over her expression.

I gaze at her for long moments, understanding slipping down my spine, panic gripping me. Someone has told her about my tattoo. Who? What else have they told her? I need to be the one to explain this. I need to be the one to make her understand. This is not how I wanted to start. I close my eyes, willing time to stop. When I open my eyes, I gaze into hers, full of pain and confusion. The look on her face guts me. "Evie, who did you talk to? Baby, let me explain first."

"No!" she screams, voice shaking. "Show me your back, Jake!"

Please don't let this be happening. I close my eyes again, resigned now, and drop my head and then lift it to look her in her eyes. It doesn't matter who told her. I wanted to do it gently but fate has stepped in and this is the way it's going to happen now. I reach down and lift the hem of my shirt, raising it over my head. I stand in front of her, bare chested, as I've been many times before. I stare into her eyes again, imploring her to understand. Her large, panicked eyes stare back at me, waiting for me to explain in some way.

Slowly, I turn around and give her my full, naked back. I hang my head as her stare burns into me from behind. Blood pumps through my brain, the sound of my own heartbeat echoing loudly in my head.

I hear her gasp but I don't move. Several long seconds stretch out, and I still don't move when I hear a strangled cry and her feet stumbling backwards.

My mind blanks and suddenly I'm back in San Diego, months before Evie's eighteenth birthday. That date had beckoned painfully to me on the calendar, the thought of the date alone causing a heartache like I'd never known before, even that first week when I knew that what happened with Lauren meant that she was lost to me forever. I felt like I had already died inside, like I was a shell of a person walking around, empty, gutted. I didn't admit it to myself at the time, but looking back, I know that, more than ever, I needed the pain to end. I was done. It was excruciating. I couldn't hang on. Life felt like a burning building and the only thing I could think to do was jump. I was suffocating from where I was, the flames licking at me from every side. Death felt like it would provide the sweet, clean air that I couldn't access from the hell of the inferno in which I was trapped. It didn't feel like an option—it felt like survival.

I wanted to die, but I wanted her to be with me when I went. I needed to hold on to her, to take a part of her with me. Something inside of me longed to tell my own story, *the story of us*, the story of how I destroyed everything beautiful that I ever had, and then destroyed myself.

And so I sought out a tattoo artist. He helped me design the artwork I described to him, remaining silent as he sketched out the first basic concept, looking at me finally when it was all done and saying quietly, "This your story, man?"

I had studied it for long minutes, finally looking up at him and replying simply, "Yes."

Willow was there, walking a tightrope, the likelihood of falling always present—no safety net beneath her, just the ever-present harshness of the empty ground below. It was Willow, but she represented so many. Always living with fear and loneliness, nowhere soft to land.

And then the clowns. All of those heartless people who were supposed to protect us, to make us laugh—to be an escape from the harshness of life. But instead had turned out to be anything but, the worst of the worst, cruel jokes in and of themselves.

And myself, half lion, half boy, just like Evie had believed me to be. And I thought she was probably right, because half the time I felt rageful, wild, untamed, and the other half I felt overly soft, too sensitive for this fucked up world. I didn't know how to merge the two into one capable person—I didn't know how to be both and not one or the other.

She had tried to show me, my Evie, my lion tamer, but I wasn't enough. Even for her, the person I loved most in this world, I wasn't enough. *I'd never be enough.*

In the background, the master of ceremonies. Overseeing it all, orchestrating the show. He had put the clowns in the act, *so many* of them. He had put Willow on a tightrope with no net beneath her. He had made me half damaged and half wild. But . . . *but*, he had given me a beautiful lion tamer with eyes as deep as forever, and Willow friends who wanted to catch her if she fell, and he had made me brave enough to love them both once upon a time. How did I make sense of that? How could I understand him when I couldn't understand any of the show he had cast me in? Was he kind or was he cruel? I didn't know. It seemed an impossible question to answer.

I paid the tattoo artist extra to do my tattoo all in one day, and when he said it would hurt too much to do a piece of art that large all in one sitting, I told him I didn't care. And as the needle plunged in and out of my skin, I relished the pain. *I deserved the pain.* The physical pain made the emotional agony take a backseat, and I finally felt a peace that day that I hadn't felt in a long time.

Later that night, alone and drinking myself into a stupor, I stared at the picture of that artwork on the piece of paper that had been used as a template for the story now etched into my skin. I had stared into the depiction of Evie's eyes, and even the copy of a copy of the large, dark windows to her soul, I had felt my heart flutter back to life and start beating in my chest. Staring into her beautiful face, something in me decided it wanted to live. I didn't know what it was, but something whispered in my ear to *hold on*. And so I had. For a little while.

I come back to myself when Evie lets out a quiet, strangled cry, and I jolt at the sound, but otherwise, remain still.

She walks around to my front now and takes my chin in her shaking hand, lifting my face so that I'm forced to look into her pain-filled eyes.

"Why are you looking at me?" she asks, void of any expression in her voice, but her eyes wild with panic.

My eyes search hers for long seconds, looking for anything resembling love or understanding, but finding none.

I know what she wants from me though and so I give it to her.

"Because I like your face."

She stumbles backwards, letting out a strangled cry as understanding fills her eyes. Then, just as I knew she would, she turns and she runs.

I think I'm frozen, but without even thinking about it, I follow her, choking out her name as she stumbles onto the elevator, and the door closes between us.

And just like I knew she would be if she knew the truth, she's gone. And I do the only thing I can do—I drop down to my knees in front of the closed elevator doors, my head in my hands, my heart shattered.

CHAPTER TWENTY-SEVEN

I don't know how long I stay in that position until I find the strength to stand up and go back inside. I'm utterly numb now. I pull my shirt back on over my head and stand at the windows overlooking the city, and I face the truth of what I've done. I think about how she must be feeling right now. Is she crying? Hurting? Does she hate me? Yes, probably. The look on her face as the elevators closed between us told me she does. I betrayed her trust, *again*. I abandoned her and then I deceived her. *She hates me*. But not as much as I hate myself.

Where is she? Is she alone in her apartment? Being comforted by the friends we were supposed to be having dinner with tonight? I want so badly to be the one comforting her. But she doesn't want me. I did this.

What if she's hurt? She took off running and I don't even know where she ran. I need to know that she's all right. I pick up my phone and text her, asking her to please let me know she's okay. New panic grips me as I consider the state she was in when she ran out on me, and the number of sketchy areas she could have ended up in if she ran in the wrong direction.

I can't sit still, and so I grab my keys and I leave my condo. I drive around for a while, dialing her number a couple more times, trying to pretend I don't have a destination. But eventually, I wind up where I knew I would wind up all along. I park in front of her building and text her again, and then call her number. Still no answer. I get out of my car and ring her apartment. No answer. She could be in there, ignoring the buzzer. I just want to know she's safe.

I get back in my car and drive around a little more, calling her a few more times, sending a couple more texts. Finally, I leave her a voicemail. "Evie, God, I . . . please call me. I'm going crazy here. You ran and I don't even know if you're okay. Baby, please just let me know you're okay. At least that. Even if you don't want to talk to me . . . or, even if you don't want anything to do with me, please just let me know you're safe. I went by your apartment and you weren't there and it's late and I . . . please be okay."

I take a shaky breath and disconnect the phone. She's probably okay—either in her apartment not answering or with her friends. *She has to be okay.* I drive around a little bit more, the sky dark now, once again, no particular destination in mind. I'm almost shocked when I find myself driving down the block where I grew up, pulling up in front of the house where I spent the first eleven years of my life. Why did I unconsciously come here of all places? What lead me to the place I never wanted to see again?

As I park, it occurs to me that this place is only a few short miles from Evie's apartment. Our foster homes were only a mile or so from here, too. So close in physical proximity, and yet she's come a million miles. We both have in some ways, I suppose, but she did it all on her own.

I sit there staring at my childhood house in the light of the streetlamp, sick memories flashing through my mind. I put my head in my hands, and I let the onslaught of visions do their worst—a lot of bad things happened under that roof, a lot of things had fucked me up forever between those very walls. But somehow, sitting here, the bad memories don't seem to have the power I expected them to have. Instead, the strongest memory that comes to me is sitting in the tiny bathroom on the second floor with Seth. For some reason he seemed to like that small space, and I would take him there when I got home from school, sometimes for hours, and I'd do my homework on the floor and try to teach him the things that I'd done in school that day. Mostly, it didn't seem to penetrate, but every once in a while, and only ever there, his eyes seemed to clear, and for a minute or two he would be present. It was the most breathtaking thing.

The sound of a door slamming jolts me out of the past, and I look up and an older black man steps out onto the porch and lights up a cigarette.

I knew they didn't live here anymore. I have no idea where they live, or even if they're still alive. I have no desire to know. But seeing someone else come out the door still shocks me a little. I start up my car and drive away.

I would have thought that today of all days, seeing that house would have done me in. But for some reason, it doesn't. In fact, on the contrary, I feel better for having gone to see it. *Stronger.* Like maybe, it doesn't hold the power over me I still imagined that it did. I'm not sure what to make of this, but I'm grateful.

I find myself pulling up in front of the foster home where Evie lived when I said goodbye to her. It looks abandoned, the lawn overgrown with weeds, the structure dilapidated. I park on the side street and gaze up at the roof where I climbed to meet her so many times. *The place where we fell in love . . . showed each other our hearts, dreamed so many dreams together.* A lump forms in my throat. *Please don't let it be too late.*

After a few minutes, I pull away and drive to the cemetery where Seth is buried. This time, I walk straight to his grave, where the headstone that I ordered for him is now standing. I sit down on the damp grass, but I don't say anything. I just need to be with my brother. After a little while, my phone dings and I pull it out of my pocket. It's Evie with a two-word text message. **I'm safe.**

I exhale and sit there for a while longer. *Fight.* My head pops up. I don't know if that single word was my own thought or something imagined, but suddenly, it is the only thing repeating through my head, filling my brain, giving me strength. *Fight.* After a little bit, I stand up and walk back to my car, and drive home.

****

I wake up early. I slept like shit, but I feel a renewed energy. I'm going to fight for her. I fucked up. Badly. I was selfish and deceptive, and I owe her so much, an apology, an explanation. I'll grovel for the rest of my life if that's what she wants from me. I'll do anything to make her understand. And then if she can find it in her heart to forgive me, I will spend the rest of my life proving to her that she didn't make a mistake.

I shower and pull on clothes, and drive to her apartment. I know I look like hell but I guess I don't much care. I ring her bell and as I'm standing there, Maurice comes out of his apartment and through the front doors. "Saw her go out almost an hour ago." Then he brushes past me and is gone. Again, a man of few words.

I lean against the outside of her building, and decide to wait for a little while, hoping she's coming right back. A few minutes later, I see her turn the corner onto her street, a cup of coffee in one hand and a small brown paper bag in the other.

I see her spy my car and start walking slowly. I walk to meet her, hands stuffed in my pockets, and when she sees me, she stops.

A myriad of emotions fly across her face, lightening speed, surprise, hurt, *love*. I see it and it gives me hope. She settles on a frown, her eyes still slightly panicked as we stare at each other on the street. And then she tries to run around me, dodging me as I turn. But I'm faster and I reach her easily, scooping her up from behind. She doesn't have to forgive me, but she's going to listen to me. This moment has been eight years overdue, through no one's fault but mine, but it can't go on one minute longer. She struggles against me weakly, but I hold on to her more tightly, and when we get to the door of her building, I growl in her ear, "Give me your key, Evie." She hands them over, glaring at me. That's okay, too. But she's going to listen.

I open her apartment door and carry her inside although she's not resisting me anymore. I set her down and close the door behind us. We stare at each other, my eyes narrowed and hers glaring for a good, long minute. I look away first, breaking eye contact and running my hand through my hair. "Evie, we need to talk and we need to talk now."

"Why do you get to decide when we need to talk? Isn't it my call, *Jake*? Or should I call you Leo? Do you go by both? Please, clue me in here."

I close my eyes, gathering patience. I get her anger, but she's gotta know that we need to talk. She can hate me afterwards. *God, I hope she doesn't hate me afterwards.* "Evie. Please. Can we talk? Will you listen to me? This has been hell on me. Please. I just want you to tell me you'll *listen* to me—really listen to me."

"Hell on *you*? Oh, please, Jake. I don't want to make things harder on *you*. Please, sit down. Can I get you a beverage? A foot rub?" She glares at me some more.

I sigh. "Sit down, Evie. Now."

She stares at me for a few beats longer before she sinks down on the couch, looking resigned while I stand above her.

I sit down on the couch, too, but make sure to give her plenty of room. We're practically on opposite ends.

"If you need something, go get it now. We're going to talk and this could take a while. Get what you need to make yourself comfortable, and then plant yourself on the couch."

Her brows snap together but she finally exhales saying, "I'm fine, Jake . . . Leo. Please, let's get this over with." She pinches the bridge of her nose as if she feels a headache coming on.

I hesitate for a second. I know we need to talk, that I have to tell her *why*, but my heart is beating loudly in my ears at the thought of what comes next.

I move closer to her, and for just a few brief seconds she stares ahead stoically before her expression crumples and she brings her hands to her face and starts sobbing. *Oh, fuck, Evie, baby. I'm so sorry. I'm so, so sorry.* I gather her in my arms and cradle her to me as she cries. I can't make this better. *I did this.* I bury my head in her hair and try to will all her grief into my own heart. I would gladly take it if I could. Only it doesn't work that way. I knew it eight years ago and I know it now.

Her hands come away from her face and she chokes out, "I *waited* for you! I waited and waited and you just disappeared. I didn't know if you were dead or alive. I didn't know if you had just decided to start a new life and written me off or *what*! And still I waited. And truthfully, even though I didn't even admit it to myself, I was *still* waiting until the day you walked back into my life, calling yourself by another name! I never stopped waiting for a boy who threw me away like I was nothing!"

Her sobs pick up in intensity, gutting me completely. I pull her tight against me and rock her and although I expect her to push me away, she clings to me, letting me comfort her.

Her sobs subside after a little while, and she tilts her head and looks up at me, so incredibly beautiful even in her sadness. She studies me for a couple minutes, and then she takes her thumb and runs them over my cheeks, spreading wetness. Was I crying, too? I hadn't realized.

Her hands still, but her eyes continue running over my face, taking in every part. Then she uses her hands to explore every feature, sweeping her fingers over my brow and my cheekbones, my nose and my jaw. Her eyes follow the movement of her own hands. I don't say anything. I just wonder what she's thinking, wonder if she's seeing me as the boy she once knew. Her eyes meet mine and that live current rushes between us. I'm not sure what to do. I'm not sure what she needs right now. And so I remain still.

But when her eyes settle on my mouth and she moves her face toward mine, I meet her halfway. She seems wild, needy, and in minutes we're both moaning into each other's mouths. When I drag her sweater over her head and pull her bra down so that I can lick and suck her nipples, she gasps out, "Leo!" and I can't help the satisfied growl that rises, unbidden from my diaphragm. No one has called me Leo in eight years and something about it fuels my lust for her. Something about it feels like starting over, like I can finally be myself, but unhampered by the emotional baggage that I collected in San Diego. With that one word, the unsure boy has taken a backseat. I'm all beast and it feels fucking great.

"Say it again," I order, and she knows just what I mean, chanting, "Leo, Leo, Leo," as I lay her down, and she wraps her legs around me. "Make love to me, Leo," she says, her eyes looking deeply into my own.

I pause briefly when I see the look on her face. She wants this but not because she knows she can forgive me. She wants this in spite of the fact that she might not be able to.

I lower my head back to her breasts, kissing and sucking them until she's writhing and rubbing herself against me. I know her body almost as well as I know my own now and I give her what I know she loves. She whimpers, arching her back and offering herself to me as I continue to worship the rosy peaks, focusing on one and then moving to the other.

"Please," she begs, "I need you."

"My Evie," I breathe, leaning off of her and undoing her jeans so that she can help me as I push them, and her panties, down her legs. Then I bring my hand back up between her legs and move my finger slowly against her swollen nub as I return my mouth to her breast. I move my finger on her in matching rhythm to the pulls I take at her breasts, and very quickly, she's panting and breathing my name again, "Leo."

A bolt of pure arousal surges straight to my cock, and I jerk at the strength of it, feeling my balls draw up tightly to my body. I'm in serious danger of coming simply from touching her, hearing the sounds she's making. We're speaking in the simplest language, without using a word.

I plunge one finger inside of her and she's slick with desire, practically dripping. I bring my thumb back up to her swollen clit, and her leg falls to the side, making sure I have plenty of room to pleasure her.

She opens her eyes to watch me with heavy lids, and gasps out another moan as I continue to stroke my fingers in and out of her, rubbing my thumb in circular motions. Watching her face is almost too much and I feel myself impossibly grow harder.

I rub and thrust with my fingers, watching her face and changing tempo just when I think she's about to fall off the edge. I draw out her pleasure so that when she comes, she comes harder than she's ever come before.

"Leo!" she begs, when I slow the tempo again. She raises her hips to claim her own pleasure.

I add another finger and pick up the pace like I know she likes, rubbing and thrusting rhythmically now. She moans and at the sound, so do I. I can see by the expression on her face that she's right there.

"Come for me, Evie," I growl and her body tenses as she arches up off the couch, crying out my name over and over again.

I pull my own jeans off and as she's opening her eyes, I flip her over. The need to claim her feels primal, almost animalistic. I don't think, I just feel, acting purely on instinct now.

I pull her up and position myself at her entrance and plunge in as we both moan together. I begin thrusting, slowly at first but then faster as I say her name, and she answers back, "Leo, Leo, Leo."

I hold her hips for leverage and watch myself move in and out of her, shiny with her juices.

I grunt on every thrust. Evie is my world right now—the smell of her, our combined sounds, the feeling of her tight heat around me.

I hear her breath turn to pants and I reach around her and press my finger to her clit. She bucks beneath me, throwing her head back and thrusting her ass into me so that I go as deep as I can possibly go. My own climax explodes, so intense, it looks like fourth of July sparklers are being lit behind my eyelids.

I take several more strokes, drawing out the pleasure and then I stop, laying my head against her back as we both catch our breath.

After a minute, she starts sinking to the couch and I catch her, pulling out and turning her over as we cling to each other.

I sit up, bringing her with me and placing her on my lap, our naked, sticky skin against each other, our breathing slow and steady now.

I lean back and take her face in my hands, finally able to say the one thing that I've been longing to say for eight, long years. "I love you, Evie."

She gazes at me and I go on, "Whatever you think about what I'm about to tell you, you have to know that. I've always loved you. I've never stopped. Not for one second in eight years."

CHAPTER TWENTY-EIGHT

We clean up quickly and she's back on the couch next to me. We both seem to be in a little bit of a daze over what just happened. It was like our bodies took over, claiming something from each other that was necessary, but that we both knew wouldn't change the situation at hand. It's still in front of us. The first question she asks me is why I changed my name. I pause before starting. *Here we go.*

"Lauren asked me if it would help me to get a new start if I started going by my middle name, and of course, my new last name. I said no at first, but after that first week, I agreed. I wanted to become someone else—truthfully, I wanted to escape myself. Of course, a name change can't do that, but it seemed like a start at the time. I registered for school as Jake Madsen and no one has called me Leo until now." And it feels right that Evie be the first one to use my real name, as if I've been hiding behind Jake Madsen for eight years. Maybe somehow, unconsciously, trying to keep the *real* me safe, tucked away. I realize now though, that Evie is the only one I *need* to be completely exposed to, and the one that I'm the most *terrified* of being exposed to. It doesn't justify my lie, but it was the motivation behind my dishonesty. *Fear.* Hers is the only judgment I really, truly care about, the only judgment that can flatten me completely. I'm beginning to think that maybe there's a chance that I'll be okay when it comes to my past and all the demons that I've carried around for as long as I can remember. But will I survive it if Evie deems me unforgivable? *God, I don't know.*

With fear in her eyes, she asks me what happened that first week.

And that's how I start telling her my story, filled with secrets and shame, and mistakes and maybe, just maybe, some redemption. From that first flight to San Diego, to the flight back to Cincinnati.

She listens to every word I say, her expression going from horror to pain, to anger, to sorrow—my Evie, her emotions right there for me to see. She doesn't know how to hide, or maybe she doesn't try. But either way, the beauty and strength in that is even more apparent to me in the midst of my own story. I had hidden in every way possible. But in the end, the demons had found me behind every effort anyway—they're industrious like that.

I tell her about that terrible day in the basement of my new home in San Diego. The horror on her face is devastating and I almost decide I can't go on. But I pull it together and I go on anyway. I owe it to her. But my own shame is scalding me from the inside, burning me alive. I'm reliving it as I tell Evie about the moment that affected us both, the moment that changed our course, maybe forever. That moment wasn't just about me. It was about her, too. I take responsibility for that. She calls Lauren a pedophile, and maybe she's right. But I cooperated. Even if she manipulated me, I played right into her web. I accept that. I have to.

I've learned a lot, and I've looked at Lauren's actions in a new light since talking to Dr. Fox. And he's helped me understand why I played the part that I did. But I still haven't been able to let go of the searing shame that the memories bring. Maybe it's the last piece of my puzzle. I've made some peace with my past, allowing me to let go of some of the pain, and I've told Evie the truth now. Maybe Lauren is the one thing that I need to let go of before I can fully heal and be that complete man that Dr. Fox talked about. Why does it still feel like such an impossible feat?

"You didn't think you could trust me enough to tell me?" she asks softly, a sob making her voice hitch, and my heart squeeze painfully.

"A million times I thought about how I could explain to you what happened. I needed you so desperately; I thought I would die of the longing. But what was I supposed to say? I couldn't even make sense of it myself, much less try to explain it to you. I was just so deeply ashamed.

"And eventually, I considered the longing for you my penance for being *me*, someone who destroyed the people he loved. The thing I couldn't get around was what my silence must be doing to you."

I pause for a minute, considering my words, listening to my own heart. "Eventually though, I convinced myself that being apart, you had a fighting chance. I figured I was broken and that some people can't be fixed, or if they can, it's only by love so big it destroys the fixer. I couldn't destroy you any more than I thought I already had, Evie. I convinced myself that knowing the truth about me would have hurt you more than leaving you alone."

When Evie looks at me with empathy in her eyes and holds herself back from touching me, I know it is more a testament to her innate kindness than that I'm worthy of her forgiveness.

Telling Evie all my truth is the hardest thing I've ever done. It's the hardest thing I will *ever* do. To sit and look Evie in the eye and explain to her what a wretched person I had been. I had turned into everything that I had always promised myself I would never be—a coward, a user, a liar. I had turned to the very thing that had hurt me so much as a boy, numbing myself with substances instead of facing my own pain. And as I reveal myself to her, I wonder how she'll ever be able to love me again, *if* she'll ever be able to love me again.

When I tell her about my accident, she grabs my hand and squeezes it, and it's almost too much. I put my hands back in my own lap, knowing I don't deserve the comfort.

I tell her about my dad's heart attack, about Dr. Fox, about all those months lying there self-reflecting, wanting her back in my life so badly, it was a physical pain.

I tell her about following her, about blurting out my lie and then letting it continue. I cringe. I'm sickened by my deceit, but at the same time, a part of me is not sorry that it gave us the chance to find out who we are together before having to deal with all the issues my identity would have immediately brought up. I'm not sure how to reconcile these conflicting feelings, and so I don't try. I just confess. I confess it all and I don't hold back.

"I almost told you so many times. I was almost sure you realized who I was the night I drove you home from our first date and we sat in the car forehead to forehead, just exactly like that night I first kissed you on our roof."

She studies me quietly, looking sad and thoughtful for a few minutes, before saying, "I've always been good at pushing things aside that I didn't want to think about, good at losing myself in my own head. It's why I'm good at making up stories, I think. Being able to escape to a dreamland was a survival instinct for me. Maybe I did that with you, too. Inside I knew that there was something I wasn't allowing myself to think about. I *let* you lie to me because the lie felt good. I admit that now."

God, that's just like Evie, trying to take responsibility for pushing the knowledge of who I am to the back of her mind, but I reject that. Maybe she did, maybe she didn't, but this is not on her. I'm the one who lied.

"I won't let you take responsibility for any of this. Maybe you made some unconscious choices, but you can't blame yourself for that. I made all the conscious decisions. I'm the only one at fault in this situation. I understand that you need space to digest it all. But please, please, Evie, I can't lose you again. I'll never survive it twice. Can you at least try to forgive me? To understand why?" I choke out.

She pauses, and says quietly, "I don't know. I just need some time, Leo. You've just caught me up on eight years of life . . . a really fucked up life . . . for both of us." She laughs humorlessly. "Can we . . . can I have some space to think? Please?"

She's sat here and listened to my whole fucked up story, and gone through every emotion it brings up, right along with me. I'll give her whatever she needs.

I feel emotionally exhausted, numb, terrified that she won't be able to forgive me. But I've stepped back on to the right path—*I know I have*. I feel it. Now, I just have to pray that she'll join me, that it's her path, too.

As I'm about to open her door and walk out, perhaps for the last time, I say quietly, "Your gift with storytelling, Evie? It's not about you getting lost in your own mind, or living in a dreamland. It's about the beauty of your heart. It's about being able to rise above even the worst of situations. It's one of the reasons I've loved you every single day since I was eleven years old." I want the last words I say to her to be words of love.

I open her door and walk out, closing it quietly behind me.

CHAPTER TWENTY-NINE

I spend the next couple of days in a state of quiet desperation. But I make it through the days without trying to numb the pain in any way. Instead, living with it and processing it the best I can.

I go to the gym, I bury myself in my work, and I come home at the end of the day, exhausted from all the emotions I'm dealing with, but feeling a glimmer of satisfaction for *holding it together*. I take this as a sign that I'm healthier than I was and I allow myself to feel a small shred of pride. I don't know exactly what the difference is this time. Maybe it's the time I spent with Dr. Fox, maybe it's that there is a peace in finally telling the truth. Maybe it's that Evie, whether she wants to move forward with me or not, didn't look at me with disgust or hatred. Hurt, yes. Disgust, no. The relief in that alone is humbling.

My plan hasn't changed. I'm going to fight for my girl. But I know instinctively that fighting for her means giving her the space to process everything I've told her.

****

A few days after my talk with Evie, I head to the airport bright and early for some business in San Diego. Preston and I hired a new Vice President of Operations for the California office and I want to be there to welcome him. It's not a mandatory trip, but getting out of town will help me distract myself for a day, and stop pacing in front of my door, wanting to run to Evie.

As I'm waiting for my flight to board, I listen to my messages. There's one from a number I don't recognize and when I listen to it, it's Lauren.

"Jake. I need you. I've been arrested. Falsely, of course. These incompetent people have taken me to *jail*, Jake. This is unbelievable! I need you to bail me out—" Shocked, I listen as she seems to put her hand over the mouthpiece and talk to someone. Then she comes back on the phone. "Jake. Just please, get me out of here. My arraignment is on Monday morning. Book a flight! I can't even fathom that I have to spend the night here. Have the money ready, honey. I'm at the San Diego central jail."

I stick my phone back in my jacket pocket, frowning and completely confused. Arrested? For what? I can't believe she called me of all people. Or, I guess I can. I look up, suddenly realizing that first class boarding has started. I grab my bag and head for the plane.

When I touch down in San Diego, I head to the rental car counter and am quickly in a car, pulling out of the lot. I Googled the police station while I was waiting and so I dial the number now. After being switched around to several lines, I'm connected to a Detective Peterson.

"Detective, this is Jake Madsen. Lauren Madsen is my mother. I got a message from her that she's been arrested—"

"Yes, Mr. Madsen," he says solemnly. "I'm the lead detective responsible for the sting operation that led to your mother's arrest."

"Sting?" I ask incredulously, laughing a humorless laugh. "That sounds serious. I thought she might've had a few too many glasses of wine and got in her car."

"No, Mr. Madsen. I can't really give you any more information over the phone, but if you're close by, I'd be happy to meet with you now and explain the details of your mother's case."

I pause. "Actually, I am. I don't live in town anymore but I happen to be here today. I can head there now if that works for you." *What is this about?* Do I even care? No, not about Lauren. But curiosity has the best of me now. Plus, what if this somehow affects the court case she has against me?

"Right now is fine." He tells me he's at police headquarters at the moment, and gives me directions and we hang up.

I call my office and tell them I'm going to be a little later than I thought and head to meet Detective Peterson. What the hell can this be about? *A sting operation?* The only sting operations I've ever heard of are drug related, or those ones I've seen on Dateline where the reporter surprises the guy who's set up a date with the underage girl he met online—the steering wheel jerks in my hands and I veer a little too far over into the lane next to me, an angry horn blaring and jolting me back to myself. A cold dread settles over me. *Oh, fuck. No. No way. No fucking way. It couldn't be, could it?* I blank my mind and drive the rest of the way to the police station.

When I get there, I ask for Detective Peterson at the front desk and after five minutes, a tall, middle aged man with thinning blond hair and tired looking eyes comes out and shakes my hand.

"Mr. Madsen. I'm sorry to be meeting you under these circumstances. Please, follow me. There's an empty office back this way."

I nod and follow him through the station, thinking that I was lucky to avoid this place on many occasions during my teenage years, but not for lack of trying. All the underaged drinking, driving with way too many drinks in me, stupid, stupid fuck up. I feel the shame spearing through me at the brief flashes of memory.

He shows me into a drab little office on the far side of the station, the bright blue California sky outside the one small window a startling contrast to the dull box we're sitting in.

He sits down behind his desk and I take a seat on the brown vinyl chair in front of it. There's the famous poster of the kitten with the "Hang in There" tagline. Something about it strikes me as funny and I almost laugh, but catch myself.

"Mr. Madsen, your mother was arrested yesterday in a sting operation that was set up to catch her arranging a sexual liaison with an underage boy. The charges against her are Enticing a Minor for Sex and Traveling to Meet a Minor for Sexual Purposes."

Everything around me seems to close in until the only thing I see is a bright point of light. I close my eyes very briefly, gathering myself, and attempting to bring my racing heartbeat under control.

I take a deep breath and open my eyes as Detective Peterson goes on, "Mr. Madsen, I'm very sorry to have to give you this news. I know this is your mother we're talking about." He pauses briefly before continuing. "This must come as a shock and I can imagine that it's very, very upsetting. But you have to understand that this type of offender is very good at keeping their secret. And most often, women don't *only* show interest in teenage boys. Often they're married, have children of their own . . . It's common that people who know them, even those who know them best of all, are still shocked when they find out what they've been doing."

I run my hand through my hair and Detective Peterson continues, "We work with a psychologist who helps us out on many of the personal crimes involving a sexual element. If you're interested in talking to him about this, I can put you in touch. He's an expert on the subject. He could shed some light. Sometimes that helps."

I nod, but only for show. I'm already educated on the subject. Unfortunately.

I remain quiet, Detective Peterson studying me as I gather my thoughts. "So she just happened upon this website where you had set up a sting?"

He studies me again for a minute. "No. Actually an anonymous tipster let us know that these conversations were occurring between an older woman and underage boys. We can only imagine that it's someone who knows Mrs. Madsen as they were able to identify her by name, and they had specific information about her online activity. She was having sexually inappropriate conversations with up to five boys, ages thirteen to sixteen. We were lucky that this person knew precisely what information we'd need, to look into the conversations that were occurring. Once we verified the information, we contacted the boys involved and their parents, and then one of our officers posed online as one of the teens and arranged the meeting. Once she was arrested, we seized her phone and computer, and found all the evidence we need to prosecute, not only for the crimes she was arrested for, but for child pornography found on her hard drive as well."

"Oh, Jesus." I feel my breakfast threatening to come up my throat.

"Jake, I'm sorry to tell you that your mother *is* going to serve jail time. And she'll have to register as a sex offender when she gets out. Thankfully, she was caught before anything physical happened with the boys, but she will still be prosecuted for the attempts she made." He looks at me with the practiced look of someone used to delivering bad news—a mix of empathy and resignation.

"Are you looking into the anonymous tipster?" I ask.

He shakes his head. "No. There's nothing to look into. The tip was mailed to us with all the information we needed contained in a letter. A lot of people wouldn't give us tips if they couldn't be anonymous. We have no reason to investigate that."

I nod and then start to stand. He stands as well. "Detective, I appreciate you meeting with me in person. I don't mean to rush out of here, but this is a lot to handle." I hold out my hand to shake his over the desk, and he grasps mine in a firm hold, shaking twice and letting go.

"I know this is a shock, and so if you think of any questions later, please don't hesitate to call me. If you're planning on posting her bail, you can call the courthouse to get instructions from them on doing that. Her arraignment is Monday morning. But, Jake, I can tell you, the evidence we have on her is foolproof."

I nod, but I have no intention of bailing her out so I don't ask for any more details.

"Thank you again, Detective." He hands me his card, nodding again, and I leave.

I walk out of his office, weaving through the station, emotions warring within me. I feel sickness and disgust at the knowledge of what Lauren was trying to do, start a relationship with another fifteen-year-old? Or a thirteen-year-old? Jesus. Vomit threatens, and I swallow it down. But something down deep inside of me feels a sort of *vindication*, too. Almost like I couldn't truly believe she was sick until this very moment. I realize suddenly that I have always believed that my participation *allowed* her to be sick, not that she was sick *despite* my participation. Walking through the San Diego police headquarters, it's like a weight that's been sitting on my chest for eight years, gets just a little bit lighter.

I climb in my car and sit there staring blankly through the windshield. I roll down the window and take a deep inhale of the fresh, warm, morning air.

I think about everything the detective said to me again, going over the information in my mind. Fuck, what if that anonymous tipster hadn't gotten the information he or she did? I scrub my hand down my face. I picture some other teenager meeting up with her . . . *Oh, Christ.* If I could call that tipster and thank him or her, I would. *But, an anonymous tipster?* Really? I wonder at how someone could have identified her by name and known about those conversations. There is no way in hell Lauren told someone about that. It wasn't like she was the type to get drunk and brag to someone in a bar somewhere about her latest underage sexual conquest. I sit there pondering on this for several minutes, thoughts racing through my brain, going in every direction.

You might be surprised to know that I used to work with computers when I was your age. Was good at it, too. I still do it on a consulting basis here and there.

I freeze. *No, no, that's too crazy.* It can't be. I shake my head to clear it, almost laughing at my own ridiculous thought. But if someone good with computers didn't access hers, how did that information get to the police? And who would want to keep tabs on Lauren's internet activity?

Detective Peterson had said that they were lucky that the tipster knew exactly what information they'd need to be able to look into the online conversations that were occurring.

So, the tipster is someone who is not only good with computers, but is an expert on sex crimes, and works with the police, and therefore knows what specific information they'd need to move forward on an investigation?

I grab my phone and the card Detective Peterson handed me on my way out. I dial his number and when he answers, I tell him who it is and then, "Detective, you mentioned a psychologist you work with who might be able to shed some light on the nature of my mother's crime. Can I get his number from you, just in case I decide to call him?"

"Oh sure. Hold on, I have his card here." I hear him rifling through what sounds like a pile of papers. "Okay, got it. His name is Dr. Fox and here's his number." He reels it off but I don't bother writing it down. I already have that number.

I thank him and hang up, not knowing what to feel. None of this is a coincidence.

As I sit there unmoving, my mind racing, I see two familiar figures get out of a car. *Preston and Christine.* They close the car doors and start walking across the street toward the station. I get out of my car and call out to them.

"Jake!" Christine rushes toward me and grasps my hands, her eyes flying over my face as if I should be showing some form of physical wound. "Are you okay? Lauren called Preston this morning to post her bail and then we called the station to talk to the detective on the case. One of the officers told us you were meeting with him. We came straight from the airport."

Preston flew in this morning for the same reason I did and he brought Christine to help out with some of the presentations we had today.

"Yeah. I just did. Can we go somewhere and talk about this? Get some coffee or something?"

Preston has walked up now and he says, "Yeah, sure, Jake. But we don't have to talk about it if you don't want to. We're just here to make sure you're all right. You're the one we're concerned about."

The air whooshes out of me and I clear my throat, feeling suddenly like they've given me something that I didn't even know how much I needed until it was offered. *Support.*

"Thanks. I appreciate that. Are you going to post Lauren's bail?" *Please say no.*

"No, I'm not. We don't need to have a conversation about why. But, Jake, I want you to know that no. I'm. Not." He looks at me pointedly and then looks away, continuing, "Maybe she'll make bail eventually but hell if I know who'll help her." Something in his expression looks pleased.

We're all silent for a minute and then I gesture to my car. "I can drive somewhere close and then drop you back off at your car."

We all get in my rental car and stop at the first coffee shop we see. We order coffee and sit down.

After we've all taken several sips of our drinks, I tell them everything the detective told me. Preston sits there shaking his head, a sorrowful look on his face, and Christine just looks horrified. I wonder if she's thinking about her own son.

"This isn't going to reflect badly on the company, is it? On Phil?" I direct my question to Preston.

"I don't see why it would, Jake. Phil's been deceased for over a year. Clearly, *he* wasn't involved in any aspect of what Lauren's been doing. In fact, if anything, it looks like this was something she decided to do once he was gone. There's just no reason to question otherwise. Also, you're the one running the company now. And obviously, you have nothing to do with this either. However, if it makes you feel better, I can make our lawyers aware of the situation. If anyone prints a word that we don't like, we will sue for slander. And we'd win."

I nod.

"I don't anticipate this affecting the company at all. But, Jake, if it does, we'll face it together, okay?"

I'm silent for a minute, thoughts whizzing through my mind again.

"At least we won't have to worry about her contesting Phil's will now," Preston says. "She'll have to drop that lawsuit. She has other more pressing concerns." He lets out a shallow laugh.

Preston, Christine and I talk through the situation for the length of time it takes for us to finish our coffees, and then Preston tells me to catch an earlier flight and get back home. Clearly, I'm in no frame of mind to be at the office today. I take him up on it. I thank both of them, hoping that they see how much their support means to me, and drop them back off at their car.

As they're walking away, Christine pauses and I hear her tell Preston she'll meet him at the car in a second. Then she walks back to where I'm standing and says, "Jake, I haven't asked you how things are going with Evie? Have you reminded her yet?" She smiles.

She's talking about our conversation at that clusterfuck of a benefit where Gwen got her claws in Evie. I take a deep breath, looking Christine in the eye. "I fucked up, Christine. I don't know. I'm still working on it."

She tilts her head, studying me. "Well, then, you have more than one reason to hurry back to Cincinnati, don't you?" She puts her hands on her hips. "And just a tip, if she won't listen to you, write your feelings down. Girls like letters." She winks and I can't help grinning at her. She gives me a quick hug and hurries off to join Preston.

I return to the airport and luckily, there's a seat on a flight leaving in an hour. I sit down to wait and pull out my phone. I dial Doc's number. He doesn't answer, but I leave a brief message, letting him know that I just met with Detective Peterson, who he apparently works with, and asking him to call me.

An hour later, I'm sitting on my seat on the plane when I hear my phone ding with a new email. I pull it out, the ding reminding me that I need to shut it off before takeoff.

When I open the email, I see it's from Doc.

Leo,

I got your message and understood the reason for your call. I'd like you to hear what I have to say without having to respond.

Sometimes people are unpredictable. But often times, they're not. Over the years, I've gotten good at knowing who is likely to surprise me, and who isn't. People who have certain propensities don't generally let them go, especially when it becomes clear that a relationship with the object of their obsession is becoming more and more unlikely. Those people generally look to replace that person. You had no way of knowing that and I wasn't going to put that on your shoulders. But I hope you see why I couldn't let that happen. I hope you see why I monitored the situation and used my knowledge to intervene.

You fought for other people your whole life, Leo. Despite the fact, that no one ever showed you how to do that, or taught you why that was noble and brave. And then when you needed it the most, no one was there to fight for you. I hope you understand my reasons for doing so now, despite the fact that I've overstepped my bounds.

And it's my hope that you will see, that I fought for you because you're worth fighting for.

Doc

Ten minutes later, as the plane rises into the sky, I look out the window at the sparkling blue water disappearing through the clouds. Emotions are threatening to come up my throat, the will to fight stronger than ever. As I lean back in my seat, taking a deep breath and closing my eyes, it registers that for the first time, Doc called me Leo. Somehow, he knew I was ready.

CHAPTER THIRTY

When I get home very late that night, I throw on just a pair of workout pants, and go out on my balcony. I sit down on one of the two chairs out there and put my feet up on the ledge, staring out at the city lights. I just sit and let my mind wander. I think about where I came from, all the miserable things I went through to end up in foster care. I think about my mom for a long time, something I've never really allowed myself to do.

She had tried to get clean a couple times. It never took, but when she was trying, I had gotten glimpses of who she might have been if her life had been different, or maybe if she had been strong enough to lift herself above her circumstances, even a little bit. She had tried to bake cookies with Seth and me one time when my dad was out. I got the feeling that she was trying to do something "mom like," trying to be someone she knew she had failed at being so far. She was trying too hard, humming and chatting a mile a minute. But I didn't care. At least she was finally *trying*. While they were baking, she got out the cards and asked me if I wanted to learn how to play poker. So she taught me the basic rules and we sat at our small kitchen table and played for toothpicks while Seth watched. It was one of the only times my mom paid us any real attention and I was so happy, I couldn't stop smiling. But then we smelled something and black smoke started wafting up out of the oven. The cookies were burning. She pulled them out, shrieking, and tossing them on the stove. And then it was like something just died in her eyes, and she retreated back inside to that place that she usually lived, vacant, unavailable. "I always ruin everything," she had said, emotionless. "I never get anything right." And then she had gone to the couch and sat there watching TV and drinking for the rest of the afternoon.

She didn't get it though. She missed the whole fucking point. We didn't care about the cookies. We just wanted *her*. So badly, it was like an ache inside that never, ever healed. Having her for that brief time just made it hurt all the more when she turned away from us again. And I had hated myself because I felt like I wasn't enough to make her want to stay.

She was always so checked out, so absent, so seemingly unconcerned with the horror her sons were living through right under her nose. I always told myself that I didn't love her because she had never shown any love for me. But the truth was, I did love her. I could admit that now. I wanted so badly for her to love me back and she never had. I wonder for the first time what happened to her that she gave up so completely, gave up her very soul. I let myself feel the hurt that washes over me when I recall the blank look on her face as my stepdad wailed on me, day after day after day.

But sitting here alone on my balcony, it suddenly seems as clear as day that it wasn't about us. Nothing we could do would ever have been enough for her because she had already given up. She had given up so completely that she was empty inside, just like Evie had told me in her story all those years ago. But now I understood that that emptiness had everything to do with her, and nothing to do with me. Sitting here in the middle of the night, staring up at the sky, a feeling of peace washes through me, and I can breathe a little easier.

I think about my dad, my stepdad, although he always *called* himself my dad. Claiming me on one hand, but then never missing the opportunity to remind me that I only existed because my mother was a whore. I had taken that inside and made it my truth, replaying his words again and again whenever I felt weak, seeking for some reason to confirm to myself that I was worthless. I think about it for a long time and realize that I no longer have a burning desire to prove him wrong. I don't need that anymore. The only person I want to prove anything to is Evie. She's the only one who ever deserved it.

I think a lot about Evie. I think about how I was always so in awe of the fact that she was so much more than where she came from. But maybe I am, too. Maybe we *both* ended up being better people than the people who raised us, or didn't raise us, as the case was.

And that's gotta be rare. Almost as rare as those counterclockwise whorled snails. The thought makes me smile.

I had told her that some people just know things in their heart. Maybe I know a few things in my heart, too. Not as many as her, not by a long shot. But perhaps I have something to offer if I work really hard at it. I want so badly to be given that chance. Once upon a time, she had saved me by loving me, by believing in me. Will she be able to again? Even after everything? I hope to God the answer is yes.

I think about the unbelievable turn of events with Lauren, still a feeling of sickness rising up in my chest when I think about how close she came to putting someone else in the same position she had put me in. And Doc . . . what he had done for me. I still couldn't wrap my mind around it.

. . . it's my hope that you will see, that I fought for you because you're worth fighting for.

As the sun comes up in the sky, I go and get some paper and a pen and a book to write on, and I return to the balcony and write Evie a letter, pouring out all my thoughts on paper. Pouring out everything she was to me, everything she is to me, and everything I want so badly to be for her, asking her to please, please choose me again.

After I fold it up and put it in an envelope, something occurs to me. I go into my bedroom and reach in the back of my top drawer, pulling out the letter that I started writing to her all those years ago—the letter I've always used to remind myself what a despicable human being I was when I started to forget. A perfect instrument of self-torture, a perfect reminder of what I did to betray her. I don't think I'll do that to myself anymore. But I hope it will make her understand a little better.

I go into work late the next morning, finally falling asleep for a couple hours in the early morning. On my way in, I stop by Evie's apartment, ringing Maurice's bell. He comes lumbering out, looking at me suspiciously. I smile my most charming smile and ask him if he'll put the manila envelope I've placed the letters in under Evie's door. I want her to read them but I don't want her to have to face me until she's ready. Until it's her choice. Maurice nods and closes the door.

I close myself in my office. Several times throughout the day, Doc's words run through my head . . . *it's my hope that you will see, that I fought for you because you're worth fighting for.*

Will Evie think so now that she knows the truth?

Later that evening, I walk out to get a coffee down the street, needing the fresh air and the caffeine in order to keep myself from nodding off over the last couple of emails I plan on sending.

As I step off the elevator to the lobby, I see Gwen walking my way. I cringe internally, but keep my expression blank as she veers toward me. The expression on her face is the same one I would imagine a shark wears right before it sinks its teeth into a porpoise. *Coming in for the kill.*

"Hi, Jake," she says, a fake smile on her face.

"Gwen," I say back, moving past her.

"I ran into Evie at the spa," she speed talks.

I stop and turn to her. She's the one who told Evie about my tattoo. Not that it matters. In fact, maybe the way it happened was for the best. Except for the fact that Evie was probably publicly accosted by Gwen the land shark, noshing her way through those who dare to get in her way.

I look at her thoughtfully for a second. "I should probably thank you then, Gwen. Evie needed to see my tattoo and I had hesitated too long. She needed to see it because it's *her*. It's our story."

Gwen draws back, her brows snapping down. "What? *She* is the girl you had tattooed on your back?" She keeps frowning, pausing for several seconds. "I just always assumed that girl was dead."

I shake my head. "No, not dead. Very much alive. And very much loved. And I pray to God, very much mine. Have a nice life, Gwen." And I turn and walk away.

I return to my building fifteen minutes later, caffeinated and feeling more alive. I wonder if Evie has read my letter yet. I wonder what she's thinking for the hundredth time since she ran out of my condo. I wonder if she'll respond to me, and if so, when. *Fight for her.* Oh, I intend to.

You're worth fighting for.

Maybe I'm getting there. Maybe I'm not the bad bet that I believed myself to be for so, so long.

I step on to the elevator and wait as the small group of people step on with me. As I'm waiting for the doors to close, a man next to me taps me on the shoulder, and when I look over at him, he points at the glass behind me. I turn around and there she is. *My lion tamer, my Evie, my love.* For a second, I don't understand. She's smiling up at me and she mouths, "I choose you." Time seems to slow and the background noise fades out around me. I suck in a huge breath, the sudden lump in my throat threatening to choke me.

You're worth fighting for.

I yell out, "Stop the elevator!" and push through the people in front of me, the door opening at the next floor so I can step off.

I run toward the escalator to the left of me, and even though it's going in the wrong direction, it's a way down to Evie and so take it, jumping three and four stairs at a time, ignoring the people swearing at me and giving me dirty looks as I push past them.

You're worth fighting for.

She's the only thing I see, the only thing in focus as I leap over the railing once I'm close enough to the bottom.

We run to each other and I pick her up, spinning her around, pressing my face into her hair, trying desperately to stay in control of the emotions that are steamrolling over me—joy, thankfulness, hope, love. She continues to chant, "I choose you. I choose you, Leo. Always."

You're worth fighting for.

The sounds of people clapping and whistling breaks through the haze of joy around me, and I look around to see people staring at us. I laugh, an unbelieving laugh, and look back at Evie who is grinning, too, her face full of love.

"I love you, Evie," I say, my voice deep with emotion, even to my own ears.

"I love you, Leo, my loyal lion."

"You still believe that, after everything?" I look deeply into her eyes and see that she does.

You're worth fighting for.

She nods. "Even more. You found the courage to jump through fire for me. You found yourself on the other side, didn't you?"

I look at her, thinking that yes, I think she's right. I think that the fire turned out to be my own fear, my own sense of worthlessness. "I guess I did. But you were the one holding the ring." *You were the one who always believed in me. You were the one who always thought I was enough.*

"That's the easy part, my beautiful boy. Believing in you is effortless. It always was."

God, I love this beautiful, beautiful girl. I grin. "I'm going to take you back to my den and maul you now."

She grins right back. "Yes, please."

I take her hand in mine, our future stretched out in front of us, the promise to give her a beautiful life is a vow etched on my heart.

EPILOGUE

Two Months Later

Leo grabs my hand between our seats, bringing it to his lips and kissing it. He smiles over at me, and I lean my head back on the headrest and give him a smile, too. As he turns back to the road, I drink in the beauty of his profile.

It's been two months since that day in his office building lobby, the most beautiful two months of my life. We've spent it reminiscing about both good and bad times, falling more deeply in love, just being *us* together, no secrets between us, no fear, no guilt or shame. I tease him that *Jake* is my lion, and *Leo* is my boy. I love both, I *need* both—just one or the other doesn't add up to the complete person that he's become. My fierce, loyal man and my sweet, tender, protective boy. Both scarred, but both finally able to find the strength to accept that even life's worst experiences can be valuable gifts.

Oh and also, both of them like to maul me, *frequently*, and that's a good thing. A very, very good thing. I grin over at him. "What?" he asks.

"I was just thinking about this morning," I say, grinning more.

He chuckles back. "Yeah. We really missed out on the showering together in the beginning, didn't we? I'm glad we're making up for lost time." He winks and grins back.

I laugh. "Definitely. So where are you taking me?" I tilt my head and look at him suspiciously. When we had gotten in the car, he had said he wanted to show me something, but wouldn't tell me what.

"You'll see in a minute."

We both look ahead as he makes a turn and that's when I realize that we're on the street where I used to live, the street of my old foster home. I frown slightly. *What are we doing here?*

As he pulls up in front of the house, I look over at Leo, and he has a nervous expression on his face as he studies me. "Trust me?" he asks.

I don't even take a second to think about it before whispering, "Yes. Completely."

He smiles as he shuts off the engine and leans over and kisses me softly. "Come on, then."

He gets out and comes around the car to let me out on my side. He takes my hand in his as I step out and pulls me against him, before shutting the door.

It's a cold December day and his breath plumes in the air as he says, "I love you, Evie."

I look up into his warm brown eyes and whisper back, "I love you, too."

He kisses my forehead and says softly, "I'll never, ever get tired of hearing that."

Then he pulls me gently and we walk toward the house. It's in terrible condition, garbage strewn all over the front yard, paint chipping everywhere, windows broken. Obviously it's been abandoned for quite some time.

As he pushes open the front door, and I peek inside, memories wash over me. For just a minute, I feel like a frightened young girl again, emptiness consuming me. But then Leo squeezes my hand and I look up into his love-filled eyes, and I'm okay. *But why did he bring me here?*

He pulls me gently again and I follow him as we climb the stairs to the second floor. I know where he's taking me now, and suddenly my heart lifts and a smile tilts the corners of my mouth. *Our roof.*

We climb carefully through the broken window and I rub my

hands together when we step outside. He wraps his arms around me, and we simply stand there holding each other for several minutes on the very slightly slanted surface.

When he lets go of me, I move to sit down, but he stops me, saying gently, "No. Stay there. Please." I look at him in confusion, but as he drops down on one knee, I understand and a breath hitches in my throat.

My Leo reaches into his pocket, and brings out a ring box and opens it to show me the most beautiful platinum, vintage style engagement ring I've ever seen. I stare at it, mesmerized for a couple seconds before my eyes move back to his. My vision blurs as I see the emotion on his face.

"Evelyn Cruise," he says, pausing before taking a shaky breath and continuing, "I wanted to bring you here to ask you to spend your life with me because this is the place where I first knew that I'd love you forever. This is the place where I learned what it feels like to *be* loved. And this is the place where my lips first touched yours." He smiles up at me as I let out a half laugh/half sob and bring my hand to his cheek. He leans into it and smiles again before looking up into my eyes and saying, "Will you do me the great honor of being my wife? Will you marry me?"

Tears are streaming down my cheeks now and there is a lump so big in my throat that I can't speak. So I nod again and again, going down on my knees with Leo so that I can kiss him through my tears and my vigorous nodding. We kiss and he laughs against my mouth, and finally, I collect myself enough to laugh, too. He pulls back slightly, smiling, but then going serious as he says, "I need to hear it, baby. Let me hear you say it."

"Yes, yes, yes," I whisper between more kisses. "A million yesses. Infinity yesses." I smile through my tears as he slides the ring on my finger.

I take his beautiful face in my hands and bring my mouth to his again. This kiss goes deeper, our tongues flirting, caressing. I feel the air shimmer around us and I tilt my head so that he can go deeper. He moans and pulls me closer and I revel in the heady taste of him, the feel of his body pressed against mine.

Suddenly, it registers that something cold and wet is hitting my cheeks. I break away from Leo, both of us breathing heavily. We look up at the same time and I suck in a breath when I realize it's snowing! We look back at each other and both burst into wondrous laughter. It's really snowing! Just like the first time we kissed. Only this time, we aren't saying goodbye. This time, we're starting our life together. The magical quality of the moment hits me and I start crying again, and Leo pulls me close, wiping my tears away. We hold each other for a few minutes before it occurs to me that we're standing on a roof on someone else's property.

I look up at him. "Um, Leo, we should probably go. Aren't we trespassing?"

He smiles, taking my hand and pulling me up and toward the house. "Actually, no. Come with me. I have something to show you."

I follow him back downstairs, confused. He leads me into what used to be the living room and leaning up against the wall is something under a draped sheet. He pulls the sheet off and I take it in for several seconds before clapping my hands over my mouth to keep myself from sobbing *again*.

It's a sign, and it says, "The Willow House," and has a beautiful Willow tree surrounded by children running and playing and reading beneath it.

"I bought this property, Evie, and the empty lot next to it," he says quietly, watching my reaction closely and bringing his arms around me. "I thought we could open a community house for kids who are in the foster care system and could use a place to come after school and on weekends. A place for them to belong that's stable and unchanging. I was hoping you'd run it."

I gaze up into his warm brown eyes and in this moment, fall even more deeply in love with him, something I didn't think was possible.

Nine Years Later

I put the last chrysanthemum in the window box and scoop dirt around it with my hands, filling it in and then arrange the ivy between the bright yellow and burgundy flowers, making sure it drapes just so. I stand back and smile, admiring the beauty of the fall plants. I brush my hands off and then gather my gardening tools together. The kids and I had spent the day planting and doing yard cleanup, and that window box was the only thing we hadn't gotten to. I had promised them I'd finish it tonight.

I walk inside and just as I'm drying my hands off, I hear Leo's voice calling my name. I rush to the front excitedly. "Hey, baby." He smiles when he sees me, a large pumpkin in each arm.

"Hi." I grin, going to him and tilting my head up to kiss him on the lips as he leans down to meet me.

"Did you find enough?"

"Yeah. We had to go to five different grocery stores, but I think we rounded up at least one for everyone. There are over fifty in the back of the truck."

"Thank you." I smile, putting my hand on his cheek and gazing into his eyes, so easy to get lost in.

"You're welcome. But baby? These pumpkins aren't exactly light. Where should I put them?" He's grinning at me though.

I blink. "Oh! Sorry. Here. Put them here." I indicate the large table that I've decorated with a fall themed orange, plastic tablecloth. Perfect for messy pumpkin guts.

Leo sets the two pumpkins down. "Are the boys with Mr. Cooper?" I ask.

"Yeah. I dropped them off at his place after we picked up the last batch of pumpkins. I told him we'd be by to pick them up on our way home. They were a big help with the pumpkins, even Cole."

I nod and smile, happy that our boys are spending time with the man who is like a grandpa to them.

I do the last of the cleanup as Leo brings the pumpkins inside.

When I walk back out to the main room, the table is crowded with pumpkins of all sizes. We'll have a fun day carving them tomorrow.

Nicole and Kaylee and her little brother, Mikey, are coming by to help. Nicole is pregnant with her and Mike's third child, a happy surprise. I know that seeing her teeter around here in her crazy heels and big pregnant belly is going to give me a heart attack. And I know she'll tell me to stop being silly, that just because she's pregnant, there's no reason for her to wear the frumpy, orthopedic wear that I'd have her in if I had my way.

Leo grabs my hand and pulls me toward the stairs and I follow, knowing where he's taking me. We enter the small room at the back and he opens the window and helps me climb through, onto the roof. I walk a little ways to the side and sit down. He sits down next to me, and I put my head on his shoulder as he pulls me close to keep me warm.

"This is my favorite place in the world," I whisper in his ear.

He smiles and brings my arms up and around him. "*This* is my favorite place in the world," he says back, smiling.

I nuzzle into his neck and smile against his skin, kissing him there and then laying my head on his shoulder again as we both look out across the night.

It was nine years earlier that my Leo had proposed to me on this roof. We were married two months later in a small ceremony with our closest friends, *the family we had chosen*, in attendance.

Right after our wedding, Leo had hired a construction company to come in and re-hab the entire property, it being important to both of us that we fix it up rather than tearing it down and starting from scratch. The roof of the house was re-shingled, but other than that, it remained unchanged, *ours*.

Several months after that, when The Willow House project was in full swing, I had taken my husband's hand and led him out to our roof, and under a warm summer sky, I had told him that I was expecting his baby. He had stared into my eyes, frozen for several beats before that beautiful smile that I love so much spread across his face, and he pulled my shirt up and kissed my belly again and again as I laughed. Then he had pressed his cheek there and looked up at me, and I had seen my beautiful, uncertain boy in his expression. I had run my fingers through his hair and whispered, "Yes, Leo, you're going to make an amazing dad. Some people just know things in their heart."

He had smiled at me and then suddenly looked panic stricken as he practically dragged me back to the window. "What are you doing?" I had laughed.

"No way my pregnant wife goes out on a roof," he had said. "I don't care how safe this one is."

Later, baby Seth slept in a pack and play in a quiet corner upstairs in what had been my old room.

When Landon got his degree a year after we opened, we offered him the job of Director and he accepted. I was here as often as I could be but I was a busy new mom, and I knew I needed the help. He brings life and enthusiasm and fun to the place and everyone loves him. How could they not? He's very loveable.

Several years after that, when I was nine months pregnant with Cole, my water broke in the front room as I was hanging artwork from a project I had done with the kids. Later, Cole took his first steps in The Willow House as the kids cheered him on.

We have a big garden in the back where the kids help plant vegetables and then collect them when they're ripe. What was once the empty lot next door now has a basketball court at the front and a big grassy space at the back for the kids to run around and play. We planted a Willow tree in the middle and put several picnic tables around it. It was still small, but someday it would grow big and strong, its branches bending and swaying in the wind. Sometimes the wind would be bitter cold, and sometimes it would be warm. I thought that sturdy tree would be okay either way.

Inside, we created art centers, a music room and a whole library dedicated to books and reading. It's where I tell stories if the kids ask. When my own book was published, Leo bought about twenty copies for that room alone. I just shook my head and laughed. But when I saw the way some of the kids looked at that book and asked me if I really grew up in the foster care system just like them, I decided to let them stay. I want the kids to know that their situation doesn't need to limit them—that if I could find the courage to reach for my dreams, so can they.

We also have computers and tutors who help with homework. We have a big kitchen where volunteers teach the kids how to cook and prepare meals.

Preston puts on a science fair every year for The Willow House and the winner receives a college scholarship to be used for a science or engineering major. Christine retired early to be a full-time mom as her kids started high school. She and her family volunteer often, and we have become very close. Christine is like a mother to me. To us.

We had planned and dreamed and loved on that roof of ours. We didn't know that the journey that would finally bring us to our happily ever after would be full of detours and pitfalls and pain. We didn't know how much love and forgiveness and understanding would be required to make it back on the path we were meant to be on, together. But what we did know was that we were here because we had both been willing to fight; to fight for each other, to fight for *ourselves*, to fight for the kids who needed a place to belong, to fight for love. And that means that despite all the pain that we had endured to be where we are, in the end, *love won.*

Acknowledgments

Special, special thanks from the bottom of my heart to my Executive Proofing Committee, Angela Smith and Larissa Kahle. Thank you for reading my book multiple times, giving me constant encouragement, and for telling me truthfully when Leo was being a "dorky narrator." I know he thanks you, too.

Thank you to my family as well, especially my endlessly supportive husband.

About the Author

Mia Sheridan is a *New York Times*, *USA Today*, and *Wall Street Journal* Bestselling author. Her passion is weaving true love stories about people destined to be together. Mia lives in Cincinnati, Ohio with her husband. They have four children here on earth and one in heaven. In addition to Leo's Chance, Leo, Stinger, Archer's Voice, Becoming Calder, Finding Eden, Kyland, Grayson's Vow, Midnight Lily, and Ramsay are also part of the Sign of Love collection.

Mia can be found online at www.MiaSheridan.com or www.facebook.com/miasheridanauthor.